Linda Regan is a successful a[...]n television to film, radio, and thea[...] e novels, all critically acclaimed. Her books are set in London, where she was born and brought up. She has shadowed police and seen, first hand, crime being committed. Her books have been described as 'strong crime'. She writes about what is happening currently and weaves her stories around that. Some have a theatrical flavour too, because this is another area she knows well. She believes books should be entertaining, truthful, and page-turning. Reviewers often mention how well her characters are drawn. Characters take the story along and, with her acting experience, she has spent her life inventing them.

Praise for Linda Regan:

'Regan exhibits enviable control over her characters in this skilful and fascinating WhoDunnit' Colin Dexter

'One of the best up-and-coming writers' Peter Gutteridge, *Sunday Observer*

'Regan continues her sure-footed walk on the noir side. Entertaining stuff, but not for the faint-hearted' *Kirkus Reviews*

'A sound debut; I look forward to Linda Regan's next book' *Tangled Web*

'For a first novel it is extremely well written' *Encore Magazine*

'This is a book you can't put down' *Eastbourne Herald*

Also by Linda Regan and available from Headline

The DCI Banham series

Staged Death
Soho Killers
Monroe Murders
The Terror Within

The DI Johnson and DS Green series

Brotherhood of Blades
Street Girls

The DI Johnson series

Guts for Garters
Sisterhoods

THE TERROR WITHIN

LINDA REGAN

Copyright © 2019 Linda Regan

The right of Linda Regan to be identified as the Author of
the Work has been asserted by her in accordance with the
Copyright, Designs and Patents Act 1988.

First published in 2019 by Headline Accent
An imprint of HEADLINE PUBLISHING GROUP

2

Apart from any use permitted under UK copyright law, this publication may
only be reproduced, stored, or transmitted, in any form, or by any means,
with prior permission in writing of the publishers or, in the case of
reprographic production, in accordance with the terms of licences
issued by the Copyright Licensing Agency.

All characters in this publication are fictitious and any resemblance
to real persons, living or dead, is purely coincidental.

Cataloguing in Publication Data is available from the British Library

ISBN 978 1 7861 5 7485

Typeset in 10.5/13pt Bembo Std by Jouve (UK), Milton Keynes

Printed and bound in Great Britain by Clays Ltd, Elcograf S.p.A.

Headline's policy is to use papers that are natural, renewable and recyclable
products and made from wood grown in well-managed forests and other
controlled sources. The logging and manufacturing processes are expected
to conform to the environmental regulations of the country of origin.

HEADLINE PUBLISHING GROUP
An Hachette UK Company
Carmelite House
50 Victoria Embankment
London
EC4Y 0DZ

www.headline.co.uk
www.hachette.co.uk

For my hubby, Brian, my rescuer in life

Chapter One

It was supposed to be a simple civic wedding, taking place in the local town hall. Alison had said she didn't want a fuss. Detective Chief Inspector Paul Banham, having been married before, was in full agreement.

His twin sister, Lottie, however, was having none of it.

Lottie had nine-year-old twins of her own, and argued they should be included if their favourite uncle was getting married. 'After all,' she reminded him, 'they weren't born when you got married the first time.'

Bobby wasn't greatly interested in weddings. 'That's cool,' he'd muttered as Lottie excitedly told him the news, his head nodding like a dog toy in the rear of a car. 'Cool. Yup. Yup. Alison's cool. She likes football.'

Bobby's twin sister Madeleine however had been the complete opposite. She had become overexcited, jumping up and down then hurling herself at Alison, wrapping her long arms tightly around the shocked woman's neck. 'Will I be a fairy bridesmaid, and get a pink twinkly dress?' she'd shrieked while clinging and swinging, leaving Alison speechless.

Lottie had quickly come to the rescue, unwrapping the child's arms from Alison's neck and placing Madeleine back on the ground. 'Calm down,' she scolded her hyperactive daughter. 'This is about Alison, not you.'

Detective Inspector Alison Grainger had been thrown by the outburst. She hadn't planned on having any bridesmaids, let alone twinkly fairy ones. She hated pink, but she had grown to love Madeleine, as she knew Paul did deeply. So, as the child clung to her neck, pleading for a pink dress, Alison had remained silent.

If Madeleine was to be dressed like a pink, glittery fairy, then Alison knew the child would talk her into donning a frilly dress herself, and she'd have to grin and bear the fact she looked and felt like a cross between a meringue and a poodle – and in front of half of the murder team that she and her fiancé worked so closely with, which she would never live down. And all because Banham adored little Madeleine and would do anything to make her happy.

As Madeleine had stood, scolded and sobbing, with her back to Alison, Alison caught Banham giving the tiniest of smiles and then a shrug. Both had felt that, despite their wishes, this was a request that couldn't be refused. Banham, and now Alison, loved Madeleine dearly – so as always, Madeleine got her way.

Now it was the big day. Alison comforted herself with the fact it was going to be a quick service. She had won on that score. Then a meal at the local Italian, with the dreaded itchy and uncomfortable dress removed and placed out of sight. That would be bearable.

And then it was off to Mykonos. That would be just what the doctor ordered. Two weeks alone on a Greek island, with Paul Banham. That would be their time. The wedding ceremony was now all for Madeleine.

Banham's own beautiful baby daughter had been murdered horrifically, along with his first wife, Diane, thirteen years earlier. The killer had never been found. Alison therefore understood why Banham doted on his niece, and pandered to her every whim. Alison had found it easy to adore her too. She had the same large blue eyes as Banham and his fair hair. So she had let Madeleine talk her into wearing a cream, meringue-shaped dress, trimmed in pink, and accessorised with cream satin high-heeled shoes that she could barely stand up in, let alone wear up the aisle of the town hall. Madeleine had also insisted they wore tiaras in their hair, as all fairies did, and Alison had agreed, but made sure her own was so tiny it was barely noticeable.

After the ceremony, when she and Banham were alone, it would all be history, and she would know she had done the right thing by agreeing to marry him. Right now, sitting in the back of the white Mercedes, in between her fat ex-army father and her fidgety, over-excited fairy bridesmaid, doubt was burning into her brain and fast turning to panic. She hated being the centre of attention, and she hated looking like a show poodle.

Why couldn't they have just set up home together? There hadn't been any need for legalising their relationship in marriage. Why on earth had she agreed to this pantomime?

As the pink ribbon-adorned Mercedes turned the corner, and onto the road that led to the town hall, she was seriously thinking of asking Barry, her police colleague and driver, to stop the car so she could get out and leg it. Deep down she knew that not only could she not run in the ridiculous satin stilettos, she loved Banham and wanted to be with him.

Or did she?

Yes, she did – it was the marriage bit she wasn't sure of. So why was she there, she questioned herself silently.

She had been so shocked when he asked her, she had immediately said yes, for no other reason than to get him off his knees in the middle of the police station corridor. When she'd thought about it afterwards, she hadn't been so sure about actually marrying him – but by then it felt like she couldn't back out.

Yes, she loved him, but she didn't need a ring on her finger to prove it to the world. Nor did she want this circus of a celebration – but she did want to keep Banham's family happy, which is why she had allowed Madeleine to take over and tell her what to wear. She just hoped this wasn't the state of things to come.

A guard of honour made up of uniformed police should have awaited her outside the town hall. Something else that had been arranged without consulting her. She was relieved to know that it had been cancelled due to the riots the previous night, where every available officer had been called in. Local gangs had started fighting and others had been breaking into shops, pilfering the goods inside.

Uniformed police had arrived but found themselves totally outnumbered, so neighbouring stations had been alerted and officers drafted in from nearby stations.

As the fighting had progressed cars were set on fire. When another forty-strong rival gang had read about it on social media, they too had come along, fuelled with drugs and too much alcohol, and all hell had been let loose. Worse fighting had broken out, more windows were smashed, and police vehicles had been set alight as the police themselves became the targets. It had got almost out of control: looting was rife, fireworks and petrol bombs were let off, and weapons were wielded as angry youths turned on the police as they attempted to make arrests. The sound of ambulance, police, and fire engine sirens had echoed throughout the night for miles around – police and civilians, as well as police dogs and horses, were high on the list of casualties.

Still it continued. The last Alison had heard, the Home Office had been alerted with a request for water hoses and the army to stand by. Armoured police vehicles too were now out in force. The station cells were full to overflowing and still the fighting and rioting was going on. A large number of the serious crime team from Alison and Banham's department had cried off from attending the wedding after the shout went out that all available officers were needed.

Alison was relieved at that news, at least it meant most of her work colleagues wouldn't see her in this ridiculous outfit. She was a respected DI in the force; it was the last thing she needed. It was bad enough in front of her few personal friends, and her own and Banham's families. They'd all just think it was lovely, as little Madeleine did. The child was in her element, sitting next to Alison in the back of the car. She kept touching her glittering, sequinned pink dress, smoothing it with her tiny hand, which also twinkled with glittering silver nails and the shiny body gel she had smothered over her hands and arms.

Alison thought the child looked like a beautiful rosebud doll, and was delighted Madeleine was bouncing with happiness, even if it meant her looking like a poodle. She would cope, she told herself, it was just for a few hours. Madeleine was about to be her niece, and she intended to be a really good auntie – and that started here. She had even bought the child glittering pink wings to attach to her dress, so Madeleine really could be the pink fairy princess she had dreamed about, for a day.

Alison had won a small victory about her own dress. No matter how Madeleine had tried to persuade her that pink was the best colour in the world, she had bought a cream dress, but pacified Madeleine by agreeing to trim it with a pink ribbon and pink net. And now she itched, everywhere, from her bra down to her hideous shoes. She was a boyish dresser normally, happiest in jeans worn with oversized, bland-coloured jumpers. It went with her job. She had to chase criminals, and she needed comfortable clothes for that, with the added practicality of flat shoes. Already, the four-inch satin shoes were giving her jip, not to mention blisters, and the day had hardly started.

As the Mercedes pulled up outside the town hall, she took a deep breath, pulled a smile, winked at Madeleine, and turned and took her father's arm to help him out of his seat and into his wheelchair.

Did someone say this should be the happiest day of her life? Well, they were wrong. This was just another day, just a short and sweet service, she reminded herself, then it would be all over and she would be off sipping cocktails in the sun – but still she wondered why she had ever agreed to a marriage commitment.

Banham was already inside, in his best grey suit with his hair freshly cut. He was nodding welcoming greetings as guests spilled into the registry office to take their seats. Beside him was tiny Detective Sergeant Colin Crowther, who he had chosen as his best man.

DS Crowther couldn't dress properly if his life depended on it. He was a first-class detective, but had been at the back of the queue when style and tidiness were handed out. The man had agreed to have his mass of overgrown black hair cut for this event, but it now looked as if it didn't fit his head properly. Previously his hair had been a mass of dark curls, usually gelled and standing alert like a hedgehog hung on a washing line. Today, the shorter curls were still gelled, but lay flat against his scalp, like a game of noughts and crosses with all noughts.

Banham was just relieved to see the sergeant was wearing the suit he had been hired for the occasion, even if Crowther's hands were completely covered by the sleeves of the jacket. And Banham was even more relieved to have checked that his sergeant had the rings, though Lord only knew how he intended handing them to the DCI when the moment came, with those sleeves in the way. Banham had rather hoped the man would have the presence of mind to at least turn the cuffs back a few inches. It had been impossible to find a decent hired suit that would fit Crowther: the man was only five foot four inclusive of the hidden lifts inside his shoes. Still, Banham had the greatest respect for this Tom Thumb of a man. As far as detective work went, there was none better.

Banham too was feeling edgy and nervous. He was also doubting his decision to get married. He thought back to the day he'd stared at Diane's butchered body, lying by the blood-splattered and mutilated corpse of their eleven-month-old daughter Elizabeth. Murdered in their own home, his home too, at a time when he should have been with them instead of taking the overtime. He had sworn to them at that devastating moment that he would find the killer and bring them to justice. He had promised he would never stop looking until the killer was found.

The years had gone by, and with no forensics or other evidence to go on, the murders slowly faded as a police priority. Eventually the case file, along with Elizabeth's yellow Baby-gro and Diane's blood-stained bedding and the remains of her nightdress, was boxed up and housed with all the other unsolved cases, in the basement of the police station.

Banham had moved into CID, and when Alison Grainger was seconded into the department, they had started working together. They had been friends for many years, then gradually the friendship had grown into a relationship, his first since the death of his beloved family.

Now, standing in the town hall registry office, waiting to marry again, he thought of that promise to Diane, and a knot formed and tightened in his stomach. He loved Alison, that wasn't in doubt, but guilt was eating at him, making him question his right to move on with his life. The memories had flooded back. He wondered how Diane would look today, and how little Elizabeth would look; she would be fourteen by now, settled in secondary school. Maybe even courting. And what would Diane think of him not tracking down their killer? Wasn't that the main reason he had joined CID and become part of the murder team? He had let her down. But he also knew he had to move on.

Alison stepped out of the car. She then found she couldn't take another step. It wasn't even the bloody awful cream satin heels, it was the fact that her father, who was twenty stone and currently sliding his way, sideways, out of the car, still sat on the edge of her dress. She had felt him sitting on it on the journey, but now as she opened the door and scrambled out of the back of the vehicle to stand up, she heard a rip. The net trimming on the satin underskirt had given way under her father's weight. She took a deep breath; it was only a bit of netting, and hardly the time, or place, to start cussing. As long as it didn't start Maddie crying.

'No worries,' she said to him, winking at Madeleine. 'Nothing that will show.'

Major Grainger was completely wheelchair-bound, so Alison had to organise putting the wheelchair out on the pavement by the car so he could haul himself, with help, into it. Philip, one of the police team who had been meant to meet them at the venue, had been assigned the job of pushing the major down the short aisle beside his daughter, so he could officially give her away – but Philip had been sent to help with last night's riot control. So Barry hurriedly left the driver's seat to help.

Madeleine too was out of the car and jumping up and down with excitement, attempting to arrange Alison's frock. Her wings were flapping around behind her, nearly in Major Grainger's face. He had to flick them away as he settled into the wheelchair.

Alison bent over to check his blanket was comfortable, and another ripping sound came as she trod on the loose netting from the last mishap. She inhaled a deep breath of air, then realising she had stuck the heel of one of her God-awful shoes through the hem of her dress as well, she rolled her eyes to heaven. How was she ever going to keep her temper in check and get into the building if this bloody dress got under everyone's feet and wheels? She wanted to pull the bloody thing off and sling it in the nearest bin, but knew to keep her famous temper under control. Madeleine always started to cry if Alison swore, and she couldn't let that happen.

It was a grey day: no rain, but everywhere was still damp from the downpour of yesterday. Autumn leaves had started to fall. She mentally noted them along the pavement. She'd have to walk carefully, the path would be slippery, she couldn't afford to go arse over tit. She had a child's hand to hold, flapping fairy wings to avoid, and more importantly, if she skidded on leaves she would over-balance onto her father who was being wheeled on the other side of her. She wasn't an elegant walker at the best of times, and it would be easy to slip. The wheelchair, herself, her father, and her fairy princess bridesmaid would all go flying. The thought of it suddenly made her smile.

She tottered on carefully, and lifted her head high as she prepared to enter the town hall. Then a pin dropped out of the French pleat that she had carefully rolled her waist-length auburn-brown hair into.

Then, as another hairpin hit the ground, a small wisp of hair touched her cheek and then fell to her shoulder where it hung. She let Maddie's hand go for a second while she flicked the stray wisp behind her ear. Perhaps the congregation would think it was meant to look like that, she comforted herself. Besides, could she really care? Just get through the next few ghastly hours, she told herself, and then you can rip the dress up, kick the shoes off, and throw them both in the nearest bin. She would be back in her comfortable jeans, carrying a suitcase full of beachwear and sun lotion, and she and Banham would be heading for the airport and that luxurious villa in Greece.

She paused as they reached the door of town hall. She could hear the chatter of the congregation. She turned and smiled at her excited niece, and then winked at her father.

As Barry was about to open the door and lead them in, and as if on cue, his radio bleeped twice. The emergency call.

'All units urgent,' the voice followed. *'PC down. Shots have been fired at police on duty. Henry Street. Assailants are armed, shots fired at officers. Emergency. Emergency. All available units. Officer shot and taken hostage. All spare officers needed to help.'* The voice was urgent. *'Armed SC019 unit on way. Backup urgently requested. We need a trained hostage negotiator urgently, DCI Banham is on leave. Can anyone help?'*

As Alison turned to Barry to tell him to go, DS Crowther shot out of the Town Hall, closely followed by Banham.

Alison looked at Banham, then herself.

'A police officer has been shot,' Banham told her urgently. 'There's a hostage situation. And I'm the only trained hostage negotiator around at present.'

'Go. Go,' she urged him. 'It's fine. This will wait.' She wanted to go too. It was what she did. A colleague had been shot and her unit needed her – but dressed as she was, it wasn't a possibility. 'I'll follow you,' she shouted as Crowther and Banham, both suited and booted, jumped into a car and shot off in the direction of the riots.

She turned quickly to Barry, who was still hovering by the wheelchair, uncertain what to do. 'Go. You go too. Go with them,' she shouted at him. 'I'll sort this and I'll meet you all there.'

She turned and noticed the registrar had arrived beside her, and was looking bewildered.

'Sorry,' she said, waving her hand dismissively. 'We're police. There's an emergency. We're putting this on hold. Can you tell the guests to go to the restaurant and enjoy themselves.'

The bemused registrar nodded her head.

Madeleine started to wail.

Chapter Two

A cacophony of emergency services sirens, all growing in volume, could be heard as Banham and Crowther sped into Burton Street, then Beacon Street, where the rioting was one street away – and which was parallel to Henry Street where hostages were being held.

Crowther had driven in record time, at one point his speedometer had hit nearly a hundred miles an hour. His BMW was practically on two wheels as he swung into the side road adjoining Beacon and Burton Streets. From this small road they had a good vision of Henry Street and the surrounding roads, which were overflowing with angry youths hurling stones, lighted sticks, and even eggs at police officers and the horses and dogs that had been seconded in. Some of the rioters were still smashing their way into shops on a mission to grab anything they could lay their hands on.

Crowther pulled up sharply. Banham leaned forward and took in a deep breath.

'You OK, guv?' Crowther asked with a wide grin, noticing Banham's flat and tense palms pushing against the dashboard.

'Fine,' Banham said. 'I just hadn't expected to be travelling at that speed, that's all – and I was expecting to be in an aeroplane.'

Jim Carter, head of the SC019 gun unit, immediately took their attention as he rapped on Banham's passenger window.

'Can't be a hundred per cent sure of anything,' he said as Banham wound down the window, 'but we believe there are two guys, with firearms, inside the disused warehouse building on Henry Street. They shot one of ours, how badly we don't know, and they've dragged him along the pavement, taken him hostage, along with others.' He pointed to the large building at the end of the road. 'They're in there.'

'How many hostages, do you know?' Crowther asked.

Carter shook his head. 'We haven't been here long. I didn't see the incident, so I don't know anything yet, for sure. We need to talk to officers who were here when it happened. There's a trail of blood outside in the road, we know that's our officer's.'

'Do we know who the officer is? Banham asked.

'We believe it's PC Martin Neville, as no one has seen him for a few hours, but as I say, sir, no one is sure of anything.'

'Anyone see it happen? Any of our boys?' Banham pushed.

'They're short on manpower out here, very stretched, and it's been a very tough night from what I hear and see. We don't know if it is Neville, or where he took the bullet, or how bad he is. Rumour has it there are more of ours taken hostage, plus civilians. But, as I say, at this moment no one can confirm anything for sure.'

'Right,' Banham said, opening his door and hurrying out. 'We need to find out which officers aren't on the street, then, and how many civilians are in there,'

'And what the gunmen want,' Crowther added.

'It's been chaotic all night,' Carter repeated. 'These men are exhausted. Things were calming down, but then this happened. We're still waiting for the army and hoses to be approved.'

Banham nodded as he and Crowther hurried on. As they turned into Henry Street, they saw for themselves the burned out cars and the burning sticks flying through the air.

'I don't envy our boys if this is calm,' Crowther said. 'It's still mad out there now. If this is calmed down, then God knows what it was like last night.'

'Doesn't look good, I agree,' Banham said, turning to indicate the angry shouts coming from the crowds and the sirens still shrieking around them. 'I'll bet our boys have taken a few knocks.'

'Lots of very low morale out there,' Carter told him. 'Everyone is well shaken up with the guns materialising. Priority now, guv, has to be to get Neville out of there and to hospital. We can't hang about on this one. Judging from that blood trail, that boy could be in a bad way. My team are in place on the roofs opposite the warehouse, and there's another team in the alleyway by the warehouse. I am happy to give the go ahead to go straight in and take the gunmen down. I believe this would be for the good of Neville's life.'

Banham cupped his cheeks and rubbed his hand across his mouth in his habitual manner as he was thinking. He took a few seconds before he answered. He had worked with Carter many times in the past. The man was a great leader and a crack shot, but had to be hauled back on his haste.

'Point taken,' Banham said calmly. 'But not knowing who's in there, or how many, or indeed what other weapons they have, I won't risk anybody else getting shot. And we don't know how many others in there have been injured, or how many hostages are in there.' He paused to let Carter take that in.

Crowther then said, 'Or how bad Neville is.'

Carter shook his bald head. 'I agree, no one can be sure of anything. But in my opinion, and judging by the blood trail there, I'd say we don't want to be hanging about.'

'Clear the streets,' Banham barked to Crowther as they headed further into Henry Street where the main rioting was taking place. 'We need all the public out of here, and out of danger. Let's get going. Martin Neville needs to be in hospital, however bad he is.' He turned back to Crowther. 'He's a good mate and a great cop. He turned my wedding invitation down, he was on duty rota, and too professional to ask to change shifts.' He shook his head. 'Too unselfish, too. Others had asked.'

'Bet he wished he had done now,' Crowther said.

Banham shook his head thoughtfully, then turned back to Jim Carter. 'Have you got a spare loudhailer? I'm unprepared. I was in the middle of getting married, as it happens.'

Carter handed Banham the hailer he had in his hand and looked into Banham's face. 'Did you say you were in the middle of marrying Alison?'

As usual Banham's face gave nothing away. 'Yes. Your team are in place, you say?'

'My unit's spread across the roofs, rifles in position, sir,' Carter told him, indicating the team on the roof facing the warehouse. 'And another team over there, by the side of the warehouse. So, is Alison Mrs Banham now? Or have you jilted her?'

Banham shook his head. 'Neither,' he muttered, as he hurried down Henry Street.

As soon as he had gone a few yards, a stick came flying through the air, missing him by inches. He ducked it, and then caught sight of Sergeant Spedding hurrying over to him. He found himself ducking more sticks and stones that were being hurled in the direction of the uniformed police and their dogs and horses. He was glad to see the officers all had riot shields and helmets and were able to use them to protect themselves, but still his temper boiled as he looked at the exhausted team, all bunched together, with just truncheons to defend themselves and their animals, as they worked to push back the last of the crowds, which had halved since the gun unit had arrived on the scene.

Crowther hurriedly followed as Banham marched up to Spedding. 'Do we know who the hostages are in there, and is it PC Neville who has been wounded?' Banham asked the uniformed sergeant.

Spedding shook and rubbed his aching head. 'I've so many men down. It's been a fucker of a night, sir, even horses and dogs have been wounded. If there weren't press around, I'd give some of these thugs a good solid thrashing, so help me I would.'

Banham gave a sympathetic nod. He knew he couldn't agree, nor could he mention his anger that the recent cutbacks to the force were causing higher crime figures and casualties. 'And are we sure it was Neville who took the bullet?' Banham asked.

The middle-aged sergeant nodded his head, then turned his dark-ringed brown eyes to Banham. He looked exhausted and desperate. 'Nevs took a bullet, that's definite.' He scratched his ear to compose himself, then shook his greying hair as he explained. 'The shot came out of nowhere. He went flying. I didn't see it, I was at the end of the road with the burning car, but that's what I'm told.' He wrinkled his forehead. Banham could see he was upset. 'A few of the boys rushed to his aid when it happened.' He shook his head again. 'But they got held back by the crowds that surrounded them. Neville was then dragged,' he paused again, then carried on, still shaking his head, 'bleeding, into the warehouse, apparently with a couple of others, maybe three others, no one is sure. Possibly Hannah, PC Hannah Kemp, but no one is sure. We're looking for her now. That's what's wrong. We can't keep together with all this going on. It's impossible. I've tried taking a roll call, but so many of us are back and forth. You can't say where anyone is.'

Out of nowhere a bottle flew through the air in their direction. Spedding, Crowther, and Banham all swiftly ducked to avoid it. Crowther turned to look in the direction it came, but it was impossible to be sure who had hurled it.

'Leave it,' Banham told him.

'Sorry not to be more specific, sir, but I just can't swear to anything,' Spedding said.

'Did anyone get a look at who took the hostages?' Crowther asked.

'No, sir, I had my eyes on the burning car, and I turned when I heard a gun firing. I hurried over, but I only caught the back of them. It all just happened so quick. I feel terrible but I can't have eyes in the back of my head. We've all been here all night. There's been fireworks going off all over the shop, so I wasn't even convinced it was gunfire at first. Jeans, tall, two of them, dark hair under hoods, and that's all I can tell you.'

'How long ago?' This was Crowther again.

'Couldn't say for sure. I've lost track of time,' he shrugged. 'An hour, maybe. My men have been here all night. They're flagging. We really need the army and those hoses. We requested them, but there's so much bloody red tape, it'll be next week till they appear. We are short of men and out of our depth.'

'I'll see if I can track down any CCTV,' Crowther said.

'You'll be lucky,' Spedding said. 'Some of my lot are just clearing the screens now. We have some, but other cameras were sprayed or masked over.'

Banham patted the man on the side of the arm. 'Your team are doing a great job,' he said. 'The crowds are dispersing now, and that's all down to you,' he told him gently.

'That's since the SC019 team arrived, but look at all the shopfronts that have been broken into, the looting is totally out of control. We were losing our grip. There's plenty been taken from those shops.'

'That'll get sorted when we collect the video footage that's there,' Banham assured him. 'We'll get footage from a mile around, and we'll get them, every single one. First things first though, and that's the hostages.' He put a reassuring hand on Spedding's shoulder. 'Finish clearing the streets as quickly as you can, mate, we need to get Martin Neville out of there and to hospital, and I can't let SC019 do anything with civilians about. I won't risk any more casualties. We have to have the streets cleared first.'

'They won't budge. We need more officers,' Spedding snapped back, shaking his tired head. 'If we've any chance of staying on top of all this and clearing these streets, we need more officers.' He raised his voice, trying to fight his anger. 'Our boys are going down like skittles. Pelted at, and kicked. We've so many injured. All very well to say, *clear the streets,* sir,' his voice had gone up in pitch again, 'but we've been trying to do that for the last ten hours.'

Banham nodded and lifted a hand defensively and apologetically. 'I agree, and I totally understand, and anyone who has committed a crime here, against our team or whoever, we will get them. I give you my word.' He turned back to Crowther. 'Check any available CCTV, try inside the shops, and organise more videos, from us, not the press. I want everyone that's left here on camera. We need clear facial images. Get someone to make a note of every CCTV camera, and every photograph taken for three miles around, get the film out, include the CCTV on all night buses, all routes coming and going up to three miles from here, for all last night. Look for anyone carrying stolen goods.'

'Guv.'

'Then phone the control room, and tell them to stay glued to every monitor photographing this area, and keep every piece of film they have from last night. I want every bit of it gone through piece by piece, no stone unturned.'

'Guv.'

'Get a good exhibits officer here, ASAP, one who can long-lens inside a window. And I want more ambulances standing by, and as many meat vans as I can have. Tell them to park round the corner, just in case any other clever bastards want to try their hand at setting fire to our vehicles.'

'Guv.'

Banham turned back to Spedding. 'I'll get onto the super,' he told him. 'I'll request she urgently chases the Home Office for the hoses, and gets an OK for the army to stand by to come in. If these hangers-on won't leave the area, they can have a soaking, and then a day in a cell. Neville is the priority right now, and any other hostages in there, we need to get them out. So we have to move on getting these streets cleared.' He turned again to Crowther, 'I'm handing that to you. Arrest anyone who doesn't move when told.' He looked around at the defiant faces, all standing in huddles or their gangs. There were, he reckoned, still a hundred or so left. He knew he could rely on Crowther to move in fast and clear or arrest, as clearly as he knew Spedding was all in. He spoke gently to the sergeant, 'Go home, mate, you're all done in.'

'I'm not leaving my mates,' came the sharp reply.

Banham didn't argue. 'Keep on to the super,' he told Crowther. 'Tell her we need the hoses and maybe the army. Anyone even stamps a foot from now on, arrest them, throw them in a meat van.'

He turned and headed off toward the warehouse.

'Bloody cutbacks,' Crowther said, talking half to himself. 'How would those Westminster bastards like to be standing out here without enough vehicles, protective armour, or manpower. I bet they're all dining in the sodding Savoy as we speak.' He patted Spedding on the back, 'Good work,' he told the tired and sad-looking sergeant.

'You've done a great job.' Then he walked off, following Banham, and clocking the SCO19 unit who were stretched out on their fronts across the roofs, rifles at the ready and pointing at the door of the warehouse.

Crowther was on his mobile already, moving on his orders. His eyes scanned the crowds as he spoke, checking for anyone who might have a weapon in hand.

Chapter Three

Alison had the boot of the Mercedes open, staring at her honeymoon case. She had handed Madeleine over to Lottie, who had also been given the task of letting the guests know what was going on and organising the chaos that would follow. Alison was now free to make a quick change from the itchy dress into her jeans and then follow her team to help with the PC who had been shot. As she reached in to open her case, her phone rang, and Banham's name appeared across her screen.

'Darling, I fear this is neither going to be swift nor straightforward,' he told her. 'So you get on the plane, and as soon as I'm done here, I will get the next flight and join you.'

'No, don't be silly, I'm on my way to you—'

He spoke over her. 'You've got loads of sun cream, haven't you? Only we know with your pale skin that you . . .'

'Banny, I'm getting changed, and I'm coming over there to help. We can go together when this is done.'

'No. Don't do that. The flight is booked. You're booked out at work, for a holiday. You need a holiday. So go. I'll get there as soon as I can.'

'No. I'd rather come over and help, and then we'll go—'

'I said no.' His tone had hardened, then it softened again. 'Darling, I know you are my wife,' he quickly corrected himself, 'or will be, but this is work, and without wishing to rub your face in it, I am your superior officer. So I make the decisions. I don't need you here. It's dangerous. I'm here because I'm the only one free in the whole of London with hostage negotiation training. I have to be here. You don't. You need a holiday. And I'd rather know you are safe in Greece.'

'No, Banny, I—'

'It's not up for negotiation, Alison.' He paused and then said in a softer tone, 'Darling, I'm up to my neck here. I haven't got time to argue. I'll see you in Greece. That's an order.'

He hung up.

Her cheeks were burning with anger as she snapped her phone shut. How dare he speak to her like that. He had told her, *it was dangerous*. She was a murder detective, her job *was dangerous*. And he had said, *no arguments,* she was to go to Greece alone. He spoke as if she was his property, and with no respect for the fact that she was a detective inspector. Or the fact that Lorraine Cory, the detective superintendent and Banham's boss, had put out an urgent call for anybody who could help, that manpower was desperately needed in this perilous hostage situation. Banham had ignored all that, just reminded her to be careful with her pale skin in the sun. How condescending could he get? What did he think she was, a sodding Barbie doll?

She was feeling pretty relieved that she hadn't gone through with a ridiculous ceremony in that ridiculous dress. She was angry, very angry. She had already been doubting her decision about marriage, but now she felt very sure. She wasn't the marrying type. This situation had saved her. It had saved her from hurting him, and also from telling little Madeleine that she couldn't be a fairy princess for a day. She had at least fulfilled that promise, and Maddie would still be carousing around in a pink frilly world of her own, off to spend the afternoon in the restaurant showing off her look.

She grabbed her jeans and sweatshirt from her case and headed speedily to the toilets of the town hall. There, she pulled off the itchy net and satin number, threw the ridiculous twinkly tiara and the unspeakable shoes into a plastic carrier, and slid into her comfy jeans and sweatshirt. She would have been ready to head for Mykonos, leaving her guests to enjoy the slap-up Italian meal with champagne – except she wasn't heading off to Mykonos. Oh no siree, she had other ideas. She wouldn't be Detective Inspector Alison Grainger if she kowtowed to Banham's bossiness. He was her senior officer, yes, but they were short of manpower down there, and the super had made a plea for all available officers to help. That request came from above Banham's head. Besides, an officer and friend had been shot and taken hostage, what kind of a colleague would sod off to Mykonos and abandon him? What kind of a person did Banham think she was? Christ, he could be a bossy bastard. Well, it wasn't going to wash with her. If he got away with it now, she would never be able to stand up to him. And that wasn't Alison Grainger.

She walked back to the car, threw the carrier bag in the boot, grabbed her shoulder bag, then hailed a passing cab.

Banham was standing adjacent to the warehouse. All seemed very quiet inside, but then he became aware of a shadow at the one small window in the front. He moved a little nearer, and noticed the shadow move back as he approached. So someone was watching the goings-on outside. He looked up; there was a long expanse of roof with a closed hatch door. Banham was sure Jim Carter would have clocked that as a means of entrance into the building.

He walked back to Carter, who was standing on the opposite side of the road. Banham was aware he was being watched and listened to by the hostage-takers, so he kept his voice down.

'What do you think?' he asked Carter, indicating with his eyes to the hatch.

'Risky,' Carter told him. 'If we went in from there, it would be one man at a time, and we don't know what's underneath. I'd like to find out the layout first, and weigh up our options. Too risky at the moment is my answer.'

Banham nodded. 'And we're still waiting to clear the rest of these crowds,' he said, looking to his left, where youths huddled in groups studying the police presence. Others had started making their way out of the area, some clutching their stolen items. He knew there weren't enough uniformed police at the moment to deal with it, so he checked the pilferers were all in CCTV range, which they were. If the CCTV was working. He recognised lots of the youths from local gangs. He made a mental note to make sure they got arrested at a later time, he just had to hope he had the CCTV evidence. Right now he needed to get Neville out, which he couldn't do till these thugs were out of the way.

Banham thought about starting to negotiate, finding out who was in there, who had shot his colleague, and indeed what they wanted. He wouldn't risk any shooting with so many bystanders around, regardless of Carter suggesting they shoot their way in.

He was very aware, too, that there were press and television cameras around, obviously having been tipped off, and now busy filming the goings-on. He decided not to stop them; he could confiscate their evidence later, and perhaps it would come in handy for future arrests.

He pulled his mobile from his pocket and called Superintendent Cory's mobile.

He ignored her first question: why wasn't he lying on a beach, sipping cocktails and rubbing sun oil into his new wife? Before he could answer her, she reminded him that she hadn't asked him to give up his marriage vows and take this on, she had put out urgent calls for anyone else with negotiation training.

He updated her on the situation. 'At least one hostage is a police officer. It's a matter of urgency. What's the hold-up on the hoses? We need to clear the streets. Police are getting shot because we are understaffed,' he added bitterly. 'What the fuck is the Home Office doing to help us?'

'Calm it, Banham,' Cory told him. 'I'm doing everything I can here to back you up. Saturday is always a difficult day to get things done at Westminster.'

Banham clicked his phone off before he said something he might regret. He then turned his attention back to the warehouse, and was again aware of the figure behind the window watching.

He signalled to Crowther to join him, then handed him the loudhailer. 'We're being watched,' he said in a lowered voice. 'Keep their attention on you.' He indicated to Jim Carter to join him in walking round the alley at the side and back of the warehouse to check possible access.

Crowther clocked the figure just behind the window, then turned in the direction of the youths who were still hovering at the end of the street and lifted the loudhailer to his mouth.

'Party's over,' he told them. 'This is now a major crime scene. You need to clear the area. A policeman has been shot. If you look over your heads you'll see a gun unit with their weapons pointed. You are being ordered to leave. Anyone not off the streets in the next ten minutes will be arrested and charged with obstructing a police investigation. If you are carrying a weapon, I suggest you drop it. There is a team of stop and search officers moving into place. If you are carrying, you will be facing a custodial sentence.'

'Fuck you,' a voice from the crowd shouted out, as an egg was hurled from the back of a large gang. Crowther saw it, and ducked quickly. He lifted his hailer to gain control, but before he could open his mouth to speak another egg came flying. This one hit him on the back of his head, cracking against his freshly cut and gelled hair before dripping its sticky yellow innards down the back of his neck and onto the collar of his hired suit.

Banham had turned back to listen when the heckling started. He caught sight of the egg running down the back of his colleague's head. If the situation hadn't been so serious, he would have found it amusing. Crowther had, for one of the few times in his life, looked half reasonable that morning, but not now. He pulled a handkerchief from his pocket and walked back to hand it to Crowther. At the same time he nodded a go ahead to Carter, who nodded to his gun team on the roof. One immediately fired a shot in the air.

'That was a warning,' Banham shouted to the youths, some of whom were now attacking the two PCs who had bravely marched into the midst of the crowd and attempted to arrest the egg-thrower. More PCs then rushed in to help, and a brawl started as more youths jumped on the officers.

Banham nodded again, and more shots were fired into the air. Some youths immediately scattered, others carried on fighting.

Within seconds a meat van roared towards the brawling gang, stopping inches from the fight. Uniformed police, decked in helmets and face shields, jumped out quickly, helping to wrestle the egg-thrower and his mates into the van. It took two of them to hold the first youth's hands behind his back, cuffing him, then lifting and nearly throwing him as he cursed, spat, and kicked out, onto the seat at the rear of the police van. Meanwhile, more uniformed PCs struggled with the other offenders. Once in charge, they turned the youths round, cuffed them, and pushed them, too, into the back of the van. Banham and Crowther watched and waited until the officers had control, and then Crowther spoke sharply again to the crowd.

'If you don't want to end up in front of a magistrate, then clear the streets and go home, now. NOW!' he roared at the remaining, defiant youths.

Banham watched as the arrested youths were driven off in the police wagon. He was pleased that the press were filming and could see the police were taking control. He was also relieved to see that Crowther was doing a good job: the man was tiny, but his authoritative voice had worked, the streets were now clearing and all was calming down. Banham beckoned again, with a jerk of his head, to Carter to walk with him round the back of the warehouse.

As they stepped into the alleyway at the side of the warehouse, a lit firework shot into the air. It seemed to come from nowhere, but had obviously been thrown by a remaining youth. It quickly fell to the concrete ground, fizzing and spitting, and spurting smoke and coloured flames like a dragon's mouth. One of the police horses, only a few feet away, immediately took fright, rearing up in the air in fear and then making to bolt.

Again, uniformed PCs who had caught sight of the culprit ran at him. After a struggle they arrested him, while other officers bravely jumped on the firework and the bolting horse was stilled, its mounted PC calming and stroking the horse's sweat-soaked neck. More ambulances and police wagons, shrieking their emergencies, sped from all directions and turned into Henry Street.

Banham had used the distraction of the firework to get round the back of the building. He was aware someone inside the warehouse would be watching the goings-on in the street. He noted the door at the back of the warehouse, a large double door locked with thick bars. 'It would take a few seconds to crack those bolts,' he said quietly to Carter, 'by that time any of the hostages could get shot.' He rubbed his hand over his mouth thoughtfully and then said, 'I'm going to try to negotiate. I can't risk your boys breaking in. Not with unknown hostages, and one wounded. Let's try and get Neville out first.'

'The blood trail looked serious,' Carter said. 'We need to get him out pronto.'

Banham turned and walked back to the front of the building. He was again aware of a figure, a tall man with dark hair, and now he could see the man was holding a rifle and standing not far from the front of the window.

He walked into the middle of the road, then up and down the trail of blood. Every now and again he flicked his eyes upwards, aware the figure in the window was watching him.

It was damp, cold, and drizzling in the autumn air, but the blood trail was clear. It started on the corner of the road at the other end of Henry Street and led to the warehouse. Carter was right, Neville had lost a lot of blood. Banham looked at his watch. It was now 11.30. The emergency call had gone out at 10.30, so it was just over an hour since Neville had been shot. He looked up, glad to see the road was finally clearing. He would wait just a few more minutes. He knew Carter was hot-headed, and keen to get in there, but this was Banham's call. He was more careful.

His hand automatically moved to cover his mouth, his habitual gesture when concentrating. He studied the warehouse again, thinking of the possibilities with its entrances and exits. No sign of the man in the window now, he noted. How was best to handle this? Carter was the SC019 sergeant, but Banham was Senior Investigating Officer. Carter wanted to go in all guns blazing. His argument to take the risk was solid, an officer's life could be in danger. But Banham wasn't a man to take chances. He wanted to find out how many hostages were in there, and if any others were hurt, and if they were police officers. He also needed to know who the hostage-takers were and why they had done what they did.

There were plenty of officers around to help with arrests, but none were armed. In some ways that was good, in other ways not so good, because they were mainly exhausted officers who wouldn't leave their colleague, and tired officers made mistakes, Banham thought. No one could blame them if they did. It was the fault of cuts, and the rise in crime, especially gang crime. He was also very sure that this story was going to make the headlines on every national TV channel within the next few hours. Something else he had to stamp on before it got out of hand – but for now he would just leave them to their jobs. They could tell this story, and let the public see how cutting back on police budgets was reckless, dangerous, and unnecessary.

This was a very tricky situation, and he had to handle it very carefully and everyone involved. Tempers were short, opinions were thrust on him, but at the end of the day he was the officer who would carry the can. Neither Mykonos nor marriage to Alison would happen for him today, that was the only thing he was sure of now. Perhaps it was fate, perhaps Diane was telling him something. But, then again, there was no question he loved Alison, and had wanted to marry her for a long time, so why was he doubting that decision now?

He put that to the back of his mind, and walked over to the warehouse. He took the hailer from Crowther, lifted it to his mouth, then changed his mind. He pulled his phone from his pocket and called Alison.

Chapter Four

PC Peter Byfield was exhausted, but seriously worried. These riots had been going on for hours. They had all come on duty at one o'clock yesterday afternoon, and been called out to the riots at the end of their shift, at about eleven o'clock last night. They should have been clocking off by midnight, but because the riots had been so intense, his team had been asked to stay on and do overtime, or even a double shift, to help out with the shortage of manpower that would be needed to get the growing rioting under control.

The extra money had been a great incentive. He was buying a house with Hannah, it was all going through any moment. All the extra things buying a house included had drained their bank balances already. Then there was the budget for the wedding. They were having a big do and a dream honeymoon in the Seychelles, most of which was saved and paid for, but spending money was still needed. They didn't want to cut corners, so all overtime was welcome. Hannah was usually partnered with PC Martin Neville, but as Peter had rushed out from the station on his first shift, with PC Shaun Levington, his usual partner, he hadn't seen who Hannah was with. He only knew she was on this shift.

At first the police had been in control of the riots, but then more youths had started coming in, and when shops were broken into and the pilfering started, things had become chaotic, with the second shift of officers rushing down to the scene while the first shift were still working there. Even with two teams, they struggled – then the rioters increased in number as word spread, and more pilferers arrived for the pickings. Backup was then called from all nearby stations and police were everywhere. The dog patrol came in, as did the mounted police, but mayhem continued. There had been no time for police recs, nor their meal break, so he hadn't linked up with Hannah. He had been at a different point of the riots to her, and wasn't sure where she was. He had seen her briefly, around midnight. She had been with a bunch of other PCs then, making a line on the corner, to stop a crowd breaking through to the open shops. He had been with Shaun Levington and some other PCs, pushing back a gang who were trying to get into the street where the broken shop windows were. Both he and Hannah had had their minds on their jobs, and he had made no conversation with her.

He hadn't seen her since. He hadn't had a second to ring her either with all that was happening. Now that there were less youths around, and he could grab a second, he had made a quick call. Her phone had gone to voicemail, but that was normal when she was working. What was more concerning was he had heard that one of the hostages was a PC who had taken a bullet, and everyone believed it was her working partner, Martin Neville. After searching all the streets where the riots were happening, and everyone he asked saying they last saw her with Nevs, he was now growing anxious that she had been taken hostage too, or worse, that she may be injured. Byfield knew DCI Banham was very approachable, so when he spotted the DCI outside the warehouse he hurried up to him.

'Excuse me, sir, and sorry to bother you.' He swallowed, and had to make an effort to keep himself calm. 'I can't find Hannah, PC Hannah Kemp.'

Banham looked round. He immediately read the concern on Byfield's face, and noted the desperation in the young man's voice. He knew that feeling of fear. It hit a nerve with him, but he didn't let it show. He kept his professional front. 'Are you saying you think she may be one of the hostages?'

'She's always partnered with Martin Neville, sir,' Byfield answered quickly.

Banham nodded, then put a reassuring but firm hand on the

young man's shoulder. 'I'll see what I can find out,' he said, studying the man's frightened face. 'You look all in, Peter. No good asking you to go home, I suppose.'

'No, sir, not without Hannah. She's my fiancée.'

'Yes, I know that. Well, we've not been here long, so I don't know much myself as yet. Go and sit in a car and take a break. I'll see what I can find out and keep you informed.'

'Sir, I'd rather not,' Byfield almost snapped. 'I'm going to keep looking for her. No one's seen her, and all those sodding petrol bombs . . . She could be unconscious somewhere. I'll keep looking, but you will let me know when you know something, won't you, sir?'

'Yes, for sure.' Banham took a beat while he studied the man, then he said, 'See if you can round up half a dozen of the team and go and search all the side streets and anywhere else she might be, then report back to me.'

'Sir.'

Banham watched the young PC walk away. He needed him as far away from the warehouse as possible. Understandably, the man wouldn't behave calmly or professionally if Hannah was inside. And Banham understood exactly how the man felt. The night Diane was murdered, he had been about the same age as Byfield, and would have thrown his career away in an instant had he set eyes on the man who killed her. And if he'd had a gun, there would have been no question, he would have killed the bastard there and then. His mind again flashed back to when he found Diane, butchered, her arm chopped and hanging from the elbow as she had obviously reached out protectively towards Elizabeth, who too had been butchered, in her tiny yellow teddy-covered Baby-gro. How must she have felt? How his little girl would have screamed, and for the millionth time, he wondered which one saw the other one die first.

He took a beat to calm himself, then put the hailer back to his mouth.

'My name is Paul Banham. Can I ask who you are, and who is in there with you?

*

The watcher was standing, his body flattened against the wall, beside the window, watching the comings and goings outside. He was holding an AK-47 rifle and listening to Sergeant Crowther barking orders. Every now and then he flicked a glance at the other hostage-taker, who was leaning against a post on the other side of the large warehouse, another AK in his hands, a pistol protruding from his waistband and a knife in the ankle of his boot. This man's dark and perilous eyes were flicking from one of his prisoners to the next, checking that all five of them were still and quiet.

Hannah Kemp had noticed his eyes, and even though the hood of his sweatshirt covered most of his face, she could read the evil in them. She was instinctive about eyes, and always read character from them. She had only been fully qualified a year, and on the streets for a year before that as a probationary officer, but eyes were ever the first thing she noted. This man, referred to by the other as Sadiq, sent a shiver down her spine just looking at him. Her instincts told her he wouldn't hesitate to hurt anyone who got in his way. She always knew her job would be dangerous, but she had never expected to feel the terror she felt at this moment.

She was kneeling, as told, on the cold concrete floor of the large warehouse. She would remember all she could, that was another thing she had taken on board on her training, observe and remember when there was no chance to write anything down. One of these men had shot her partner and best friend, Martin Neville, and she sure as hell was going to make him pay for it. Nevs lay beside her on the filthy floor, groaning in pain as he fell in and out of consciousness. She had torn her blouse in two to use as a tourniquet as soon as they were pushed into the warehouse, and now sat in her white cotton vest with her dark uniform jacket over it. She pressed the tourniquet tightly to staunch the bleeding wound in Martin's abdomen. She was concerned and frightened for his welfare, but was doing all she could to help stop the pumping blood. He needed medical help and it was up to her to talk her way into getting him out of this place and into an ambulance. She was relieved that she had nearly stemmed the flow of blood, but nearly wasn't enough, she knew that.

Hannah held his hand with her free hand, to keep him awake and talking. He mustn't lose consciousness permanently. They had covered hostage-taking in her training at Hendon, and raids and riots, but her memory of that training seemed to have disappeared and been taken over by the desperate panic that her partner and close friend might be dying in front of her. She watched his eyelids repeatedly twitch and willed herself to stay calm so she could help him. He had helped her so much during her time as a PC, and if ever he needed her to return those favours, it was now. She squeezed her lips together to stop herself crying out.

Then DCI Banham's voice came again. 'Can you tell me who you are, and what you want.'

The watcher near the window looked to Sadiq, who shook his head. 'No, Massafur.'

Neither answered.

'You have at least one injured man in there,' Banham spoke with authority and volume. 'We have an ambulance and paramedics here. Can you tell me why you are holding this man?'

Hannah took this as her chance. She looked up at Sadiq. 'Please, please,' she pleaded. 'He urgently needs medical attention. You've got me and three other hostages. You could let him go? If anything—'

'Shut the fuck up,' came the reply from Sadiq, followed by a sharp movement with the edge of his boot, which shoved her hard in her back.

She flinched, making sure her pressure stayed on the tourniquet, but she persisted. 'If anything happens to him, you will be done for murder.' She squeezed Martin's hand again, just in case he could hear. She didn't want to frighten him into knowing his wound was as serious as she suspected it was. But she was terrified something would happen to him, and she intended to do everything in her power to make sure it didn't. The blood hadn't completely eased up, and that was worrying. Time wasn't on her side, she knew that.

'As it stands, if you let him go and get medical help, then things will be a lot easier,' she said. 'I, for one, will say you cooperated . . .'

This time Sadiq kicked her harder, again in her back.

'I told you to shut the fuck up,' he spat at her.

She took an intake of breath and then felt Martin's little finger against hers. She hadn't imagined it, he was trying to tell her he could hear, and warn her to be careful. He always gave her the benefit of his many years of experience as a PC. She had been assigned to him as a probationary officer for this reason, and had requested to stay with him as her partner when she was qualified. She squeezed his hand back, very gently, and bit even harder on her lip. She couldn't let him down.

Banham's voice came again. 'I am here to help. I have told you what I want. I want to know who your hostages are and why you are holding them. Will you tell me what you want?'

Sadiq and Massafur made eye contact but neither answered the voice.

Hannah was glad the negotiator was Paul Banham. This gave her reassurance, he had an excellent reputation in hostage situations. He had, many times, got people out without problems or casualties.

She decided she wouldn't push it further. She'd had the warning from Martin, and these men clearly weren't the sort to argue with. She needed to stay with her partner. There were also three civilian hostages on the other side of the room: a very pretty young woman, early twenties at most, who looked to be of Asian origin, an older Asian woman, who was short of teeth and wore a brown shabby scarf over her head, and an older Asian man, who held a handkerchief to his head and was dabbing at a small wound he had received to the top of his forehead, presumably given while he resisted. The girl was tied to the radiator, so she had obviously fought and resisted too, but the other two were sitting untied, Hannah was relieved to notice, though looking very frightened. The man looked to be in his seventies, a sign of the insensitivity and ruthlessness of these hostage-takers. He clearly wasn't well, he looked vague and confused and coughed constantly. Hannah thought she recognised him as a shopkeeper who had come out and started shouting when youths broke the window of his grocery shop, then started pilfering his cigarettes and alcohol.

He was sitting on the floor near the older woman. Hannah wondered if the two women were related. The older woman could have been an old-looking fifties, and the girl could be her daughter. She had been aware of the terror on their faces as she pleaded with Sadiq. Again, she wanted to keep these hostages calm and she knew it would be down to her to get them out of the building safely, if the SC019 decided to invade.

'It's all right,' she said to them in a reassuring tone. 'Try and keep calm, help is around. We'll get you out.'

The older woman raised her voice and spoke in what Hannah recognised as a South Asian accent. She was shaking, and lifted her fist. 'If you make him mad, he will hurt everyone. Why don't you keep quiet, you stupid woman!'

The poor woman was clearly frightened, and Hannah understood why. She had the police training, and knew to show calm, even if she was a quivering mess inside, which she was. She so wished Nevs was well, and beside her helping.

She didn't answer or argue with the woman. She looked over to Massafur. Beads of sweat were rolling down the side of his face as he listened to Banham repeatedly asking the same question about the welfare of the injured man.

This Massafur looked the last thing from assured. That made her more nervous for all their welfare. She had seen many a young man do stupid things in a panic to avoid being arrested, including shooting or stabbing their victims. This man had a rifle under his arm, as well as a small pistol poking out from the back of his jeans. Maybe the woman was right. And what did Hannah know anyway? She had only been in the force two years.

Then Banham's voice came again.

'Hello in there. My name is Paul Banham. Will you talk to me?' His voice was calm and warm. This filled her with confidence. Banham would get them all out safely, even Martin, she assured herself. She just had to stay calm and wait.

Massafur was the one that had dragged her backwards to the warehouse as she leaned over to hold and help Martin when he took the bullet. She knew his first name, she would get the rest of it when she could. They would need his name for evidence later. He had hit her twice when she resisted him grabbing her. Assault on a police officer, for starters. She didn't know which one had shot Martin, she had had her back to them when he was shot, but she would find out and the gunman would pay. She had leaned into Martin after he was shot, and as the bully pulled her from behind she had kicked out at him, receiving blows to her head. He had then grabbed her arms, wrapping them around her back and jerking them agonisingly upwards, as he dragged her into the warehouse. Sadiq had dragged Martin roughly behind her, her partner crying out in pain. She had no idea why, or when, they had taken these other three hostages, but obviously they wanted more than just her and Nevs, so there must be a reason, something they wanted, something worth negotiating for? They were aware that Martin wasn't in a good way, she knew that, and yet they were paying little notice. Massafur was nervous, that was for sure, but not enough to help the man stay alive. So killing came easily to him, did it? She trembled at that thought.

The men still ignored Banham's voice, meaning they were not ready to negotiate. But Martin had to be in hospital. She had to help him get there.

She told herself to think straight. She weighed up the idea of taking on her police role and telling them to answer the DCI, warning them that the shooting of an officer of the law carried a very heavy sentence, and if they didn't want to be in more trouble, then her advice was to answer Banham and release Neville immediately. She had tried half-heartedly and it hadn't worked before but she had a rush of confidence now she knew Banham was doing a great job. However, these men had shot one officer, and they were holding rifles now, so maybe speaking up again wasn't such a good plan.

All her training had gone out the window now. And seeing these brutes with AKs in their hands, and her colleague lying on a disgustingly dirty floor, floating in and out of consciousness with blood still coming through her makeshift tourniquet and drying on her fingers, was terrifying her. Earlier, as she was dragged into the warehouse and thrown on the floor, Sadiq had told her any false move and he would rape her in front of everyone. She hadn't taken that in, but now she believed that he would, he was brutal enough. She wasn't risking that happening. She was getting married in a few weeks. What would that do to her fiancé? Poor Peter. He was also somewhere out there on this riot duty, and probably desperately looking for her at this moment . . .

She had to dismiss that from her mind too. Peter was safe. He was out there on the streets, with his colleagues to back him. Martin was here, and needed her if he was to survive. So for his sake, she had to hold this together. It was down to her to get herself, Martin, and the other three hostages to safety. DCI Banham was outside. With him on board, it was just a matter of time, she told herself. However, these men hadn't answered Banham, which didn't bode well. It meant SC019 would get involved and that meant a shoot-out.

Martin's coughing took her attention. She looked down to see fresh blood leak over her hand. The tourniquet was now soaked in it, and even more alarming, blood was leaking from his mouth. Jesus, this was a haemorrhage. She quickly put more pressure on the half-blouse she had tied around him. The shirt was already dark red with blood, and more was coming quickly. Her hands were really shaking now, one of them sliding in his blood, but she managed to fasten the blouse into a tighter knot around his abdomen, which did the trick and stemmed the flow. But for how long, she wondered as she bit hard again into her lip to stop herself crying out. She tasted her own blood. Then she noticed Sadiq watching her. She looked back pleadingly at him. He turned and looked the other way. The other hostages too all looked away.

'Martin, don't go to sleep. Stay with me,' she whispered, turning back to her friend and giving him a slight shake to try to keep him from slipping into unconsciousness. But his eyes didn't flicker open this time. She patted his cheek. His eyes half-opened with that, then closed again.

'Jesus,' she muttered, telling herself to stay calm, but her good intentions flew out of the window, and she shrieked, 'Please, please, help him. He needs a doctor. You need to let him go!'

Massafur looked over to his friend, momentarily concerned, and Sadiq looked back. She sensed their dilemma and quickly persisted.

'You've got me, and three other hostages. Better for you if you let him go.' She raised her voice. 'You've still got four of us to barter with for whatever it is you want. Please, you have to get him to a hospital!'

'Why don't you keep it buttoned,' the older female hostage shouted at her. 'You are making them mad, this is worse for all of us.'

'Because he could die,' Hannah shouted back, desperately choking back her emotion. She turned back to Massafur. 'Please, don't let this happen,' she pleaded.

Massafur shrugged dismissively. 'I want Devlin McCaub,' he said.

The young female hostage let out a gasp. The older woman turned to the girl and told her too, to hush up.

Hannah had heard the name Devlin McCaub, but with her head fuzzy and confused, she couldn't place where.

'Tell the detective outside,' Hannah told Massafur urgently. 'Tell him you want Devlin McCaub, and you'll swap the injured policeman for Devlin McCaub.' She wracked her brains again, but couldn't place the name. She just hoped the force could, and if they could find him, Martin could get to hospital and get the help he desperately needed.

Massafur still stood there. He said and did nothing.

'Tell him,' she yelled again, as both the older woman and the younger woman urged her to pipe down and keep quiet. 'Tell him, the injured policeman can go if you get Devlin McCaub.' Before she had time to think what she was doing, she had jumped to her feet, and ran towards the window, shouting to Banham. 'Sir, sir, they want Devlin McCaub. PC Neville needs a—'

She got no further than those words as a large sweaty hand covered her mouth and gripped her face, squeezing tightly and dragging her backwards. A knee clamped into her back, then she was thrown so her head hit the cold, damp, concrete wall. Blows followed. Her head was repeatedly banged back and forth into the wall. She didn't scream out, she didn't want to alarm the other hostages, so she took the blows and hoped they weren't going to knock her out. Martin needed her to keep pressure on his wound or he would bleed out. Those thoughts kept her strong. The hand gripped her face again, making it impossible for her to speak or scream. The other hand pulled her hair back. He then pushed against her from behind her, pressing himself hard into her.

'You want me to rape you?' Sadiq asked, releasing his grip on her face and then landing her another hard slap on the back of her head.

She felt sick and giddy.

'No, no, I'm sorry,' she said unsteadily, wishing she had the strength to bring her knee up sharply and bruise both his manhood and his pride in one hard swoop.

'You are a whore,' he spat at her, pulling at the back of her trousers.

A shiver went through her whole being at the thought of what he might do to her.

'Leave her alone,' the young female hostage piped up. 'Why don't you leave her alone? She hasn't done anything.'

Sadiq spun around. 'You shut up. One more word out of you, and I'll cut your tongue so you never speak again, got it?

'Where are we, why are we here?' the older man broke in, and shouted out. He was getting more and more distressed. 'My head hurts. I don't know where I am. I need my pills.'

The young woman became silent. The older woman had turned to the man and was telling him too to keep quiet. Sadiq turned back to Hannah. He grabbed her arm and dragged her back over to Martin Neville. He then threw her down on the ground. 'Tend to your fed friend, and shut your fucking mouth, or I will rape you in front of your dying friend.'

She hit the ground hard, and cried out with the pain. Sadiq spat at her. 'English whore,' he said as he turned his back on her.

She reminded herself she was an officer of the law, and he would pay for this. There were hostages, and her dear friend and colleague needed her to keep this together. She wasn't going to let them down. Besides, Banham was outside. He was going to get them out very soon.

'It's OK,' she said to the terrified hostages across the room, hiding her own pain and fear. 'Really. It will be OK.' She promised herself she would think before she did anything stupid again, and risk anybody's safety.

'I need my pills,' the older man shouted aggressively.

'Oh, you shut up,' the older woman told him, shrugging and turning away from him as he put his hand to his head and started to moan loudly. 'Just shut up. That is the least of our problems.'

'Try and stay calm. You'll all be out of here soon,' Hannah told them.' Then she turned back to Martin, and lifted his hand. It was cold.

Chapter Five

Detective Chief Superintendent Lorraine Cory was a tall, well-built woman with a short nose and a full mouth. Her hair was grey-brown in colour and cut into a sharp, short, tapered bob, with thick bleached streaks at the front that fell like a curtain around her wide face. Her intense brown eyes, along with her olive skin, gave away the fact that she had never been a natural blonde. She was smartly dressed in grey tailored trousers and a tan silk blouse. Her hands were large, with the long, lithe body of a tiger tattooed on the base of her right thumb, half-screened by the wide silver ring adorned with a whale that she wore over it. She was a tough, no-nonsense policewoman, well-respected, very sharp, and extremely good at her job. She had worked hard to get where she was in the force. No matter what anyone said, she was evidence that being a woman was against you when climbing from one detective position up to the next. She had been rejected for each position more than once, but hadn't given up. She had kept on trying and applying, and now had arrived, and was in a position where she called the shots and kow-towed to no one. Having personally experienced sexism in the force, she was sensitive to the female officers and the struggles they faced.

When Alison Grainger knocked on her office door and walked in, Lorraine lifted her eyebrows and offered a half-smile. 'Not flying off to the sun then?' was all she said, before dropping her gaze back to her paperwork, acting as if she wasn't surprised or interested in Alison turning up at the station when she was supposed to be heading for Greece.

'Lorraine,' Alison was slightly hesitant. 'Sorry, ma'am.'

'Oh, get over yourself.' Lorraine looked up. 'I've told you a million times, it's Lorraine, or Lorry, when we are one to one, it's only ma'am in front of the team.'

Alison smiled, feeling a little more at ease. 'Sorry. Lorraine. Look I'll come straight to the point. I need you to put me on the hostage situ. I don't want to go on honeymoon.'

Lorraine looked up. 'Or do as you're told, by the sound of things,' she said, her face giving nothing away. She leaned her elbow on her desk, and then her chin on top of her fingers, and again raised her eyebrows at Alison. 'Go on. Tell me all.'

'You asked for all available officers,' Alison pushed. 'I am available. I want to help with the hostage situation. I hear Martin Neville has been shot and is being held hostage. He's a good friend. I want permission to cancel my leave and get down there and help.'

Lorraine pushed her fingers through the bleached layer of her hair to stop it falling over her face as she looked at Alison. Now she became serious. 'It's been a terrible night,' she said. 'We've got police wounded all over the shop and, as yet, we don't know who exactly has been taken hostage. We can't do a roll call as everyone is spread all over the area. So, yes, I could do with all the help I can get down there.' Her fingers went back to her hair and repeated flicking the bleached layer from her face.

'Banham has told me I can't give up my leave and go and help. He is doing the superior officer bit,' Alison told her. 'He has ordered me to go on honeymoon, on my own.'

Lorraine frowned, then her face broke into a grin. 'Not a good start to a marriage, I'd say,' she said lightly.

'We aren't married.'

'No, I heard.' She looked down at her notes, then back up to Alison. 'Well I'm afraid, and I'm sorry too, but I can't go over his authority. It's Banham's case now. I have appointed him senior investigating officer on it. He is a trained hostage negotiator. He offered to help, and I had no one else. I would never have broken your marriage ceremony up otherwise.'

'I'm glad you did,' Alison said flatly, turning and staring out the window.

There was a few seconds when no one spoke, but Alison knew Lorraine was watching her and had taken the situation in. Lorraine was a feminist, fully aware how hard a place the force was for women. She always took their side.

'Lucky it's me sitting here, then, and not Chief Constable Mathew Glen,' Lorraine said as Alison turned back to see the super half smile and raise her eyebrows. 'As I said, Banham is now SIO on this, so I can't, and won't, go over his head and get you out on the front line. But I am still in charge here – so would you settle for working the case with me, from here in the investigation room? We're short in there too. Every available officer has come in, but we're still skeleton-staffed. We could do with your help to interview and charge as the arrested offenders are brought in. And they will need a liaison officer here to check anything they send over, and run names through the computer. They don't have to know it's you. Sergeant Seward will take any details and pass them on. Your job will be to do all the backing-up that they need from down there on the location. I've personally been on to the Home Office and I have just got permission to put the army on standby, and I'm waiting for permission to get the water hoses out there. We've had home-made petrol bombs going off. It's been pure hell all bloody night, and now we've got this hostage situation, and the big worry now is how badly our Neville has been shot, and if we have any others of ours in there as hostages. Peter Byfield has reported not being able to find Hannah Kemp. Her radio isn't picking up, and he is beside himself. So we need all the manpower that we can get in here. There are many arrests and I'd be very grateful for your help in interviewing them. The arrested may have seen something, they were all down there at the time of the shooting and they could be key witnesses, so all of them will need to be interviewed in depth.'

'Yes, I'd love to.' Alison had the smile back in her voice. 'So my leave is cancelled?'

'Certainly is. Call it an emergency request to all available officers.'

'Thank you.' Alison was smiling fully now.

'And it's on the condition we don't tell Banny you're here till this is over. Then you can fly off into the sunset together. How does that sound?'

'Not sure.'

Lorraine raised her eyebrows. 'Oh, my.'

Banham had heard a female voice shouting from the inside of the warehouse building. He clocked immediately that she had shouted *'Sir'*. That had confirmed to him that it was definitely a PC. He turned to Crowther as the DS walked up to him. 'There's a female PC in there,' he said. 'She called to me, called me sir, so as she knows who I am, she's one of us. Would you recognise Hannah Kemp's voice?'

'Probably not, guv, shall I call Byfield over?' Crowther asked him.

'No.' Banham shook his head. 'Not a good idea. He's distressed and will go apeshit. Understandable, but if he does that'll put everyone in there in more danger. Truth is, I'd rather he wasn't here. He's another liability for us, but understandably he won't go until he finds her. And it may not be Hannah.' Banham shook his head. 'No, we say nothing to him, yet.'

'Sir.'

Banham lifted his hailer to his mouth. 'OK. So, I get that you want someone. So now we have a good start. We are open to negotiating. And I can assure you, I will listen to you, but first you need to let our wounded man out of there. It is clear he needs hospital attention. You have other hostages. We have an ambulance standing by. I want that man safely in hospital before we go any further. I give you my word then I will most definitely listen to your request. And if your request is reasonable, then we can negotiate further. We will see how we can find your friend and then we can see about releasing your other hostages. Would you like some water sent in?'

No answer came.

Banham looked around. The streets were now very nearly clear, just the odd few gathered in small groups refusing to go. SCO19 were still in their prime position on the roofs opposite the warehouse. Banham glanced again to the ground, studying the bloodstains on the pavement. He turned to Ainsley Kay, the patient paramedic who was standing beside him. 'How long can we play a waiting game, do you think, judging by these blood stains?'

'We need to get that officer out of there,' Ainsley told him. 'I can't say much for sure, really I can't, sir. I wish I could, but until we see where the wound is it's anyone's guess. Let's not beat around the bush, though, that man's life is definitely at risk.'

Banham turned to Jim Carter, who was now back standing beside him, looking impatient. 'Right, so what are our options?' Banham asked him.

'I'm going to have a good look around again, around the outside of the building at the back, for all possible entrances in,' Carter told him. Before Banham had the chance to tell him he was not allowing SC019 to storm the building and risk the lives of the hostages, Carter had raised his hand and added, 'I share your concern that someone else might get hurt if we storm in, but then what's the alternative if they aren't answering you? There's a man in there who may be bleeding to death. And that man is one of ours. Time is not on our side. I'm not OK with going one at a time through the shutter opening in the roof. That's not a safe option either. My thoughts are we storm in, en masse.'

When Banham didn't answer, Carter turned and headed towards the alley at the side of the building. Crowther glanced at Banham and then followed Carter.

They had only taken two steps when a loud explosion broke the calm. A petrol bomb had landed by a car at the end of the road. The car immediately burst into flames, spitting pieces of glass into the surrounding air, with some of the burning metal and glass landing as far as ten feet away.

Again, some of the police horses who were nearby reared up in fright, and their riders struggled to calm them and stop them bolting. One horse caught the edge of a burning piece of glass in his foreleg. As the rider jumped down to check his animal's leg, a hooded youth came flying at him with a chair leg, smashing into the back of the officer's head. The officer hit the ground, and the horse took off, alone, into the crowd, heading towards the burning car.

Many police quickly sped after the hooded youth and Ainsley Kay ran to help the injured PC. Three mounted officers sped after the lone horse as the animal, hypnotised by the flames of the burning police car, headed straight towards it. A mounted officer just managed to block the horse's way and stop him galloping into the flames, while another officer, who was on foot, grabbed the horse.

It took three unarmed PCs to wrestle the hooded youth to the ground, take the chair leg from him, then cuff his hands behind his back and arrest him. TV crews happily moved in to film the incident.

Banham, Crowther, and Carter had all turned to watch, and all were coughing from the smoke that curled through the air. Aware there were camera crews filming, Carter turned back to Banham. 'If those cameras weren't here and, as we all know, happy to write up a story about police brutality, I would kick that guy so hard in the balls he wouldn't walk straight ever again. Those poor bloody horses.'

'Crowther,' Banham called out to his sergeant. 'Get rid of all the press. Tell them it's a no-go zone, and a crime scene, and we'll release a statement when all is done. I don't want to see sight of one inside the cordons until I give the word. Tell them if they attempt to come back in, we will confiscate their cameras.'

'Sir.'

A fire engine sped into the street. The officers leaped out, grabbed their hoses, and spilled their contents over the flames on the car, quickly putting it out.

As the TV crews withdrew, still filming as they went, Crowther checked all was clear, and there were no lone photographers hiding anywhere, then instructed the fire officers to soak any youths that still remained.

It did the trick: the soaked youths speedily started scattering, swearing and shrieking, and the street became empty except for exhausted police, burnt out vehicles, and broken chairs and other dismantled furniture, plus shards of glass which had spewed everywhere from the broken shop windows, which were now empty of goods and displays.

As the police began cordoning off the area, Banham walked back and stood in front of the used warehouse. He could now get nearer than he had been able to before. The emptied street also allowed the hostage-takers to get clear sights of what the SC019 team were doing. Banham wanted to distract them from seeing Jim Carter, who had slipped around the side of the warehouse, down the alley, and was checking all ways and means of getting into the building.

Banham lifted the loud hailer.

'That explosion was nothing to do with the police,' he told them, addressing the shadow in the window of the warehouse. When no one answered he continued, 'As I said, my name is Paul Banham, and I am very concerned about the welfare of any wounded hostages in there. I know that you want someone. Would you please talk to me and tell me what this is about? We all know at some time we will have to negotiate on what we both want.'

No answer.

'We know there is a police officer among the wounded. And I now know that you want someone in return for this officer, and the hostages. It would be good if you would start to talk to me. Tell me where I can find who you want, and why you have chosen to hold hostages for the reason of getting this person. I am very ready to negotiate, but I do need you to release the wounded man, urgently. Neither of us want this to get any more serious. Tell me this person's name, and where I can find them. I'll get on to it, you have my word, but first you must release my wounded officer. That is a very fair exchange.'

Banham waited, and finally the man behind the window spoke. 'No one goes nowhere till we get Devlin McCaub delivered to this door.'

'Devlin McCaub. Thank you. I'm onto it. But that may take a

while if we have to track him down and find him,' Banham said. 'Time is of an essence here. I'm concerned that this trail of blood looks pretty bad. If you release the wounded in there, now, I give you my word, I will find this McCaub. Do you have an address for him?'

No one answered.

Banham pushed again. 'You will still have others in there, and I believe you have one of my female officers, is that correct?'

'I ain't denying all that.'

'And you have other hostages.'

'Yes.'

'How many?

Silence.

'Are any others wounded?'

'No.'

'That's good. So now we know what we both want. Now, there is an ambulance waiting here, and we can send in water and biscuits if you like. Release, please, the wounded hostage, and tell me where we will find this Devlin McCaub. I would also like to know why you want him badly enough to hold innocent people prisoners in there. And please can you tell me how many others you have in there?'

'No one ain't going nowhere till I see McCaub,' came the reply.

'The wounded man is in a bad state, judging by this blood out here. You will be held responsible if anything happens to him. I'm being reasonable right now, and I will keep my word. Please just let the wounded man out.'

'I told you, no one goes nowhere till we see Devlin McCaub at this door.'

'I'm on it,' came Banham's speedy reply. 'But holding people against their will is a serious offence,' Banham spoke calmly. 'However, holding an injured police officer, whose life is in danger, carries a much heavier sentence. Have you thought of the consequences if anything happens to him? You would be facing a murder charge. Right now, if you release him, you are simply holding a person, or persons, against their will. Much lighter.'

No answer.

'Be sensible, we will find this Devlin McCaub. I give you my word. You have other hostages, so let the wounded officer out, for everyone's sake.'

No answer.

'I'm offering to help you here.'

'Fuck you, I don't need help. Just get McCaub. If you want your man.'

'Will you release him now?'

'Not till I see McCaub.'

Banham took a second, then spoke again, keeping calm but with his voice completely changed to an authoritative tone. 'OK. So here's what you need to know. There is a team of armed police just here, their weapons are aimed directly at you. They are on the roofs all around. You want to take a look?'

No reply.

'There is no way you can walk out of this building without being arrested, at best, or shot, at the worst. So let's start again. I am listening to your demands, we are on to McCaub. In return, I need the wounded hostage, as a show of goodwill, if you like, and I need to know who the other hostages are.'

Silence.

He pushed on. 'Do you have any clue to where we will find this McCaub?'

'You're a fed. That's your job, ain't it?'

Carter walked back to Banham at that moment, shaking his head. 'No help really, the roof is out, as I said, and the window hatch is too narrow. Also looks as if the roof could give with our weight, it's rotten. So, unless we peel down the roof tiles and lift the underlay, which would take a good while and we'd risk being heard doing it, then we surprise them. Otherwise it's a waiting game, time we don't have. Also, we don't know the layout in there, or who's where. So it's not something I want to proceed with slowly. Only answer is to take them by surprise.'

Banham rubbed his hand across his face in his habitual way.

'Look, guv, we all know we need to get that officer out. We can storm in from the front, with backup from the boys on the roof opposite. They have long-lenses on them.'

Banham rubbed at his face again.

Carter raised his voice. 'There's an officer in there, bleeding, for Christ's sake! He's one of us and his life's in danger. We need to get in there.'

'And that's risking others' lives, not to mention the other hostages, who are sitting targets,' Banham told him, shaking his head. 'We don't know who or how many they have in there. No. I'm not taking risks on their lives,' he told him. 'We'll keep trying to reason with them, and find this Devlin McCaub.'

'For how long? Carter snapped.

'Until I say otherwise,' Banham snapped back. He turned to Crowther. 'Chase up that forensics team,' he told him. 'Tell them to drop everything else,' he barked. 'I want them here, pronto.'

The hailer went to his mouth again. 'I think we would all like this to be amicable, but my patience only lasts so long. So are we going to come to an agreement?'

'Depends.'

'On what?'

'If you agree to give me what I want.'

'Well I can't agree if I don't know exactly who McCaub is or where he is. However, I am willing to try, but an agreement works both ways. I must insist you first release the wounded hostage.'

'You'll get him when I get McCaub.'

A Molotov cocktail came hurtling through the air and hit the ground next to Banham at that moment. The bottle smashed but the cloth carried on burning. Banham and Carter both jumped on the flame and quickly extinguished it. Both looked around. A youth stood, hood up, head down, holding another bottle and cloth in his hand. He had sneaked over a wall and back into Henry Street, determined to cause trouble. Sirens screamed as a patrol car sped towards the youth, and pulled up sharply by the wall where he stood.

The youth tried to light the next petrol bottle but, realising time wasn't with him, dropped it and started to climb to get back over the wall. The police were out of the car and running too. They quickly caught his legs and pulled him back down, cuffing him and pushing him towards a waiting meat van.

Banham watched, relieved that the police had kept their tempers. They arrested properly and professionally, even though the poor buggers were all knackered. Banham knew the national press and every television station in the area were still around, outside the cordons in the street, but hovering and watching like hawks for a chance to get a good shot. Had they not been, the youth might have been given a wallop, and Banham would have been the first to turn the other way. The police had been here all night, they were exhausted, and the troublemakers more than deserved a hard slap. Of course, Banham knew if any press saw a hint of that, the force's reputation and confidence with the public would be in tatters.

Crowther hurried back up to Banham. 'Forensics are here,' he told him. 'They're waiting in the next street.

'Bring them in,' Banham told him. 'Assure them it's safe.' He lifted the loudhailer again. 'A petrol bomb has just been thrown out here,' he said. 'The team are getting impatient. I can't be responsible for the armed officers out here. They are not patient men. I don't want them to have to storm your building, someone else might get hurt. I can assure you we are on the case of Devlin McCaub. I am asking again, please release the wounded.'

There were a few silent seconds, and then the voice boomed out, 'That was nothing to do with me. Told you, nothing happens here till I see McCaub. When you bring him here, then your fed can go. An eye for an eye an all that. So you'd better liven up.'

'You have to hope the armed police out here will agree to that,' Banham said flatly.

'We ain't afraid of threats from armed officers neither. We got guns too. What, you think I'm stupid? If they shoot in here, they will shoot your own. We got two of your pigs in here, or have you forgotten?'

Banham flicked a glance at Crowther, then brought the hailer back to his mouth. 'No one wants any further casualties. As I said, we are looking for this Devlin McCaub, but we could do with a bit of help on that front.' He nodded to Crowther. 'Get on to the station,' he told him. 'Find the bastard.' Then he brought the hailer back to his mouth. 'We need an address, or something we can start with. You must have that.'

'Ain't my problem.'

'Supposing we can't find him in a reasonable time. That wounded police officer won't get better unless we get him to hospital. Surely you don't want that on your conscience. I give you my word we are looking. You need to meet us halfway on this.'

Silence from inside the building.

Banham's temper was now building as he thought of his friend Martin Neville and the distress the man might be in. The DCI knew he had to stay calm if he was to help him. His training had taught him that. 'OK,' he said, regaining his calm, but keeping his authoritative tone. 'You already know your building is surrounded by a highly trained gun team with rifles all pointed in your direction. Highly trained, meaning they can shoot and miss the hostages, but not their targets. So you cannot escape. However, I am offering to get you what you want, and negotiate with you so you can leave the building. This is an excellent deal for you. You want this McCaub, We are showing goodwill and doing it, if we can find him. The deal is: we find McCaub, and you release the wounded officer. In what order it doesn't matter. Release the wounded officer for all our sakes. He needs to be in hospital, and you need to find your friend McCaub. And if you release my officer, it will make things much easier for you in the long run.'

No answer.

'You and I both know that there is a man in there, with a bullet in him that needs to come out.' He heard himself getting angry and frustrated, and calmed his voice. 'He should be in hospital. If you let me get him there, and you tell me who else you have in there, then we will track down this Devlin McCaub and bring him to you. My problem, you must understand, is how long it will take to find your friend. You see, if anything happened to that officer while we are looking for your friend then you will be facing a murder charge.'

'What proof do you have that I shot him.'

Banham took an intake of breath and fought to keep his calm exterior. He had to get Neville out and to hospital, whatever it took.

'Would you like me to arrange for water to be sent in? Food, biscuits, sandwiches perhaps. How does that sound? You and your hostages must be hungry?'

'What? So I'll open the door and you can storm in. You think we're stupid?'

'No. So your hostages don't go hungry or thirsty.'

'No.'

'From what I can see from the blood here, every minute counts, and I can't say how long it will take to find this McCaub. At least give us a starting point where we can find him.'

Silence.

Banham hid his frustration and pushed on. 'If you don't talk to me, and you don't let the wounded go, then you give us no choice. If it is taking time that we don't think we have, then we will come in and get our wounded officer, and more people may get hurt. So let's be sensible here. Tell us where McCaub lives, and release the wounded man. You will still have other hostages.'

'First sign of anyone trying to get in here, your other officer will get a bullet, this one in the head.'

Banham glanced at the approaching Jim Carter, who was walking back up the road having been round the back of the warehouse again, desperately studying the geography of the building. Carter raised his eyebrows and flicked his gaze towards his team on the roof. Banham knew what Carter was saying, but there were innocent civilians in there as well as police colleagues. He wasn't about to risk lives.

He checked his watch. It was now nearly two o'clock. His honeymoon flight to Mykonos would be taking off in a few hours. His thoughts went to Alison. He wasn't sure if he minded not having married her. Maybe fate had intervened and this was a sign that living with her was the better option. She could be very difficult sometimes, stubborn and with a terrible temper, but he had no doubt he loved her. She would probably be arriving at the airport quite soon. He hoped she had the right factor sun cream.

Chapter Six

Hannah Kemp was listening to the conversation between DCI Banham and Massafur. She had felt confident that all would be fine very soon, that the DCI would get them out, but now doubt was starting to set in. Martin was still breathing. A few minutes earlier she had thought he was dead. She had left pressure off his wound for seconds and he had quickly grown weaker. How much longer could it be? He urgently needed blood. Her own head was also pounding from the beating she had taken. She pushed that from her mind. In her desperation, and again without thinking, she shouted over to Massafur.

'Please, let him get medical help? Better for you if you do. They'll find your friend.'

Both Sadiq and Massafur ignored her. Then the young girl hostage, who Hannah had heard being called Farzi by the men, suddenly lost it and started shouting.

'They won't find him,' she shrieked at Massafur. 'And that man will die because of you, and you will rot in prison. And I will spit at you.'

The older woman immediately clapped her hands over the girl's mouth. 'That's enough. You are making them mad. They'll slice your neck if you say any more.' But the warning came too late.

Sadiq and Massafur both turned angrily to Farzi. Sadiq grabbed the girl, dragging her up by her waist-long shiny black hair. He struck her hard in the face, then held her by her hair, turning her to face Massafur, who kicked her in the groin. As she screamed out in pain, Massafur booted her again, 'You watch your filthy mouth. You'll be the last to die. We'll kill them one by one, then we'll burn the witch out of you. First you'll watch what we'll do to McCaub.'

Hannah took an intake of breath as she watched the girl fall back from the blow and pass out in a heap on the floor. Massafur was about to kick her again but the older woman intervened and pulled the girl back.

'Don't,' the woman warned the boys. 'She is unconscious. You could kill her. You will have your man soon.'

'Shut up,' Massafur said to her. 'Just keep yours shut.'

The old man with the bleeding head had started shaking violently as he watched the horror in front of him. Then he started sobbing, and then his sobbing increased in volume. Hannah watched Sadiq look to Massafur and touch his gun. She balanced her options very quickly. By the sound of that conversation, they intended killing all the hostages. And it was in her hands to try to stop them. She had only been on the beat for less that a year. She wouldn't forget this in a hurry – if she lived to tell the tale.

Massafur was standing in front of the girl as he spoke to the older woman. The old man and his crying and ranting had taken Sadiq's attention. Hannah was aware the window was free, and open, and Massafur had his back to it. They had spoken of killing the hostages, so she decided she had nothing to lose. She belted to the window and shouted,

'Sir, there's five hostages here, Martin is very—' But that was as far as she got. Massafur had turned back, quickly running and grabbing her. Turning her quickly to face him, his boot went up speedily, slamming into her crotch. She tried to double over as she took the blow, but he held her head firmly, so she couldn't move, then delivered another agonising strike.

The next thing she knew, she saw stars as she was thrown across the room and landed on the hard floor, banging the side of her face and head that had already taken a smacking. She was dizzy and the pain was agonising. She breathed in, remembering the previous warning: if she did one more thing to anger them, they would rape her and then cut her. The fear rushed through her. The old man was still ranting and Sadiq was dealing with him. She crawled to Neville and put pressure back on the tourniquet, but he was very still, and showing no sign of life.

'Jesus,' she cried out, all her calm leaving her. 'Nevvy, stay with me. Don't go. Nevvy,' she raised her voice. 'Stay with me. Please.' She lunged at his blood-soaked mouth, prising it as open as she could manage, and blew air into him, then her entwined fingers pressed onto his chest and she started beating hard against him. 1, 2. 'Come on, Nevs, wake up.' She blew into his mouth again, and repeated the chest pounding. 'My God, Nevvy. Stay with us, Nevs, stay with us, please, help is just outside.'

Chapter Seven

Alison had settled herself in the control room at the station. She was feeling like herself again, comfortable in jeans and trainers and her oversized khaki sweatshirt. Her hair was tied into a ponytail to keep it from her face.

She had her eyes peeled, flicking from one screen to the next. The many videos around the control room showed the riot and hostage situation in Henry Street and the roads around it, all from different angles from the local CCTV.

A pair of headphones covered her ears, and she spoke into the microphone in front of her, keeping Superintendent Cory updated. A small team of uniformed police officers were also in the room, spread out behind desks in front of their own CCTV units, each watching a different view of the now-quietening riots.

Alison could see the SC019 officers on the roofs across the road from the warehouse, their weapons pointed over Banham's head, aimed at the warehouse. She could hear the gist of the conversations from the microphone on the camera that Banham had now put on his lapel, the transmissions of which came back to the station. She watched and listened as Banham struggled to gain the release of their colleague. She was frustrated that she couldn't actually be there, but she was also concerned for Banham's safety. These were dangerous men, they had shot one police officer, so wouldn't hesitate to shoot again. Banham was standing in front of the building. He had no bullet-proof vest, he hadn't had time, having run straight out from the registry office.

As she took her eyes off the monitors, another glass bottle came flying over a wall, hitting the floor and exploded on the ground near Banham. She quickly turned back when she heard the explosion. Banham had been standing facing the warehouse, loudhailer in hand. Immediately, at Jim Carter's orders, SC019 officers fired warning shots around the wall. Alison alerted Lorraine Cory, who immediately hurried in to watch the screen. Both women turned to see the panic as the last few remaining looters started running, turning in all directions, not knowing which way was safest to escape. Most of them ran into the cordons which were guarded by waiting police, who immediately arrested the ones they could catch and piled them into the police vans.

'Our boys look exhausted,' one of the officers in the room muttered, as he watched a helmet go flying as a PC ran into the melee.

Others in the technical room were widening their screen views to take in all they could of the latest uproar. 'More arrests on the way then,' one of them said, shaking his head. 'The cells here are already overflowing, God only knows where they can go.'

'That came from the alleyway leading to Beacon Street,' Alison announced, turning back and pointing to the monitors.

She turned back to watch Banham. He had felt the vibration of the petrol bomb beneath his feet. He turned around to check the officers who were in the street. No one had been hurt.

Lorraine Cory was on the phone to Banham. 'What's going on there?' she asked. 'Was that a home-made bomb?'

'No, a lit cloth in a bottle of petrol, it wasn't very effective,' Banham told her. 'But it did frighten some of the horses. The rioters are more or less all gone,' he told her. 'Neville needs to get to hospital. They want a Devlin McCaub in exchange. Can you check that out at your end, and locate him ASAP? They are adamant they won't release Neville until they get sight of him, so ASAP.'

'I'm on it.' Lorraine turned to Alison. 'We need to find a Devlin McCaub,' she said. 'They say they will release Neville when they get him, but not before. So let's find him pronto. Then we can find out what this is all about.'

'McCaub, did you say? Devlin McCaub? I know that name. He has form,' Alison told her.

Lorraine immediately put her hand over the mouthpiece, in case Banham heard Alison's voice.

'Small-time thief. He's been done for breaking into properties before now, and street brawls,' Alison told her, as Lorraine quickly relayed back to Banham she was on the case and would get back to him. She quickly finished the call.

'It sounds to me like it could be a war over a turf. There was gang-fighting going on down there last night. Is he a dealer?' asked the Super.

'Not that I've heard. I only know him as a house-breaker.'

PC Eddie Bright had been sitting behind a computer. He had done his full ten-hour night shift during the night at the riots, but then offered to stay on and help in the station as his colleague and friend Martin Neville had been taken hostage. He had been listening, and turned around as Alison and Lorraine were talking. 'McCaub, did you say? Irish? House-breaker?'

Alison nodded. 'Yes, do you know him?'

'He's in the cell, ma'am. I arrested him myself. At the riots last night.'

Hannah sat back on the floor, relieved Martin had started breathing again, even in a heavily laboured manner. He was close to death, that much she knew, but there was still hope. She dismissed her own throbbing head and her swollen and split lip, she had to help her friend. She didn't know if the blood she could taste was her own or Nevs'. She just knew she had to keep focused. It was down to her to keep him alive until the DCI got them out, and also to keep the hostages calm, which was now looking to be a problem. The older man seemed to be getting worse. He kept shouting out. The older woman was trying to keep him calm, but failing. Farzi had woken up. She kept spitting at Sadiq and Massafur, every time they looked in her direction. This girl clearly knew McCaub, Hannah was aware she had become anxious and angry since his name had come up.

So could he be her boyfriend? These boys were jealous, perhaps? Or related? Was this what was going on?

Hannah knew she wasn't in any danger of dying from her injuries, but she could be in danger of passing out. She was feeling very dizzy, but Martin's life depended on her.

She carefully lifted the blood-soaked half of her blouse and checked his wound. The blood was coming through again, but she was almost relieved. If he was losing blood, it meant he was alive. Although for how much longer she didn't dare contemplate. She had to pray they'd find this McCaub fellow soon, so she could get her dear friend into hospital.

'Martin,' she whispered to him, rubbing his cold hand with her free one. 'Martin, Nevs, don't close your eyes. Fight to keep them open, OK? You have to stay awake. Can you hear me? We'll have you out of here very soon. I promise.' She nearly choked on the words as she spoke them. Her best friend was dying in front of her, she knew it, and she knew that he knew it. He could die on this disgusting, dirty and cold floor. She had to keep him going until help came. She owed it to him. He had taught her the ropes when she was first out of training. He was going to be the best man at her wedding, and she couldn't bear the fact that he might not see that day. But now wasn't the time to think about any of that, she told herself. Her energy must be used to keep him alive – and herself for that matter. If anything happened to her, the other hostages would have no one. No more brave attempts to plead or shout out of the window to the DCI.

She put his weak and pale hand to her cheek, and spoke quietly. 'We're getting help, Nevvy,' she told him, keeping her voice strong but quiet. 'Hang on. I need you to hang on in there. Right, my mate? I'm staying with you and I'm going nowhere.'

She looked across at Massafur. He was back standing by the window again, his body flat against the wall, a gun in his hand, but his head peeking out, just a millimetre, through the window. He was watching the comings and goings across the street.

She then turned to Farzi, who was sitting against the wall again.

Her head had lolled to one side and her eyes were closed. She was asleep. Best thing. The girl was riling these men and making it worse for everyone. These hostage-takers knew this girl well. Perhaps she was a family member who had gone off with this Devlin McCaub and the family were having none of it. If that was the case, this was going to be a tough battle for Banham, because these boys clearly meant business. McCaub sounded like an Irish name, and if he was involved with this girl, that could have broken serious religious and family traditions. Maybe this beautiful girl lying asleep against the wall wasn't allowed to choose who she loved. But where did the older woman come in? She seemed to be on the girl's side. Another victim, but one Hannah felt she could rely on in an escape situation. If the worst happened and they couldn't find McCaub, and they started killing their hostages, Hannah, with her minimal experience, would have to take charge and try and get them all out and to safety. But how? The older man was a big problem. He seemed as if he wasn't right in the head, so he would need caring for. Her thoughts turned to Peter. He was outside somewhere, out of his mind, no doubt, with worry. She told herself to stay strong.

Then she heard rumbling noises coming from above her head. Scraping sounds, like steel being dragged along the roof. She knew immediately this would be the gun team trying to find a way in, or setting up some sort of contraption to get in and get to them.

She needed to distract Massafur and Sadiq. If they sussed what was happening, they would react, and someone else might get shot. She raised her voice. 'Please,' she shouted, 'my friend is in a bad way.' She was hoping that whoever was on the roof would hear her, and realise how urgent the situation was. 'He is going to die if you don't get him medical help.'

'So am I,' the old man hostage shouted back. 'I need my pills, my head is pounding and I am going a have a stroke.'

Farzi woke up at that moment. Hannah noticed her nose had been bleeding, but felt relieved because she was awake, one less to worry about carrying if they needed to make a quick escape. Then the girl noticed her own blood and immediately started to scream out. Hannah was delighted at this, it was noisy and would distract Massafur and Sadiq from the noise on the roof, and also alert the team that this was getting very urgent.

The old woman moved in to Farzi and shook her. 'Shut up, will you.'

Farzi retaliated by screaming louder, while the old man carried on crying out. He was making no sense, but it was a godsend for Hannah, a diversion she could only have hoped for, keeping herself and Neville out of it.

'Shut your mouth,' the old woman's tone became sharp as she shouted at Farzi. 'Or you'll get it again. Is that what you want? This time it could be a bullet.'

The older man cried out louder. 'Help me, help me, he was crying. 'I am in Hell and there's many devils.'

Massafur had turned and was watching and listening to the two women arguing.

'A bullet's too good for that slut, wouldn't waste it,' was his retort.

Sadiq then joined in. 'She'll not bring his babies into the world.' He then moved over and as he attempted to kick her again in the stomach. The girl screamed in fear, then spurted a load of abuse in a language that Hannah didn't understand.

So Hannah was right, this girl was family to one or both men – and pregnant, perhaps with a baby from another religion? It was a recurring crime in the Met, and one that was rising in numbers, Hannah had already seen it many times. A girl beaten badly for her choice of man. The hostage-takers knew the girl – but were the older man and woman just in the wrong place, at the wrong time?

Sadiq, meanwhile, had become aware of the noise above them. 'Shhh,' he said, alerting Massafur, and pointing to the roof, then turning aggressively to Farzi who was crying and holding her stomach.

'Shut your noise, or he'll stab you in the stomach,' the older woman told her. 'You've got to shut up,' she repeated, raising her voice.

Hannah abhorred domestic violence against women. She felt

a strong urge to rap her truncheon hard against Massafur's head – except he had taken her truncheon and radio, which he had then jumped on, after she had been dragged into the warehouse. Anyway, she couldn't cross these men, she had seen how savagely they reacted when anyone did. And maybe SC019 were going to storm the place? She was ready, it could be any minute; if that was the case, she prayed, Martin might have a chance.

The crying from Farzi and the shouting from the old man had obviously got to Sadiq, whose fuse, Hannah had grown to realise, was short. He moved to the middle of the room, pointed his rifle towards the ceiling, and fired off a round of bullets.

The old man's hands flew to his ears and he screamed out, rocking himself back and forth. Hannah was very concerned for this man. He wasn't mentally stable and he needed his medication, but from what he was suffering, she didn't know.

'Stop, stop, please,' she shouted out. She put her hand up, and an agonising pain shot through her. She realised her arm was either dislocated or, worse still, had been broken as she was thrown back on the floor.

'Everybody, you need to calm down,' she told them, realising her voice was hardly above a whisper. She turned then to Massafur and through her swollen lips she spoke, 'They are doing what you asked. You can take my word for that. Devlin McCaub will be on his way. No need to hurt anyone any further. Please don't. Why don't you take the offer of the water outside.'

Jim Carter was back in the street, standing beside Banham, watching his men crawling over the roof and listening. As soon as the hail of bullets tore through the ceiling, the team sharply rolled, then stood up and moved to the side of the roof, squatting again. None had been injured. Carter immediately signalled them to retreat.

Banham looked furious. He turned to Carter. 'Someone else could have got shot then. That was what I call lucky,' he said in a clipped tone. 'I told you not to go in like a bull in a china shop. We've got two officers in there, as well as other hostages. And I don't want you riling them any more than necessary. Not yet, anyway. We are on to the McCaub lad, so it is just a matter of time, so just hold back, can't you?'

He then lifted the hailer so quickly he hit himself in mouth. 'What's going on in there?' he shouted over the screaming and shouting that was very audible from inside the warehouse. 'I need you to all stay calm. If you shoot again, we will come in, and more people will get hurt. Let's keep this calm. We are finding McCaub, and you need to get the hostages ready to bring out. That was the deal we made. Is everyone in there still safe?'

Peter Byfield rushed up to Banham at that moment. 'Sir, Hannah is in there. I heard her voice. We all heard it. It's definitely her, I'm not the only one. We all heard her. Sir!' he raised his voice.

Banham was quickly aware that if Hannah's head came into view, as it had done before, then either Peter or Hannah would lose their cool, putting everyone into further danger.

Banham quickly put his hand on the man's elbow, at the same time nodding to Crowther to follow, as he steered Byfield towards him and away from the front of the building.

'OK. Now, are you sure?' he asked the emotional PC.

'Yes, sir. Sure as anything. I heard her, and so did a few of the others. Ask them!' His hand flew to his forehead. 'Hannah's definitely in there. Jesus Christ. She is in such danger.'

Banham opened his mouth to speak, but the PC spoke over him. 'And I'm staying right here. You have to let me help her. She is my fiancée.'

'No. You can't stay here,' Crowther told him. 'The best way to help is to stay out of the way and let us do our job.'

'Christ.' Byfield shrugged his arm away from Banham's clutch. It flew to his head. Then he burst into tears. 'We're getting married.'

Banham put a hand on his shoulder. He knew what this man was going through. 'OK, mate, now get a grip. We'll get her out,' he told the man sternly. An image of Diane's body again jumped into his mind. How he still wondered what would have happened if he hadn't taken the overtime on that fateful evening. Would she still be alive now if he had been there to protect her? And what would have become of his tiny baby Elizabeth? A question he would never know the answer to. He more than understood this man's fear, although there was no way he would show it.

'Pull yourself together, then, if you want to stay near here,' Banham told him. 'You're no good to anyone if you fall to pieces. If you want to help her, then you have to obey orders. I understand you won't leave the street. You are to stay behind the cordon, out of sight of the window, and leave us to do our job.'

'Sorry, I'm sorry,' Byfield said. 'I can't help it. `I need—'

'You need to go home, that's what you need,' Banham now raised his voice and spoke very firmly, 'and you need to leave this to us.' Then his voice became softer. 'But I understand that you won't. So over there, stay out of sight, and don't get in the way of my operation. Or you'll be up for a disciplinary.'

'I've told you, sir,' Byfield snapped back, then immediately checked himself. 'With respect, I won't go anywhere until I know she is safe.'

'And that's fair enough,' Banham said, making an effort not to show any of the deep compassion he felt for the poor, tortured officer. 'Then you sit in one of the unit cars, and you don't move from there. We will keep you posted every step of the way. Get some coffee and have one of the team sit with you. We haven't time to waste babysitting you. Martin Neville is in there, he's bleeding, I don't know how badly, so he's my main concern at present. Hannah sounds fine, she is not hurt, and we will get her out too. Trust me to do my job.' He kept the authoritative tone in his voice. 'We will keep you informed. Got it?'

'Yes, sir.'

Banham then walked back to Carter, who had been listening and watching the warehouse and had moved his men over from the roof of the warehouse, to the roofs of the adjacent building. 'My team are still standing by, guv,' Carter told Banham. 'The roof is still covered, as you can see, but from the next buildings. We are just waiting on your say, now. My feeling is we need to get in there and get our officers and the other hostages out. Time ain't on our side but it's your call.'

'I'll get an update on that McCaub,' Banham told him. He stabbed a quick text through to Lorraine, and then lifted his hailer.

'I asked what was going on in there. Why did you fire those shots and is everyone unharmed?'

When no answer came, he spoke again. 'I need to know if anyone is hurt. We are finding McCaub as I speak. So please confirm no one else in there is hurt.'

'Get your men off the roof,' came the angry reply. 'Or someone will get hurt.'

'They are not on the roof.' Banham was about to carry on and ask, again, for Martin Neville's release, but the angry voice butted in.

'I said get them off the roof now.' Then another shot was fired from inside the warehouse. A woman screamed. 'And that's just for starters. If you want your lot to see the outside of here, move them now. You have thirty seconds, and then I will start shooting them.'

Banham stayed calm. 'They are not on the roof.'

Carter turned to Banham. He shook his head. 'You should let us go in. That man isn't stable. He thinks he's calling the shots. If they shoot those hostages—'

Banham cut him off. 'I am running this operation.' He lowered his eyes. His thoughts were with Peter Byfield, and Edna, Martin Neville's wife. Was he letting his own memories cloud his judgement? He just couldn't let anything happen to those hostages. Their lives were in his hands.

Chapter Eight

Devlin McCaub had been brought up from the cell and was now seated in interview room A.

He had his arms crossed as he leaned forward on the desk. The fingers of his left hand tapped impatiently against his right elbow as his gaze moved from Lorraine Cory to Alison and then back to Lorraine. You didn't need to be a detective to read the body language, Alison thought. This boy was agitated, very agitated. It didn't take a detective, either, to see he had traveller blood, she thought. He had that dark, handsome look about him: thick, black wavy hair that fell over his forehead, nearly masking his eyes which were bluer than a cornflower. His skin was a rich dark olive. She would have thought him deeply handsome had it not been for the fact that his hair hadn't seen shampoo in a while, and his fingernails needed an introduction to soap. His notes told her that his mother was Irish and his father half Jamaican. Lots of travellers in Ireland, Alison thought, as she watched him, nervously, still looking from her to Lorraine and waiting for them to speak. Neither did. Alison noticed he had a tattoo of a rose inside the outline of a heart, between his thumb and forefinger. It bore the initials FK. He also had a gold earring hanging from his left ear. No doubt this man was handsome. He reminded Alison of a very young Elvis Presley, or was it David Essex?

Alison and Lorraine had talked prior to the interview. The super had told Alison to take the soft approach with the interview, saying she would come in tough if, and when, she had to, but Alison would lead the questioning.

'This interview is being recorded and videoed,' Alison announced into a tape. 'Present in the room are . . .' She turned to the super.

'DSI Lorraine Cory,' Lorraine said,

'Myself, DI Alison Grainger, and Devlin McCaub,' Alison finished the sentence. 'Time two forty-five pm, Saturday October the nineteenth.' She then looked up, raised her eyebrows, keeping a matter-of-fact tone in her voice, and asked, 'Why were you rioting, Devlin?'

He uncrossed his arms and flicked his hair off his forehead. He spoke in a soft southern Irish lilt.

'Truth is, I wasn't. I was just out with my . . .' he paused and then said, 'girl.' Again his eyes moved from Alison to Lorraine, and back to Alison. 'Doesn't everyone go out for drink or two on a Friday night?'

Neither women answered. He carried on.

'I had no plans for fighting. I was just with my girl. We wanted only to have a good time, you know, drinks, maybe a smoke. Listen to some great sounds in the pub and raise a stinker. I didn't start the looting, but when it started,' he looked at Alison and half smirked, 'what would you do? I took the opportunity to get inside those buildings.'

'And now the truth?' Alison ordered, meeting his eyes.

He shook his head and looked away.

'OK.' This was the tough voice of Lorraine. 'Let's cut the crap. We don't have time to fuck about. You know, and I know, that this is about more than a good drink-up in the pub. How do you know the guys that have barred themselves inside the warehouse?'

'What guys?' he shrugged. 'I don't know who's in there.' He turned his head and looked away, but his fingers started tapping on the table again.

'Well, they sure as hell know you,' Lorraine interrupted quickly, her voice rising with her impatience. 'They are asking for you, by name. Even willing to swap you for their hostages.'

His head flew back round. 'He's got Farzi.' He almost shouted as the words tumbled speedily from his lips. 'She's my . . .' again he paused before adding, 'girl. I was protecting her. I didn't steal anything. I broke the fucking window to get a weapon. I saw him coming for us, and I had to protect her.'

'Saw who?' Alison interrupted.

'Massafur Khan. He's a bastard, and a dangerous one, and I need to get the fuck out of here. Bail me, or do your worst, but just get me out, 'cos I need to help her. She's my girl.'

'Who?' Alison interrupted.

'Farzila Khan. She's his sister.' He took an intake of angry breath. 'I need a smoke. Can I?'

Lorraine fished into her pocket for a packet of Marlboro, then pulled a cigarette out and handed it to him. 'I'll break the rules just this once,' she said.

He took it. She followed with her lighter, clicked the flame, and lit his cigarette. 'Tell me all,' she instructed firmly.

He inhaled very deeply on the cigarette, blew out the smoke, took another drag, then nodded. 'I got a call from him. He said he wanted to meet. Said he just wanted to see his sister. That it was the family, not him, that didn't want us to be together.' The man was agitated, he shook his head continually and blew smoke from his nose. 'He just wanted her happiness, all that shite, he said. Told me to ask her what she wanted, and tell her it was OK. He kept on, said she was his sister, and he missed her. He said he was OK with me and her, and it was a good opportunity with the rave an' all that was going to be going on. Said there'd be a big crowd hanging out around there. No one would notice if he and Farzi met for a few minutes.' He shrugged. 'He said no one in his family would have to know. He would keep it between us. Never to tell his family. We could make it a regular thing,' he said. 'Let's get friendly, all that shite. I wasn't keen, but,' he shrugged, 'I told her what he said. It was fair to do so. She's his sister.' He took another long drag on the cigarette, then flicked the ash on the floor. Alison opened a drawer and took a saucer out and put it on the desk. He looked at her, then tapped the end of the cigarette in it. 'Sorry,' he muttered quietly.

'Go on,' Lorraine pushed.

'Farzi was up for it, said she would like us to be friends. He was her brother.' He shrugged again. 'Fair dos, keep the lady happy. So I brought some of the boys with us to look out for her.' He took another deep drag, and Alison read the distress on his face, as he hesitated before saying. 'It was crazy out there. You should have seen it.'

'We did. Go on,' Lorraine told him.

'The crowds, and everyone, off their heads an' all. Then there was windows and shops smashed up, shopkeepers swearing as the looting started, and everyone was diving everywhere grabbing stuff, breaking more windows.'

'Yes, we know all that,' Lorraine snapped at him. 'Tell us what happened with this Massafur Khan.'

'As we walked. I saw him. Massafur. He was standing, watching us, leaning against a corner thing.' McCaub took another drag on his cigarette, then blew out smoke and stubbed the remains of the cigarette out politely while looking Alison in the eye. 'He had his cousins with him. That's when I knew there was trouble coming. I turned, and kicked a window in. I needed a weapon, I could see that, and so did the boys. I wanted to grab something quick to protect her with. I grabbed a television, I was aiming for a chair, but it was further away and I needed something quick. I figured I could throw it at the bastard fuck, knock him out of the way while we ran. I threw the television, and that's when the gun went off and your man went down. I turned back to Farzi, but she had disappeared. I just saw the blood. Your fella was on the ground, and being dragged by the leg. Your lady one was being dragged an' all. It happened so quickly.'

Sweat was running down the side of his face and Alison could see he was getting upset and worked up. 'I screamed to Farzi, told her to run. Look. I need to get out of here,' he said, half begging. 'They're dangerous bastards. I have to help her. I've told you all this. I wouldn't talk, not a bit of this, to you if I wasn't worried for her life. But I am. I am telling you that family are fucking insane, they think nothing of killing, and they will hurt her badly. It's because she is with me. Please don't keep me locked up. I need to help her.'

'That's presuming they have taken her,' Alison said. 'You don't know that for sure.'

'Oh, I'm sure,' he argued firmly. 'This is what it's about, all this. So, I've told you. So let me go now, you'll see then, I need to help her.'

When neither answered him, he protested, with a great deal of charm. 'All I did was grab something to throw at him, to protect her.'

'That's theft,' Alison told him. 'We have you on CCTV kicking the window in to the furniture shop and going in and taking the TV. You are being charged with damage to property and theft.'

'That wasn't the way it was. I just told you what happened.' His voice had risen in volume and desperation. 'I had to look out for her. He threw his hands in the air. Alison recognised the signs of the Celtic temper about to explode. It did.

'I've told you the fucking truth,' he shouted. 'So if there's any justice you're gonna let me out of here.' He pulled his chair back and went to stand. 'Bail me, will you, for the love of God.'

Lorraine then roared at him, 'Sit the fuck down. I haven't got time for your thoughts on justice. I have a hostage situation, and one of my team has been shot. So you listen up, and you hear this. This man, presuming it is Massafur Khan, is asking for you. In return he says he will free our hostages. I have a badly wounded police officer in there. Even so, I cannot, and will not, risk your life there.'

McCaub opened his mouth to protest but Lorraine spoke over him. 'We will let you go, but there are conditions, and you have to agree to them.'

'Anything. Bail me, whatever, but let me go to help her.'

Lorraine nodded. 'You can help her, but you'll have to help us too. I will wire you up with a radio mike, so I can hear every word and move you make. That way we can protect you. Then we will take you there, and you can talk to him. We will be beside you all the way, and you will not leave the car without my say-so. Got it?'

'Yes, lady.'

'We will tell you what to say, and you will negotiate Farzila's release.'

McCaub took an intake of breath. He clearly wasn't used to working with the law, Alison thought.

'If you will do this and help us,' Lorraine continued, 'then we will speak for you and ask the judge for leniency on your breaking and entering charge.' She passed him another cigarette and clicked her lighter.

He took the cigarette and then the light, and looked straight back at her. Alison thought he had kind eyes, none of the hardness in them she was used to seeing in street criminals. He blew out smoke and said very calmly, 'Of course. I'll take any condition you offer if I can get out of here. Otherwise,' he shook his head and sounded pitiful, 'dear God, I am afraid they will kill her.'

Lorraine and Alison turned to each other.

'It's an honour thing. They will kill her for sure if they find out. See,' he paused then said quietly, 'the truth is, we got married. My family thinks they found out. They believe they should pick who their daughters marry.'

'Massafur's sister is your wife?' Lorraine asked calmly.

He pushed the side of his cheek out with his tongue, took another drag and looked down at his third finger which bore a gold ring. As he lifted his hand and pointed to the ring, his forehead furrowed. He then nodded. 'Yes, and if they have found that out, they'll be planning to crucify her. She's nineteen. She's run away from home before, twice, but each time her brothers got her back. Buried her once, up to her neck, then poured ants over her head. A warning, they called it.' He looked at Lorraine, and stubbed his cigarette out in the ashtray. 'When I heard they'd done that to her, I went looking for them.' He now looked Alison in the eye. 'I was fuelled with drink, angry as fuck, and high on pills. I picked a fight with one of her brothers and gave him a good kicking. I took her away, but they found her and brought her back. Cut off her hair and burned her vagina. Then she ran away again. She phoned me to come and get her, and I took her to my local priest. He hid her in his church and then married us two weeks later. He said, as she was over sixteen, and married to me, they would have no hold on her. The law will see me as her next of kin, not them.' His forehead furrowed again, and he shook his head, his voice broke as he spoke. 'If they have found out. God knows, they will kill her. They are fucking animals.' He looked up and became angry again, although his eyes were full of tears. 'I took a TV from the shop window because it was the first thing I laid my hands on. I had to protect her. Is that so bad? The shop's insured. She isn't. This is her life we are talking about.'

'It's still stealing,' Alison said quietly. 'And against the law.'

'People are hurt, a police officer has been shot, and is being held hostage, along with other hostages,' Lorraine added.

'That's them, not me,' he argued. 'All I'm guilty of is protecting my wife. Who wouldn't do that? Have you spoke to Massafur?'

'Yes.'

'Has he said he has Farzi?'

'That we don't know,' Alison said. 'We don't know who the hostages are, apart from our officers. They are in the warehouse.'

'I know the building.'

'Are you agreeing to help us?' Lorraine asked him.

'I'm agreeing to help Farzi,' he said. 'If that means helping you, then yes, I am agreeing.'

'We don't know for sure if she is in there.'

'Nor do we know if she is wounded,' Alison added. 'But we do know time is at a premium, Massafur is offering to exchange our wounded officer in return for you.'

Devlin looked puzzled. 'Then I reckon he definitely knows she has married me.'

'Right, well then, we can't waste time,' Lorraine said. 'So let's get you wired up and we'll get down there.' Before she had the chance to even stand, her phone rang.

She checked her screen, then stood up and went outside to take the call, leaving Alison with Devlin.

'We'll wire you and you'll have police protection at all times,' Alison assured him. 'But you must do what we say, and don't try anything unless we OK it. We have to keep you safe. Have you got that?'

'It's not me I'm worried about.'

Lorraine walked back into the interview room at that second. 'Time isn't on our side,' she said gravely. 'Let's go.' She turned to Alison. 'PC Hannah Kemp is confirmed a hostage in there. She was partnered with Neville last night.'

Alison stood up.

'You can't come,' Lorraine immediately told Alison. 'I told you, you have to stay here. There's enough going on without Banham starting an internal on me.'

Devlin stood up. 'I'll help you,' he said to Lorraine. 'I'll happily kill them too, if that's what you want. They treat women like shit.'

It was starting to rain again, only spitting drops, but enough to dampen the ground once more. Henry Street was now busy with ambulances, the SC019 gun team, the forensic team, and uniformed police and plain clothes officers working on the scene. The broken windows in the shops remained broken. No unauthorised access had been allowed.

Banham was aware that, like himself, that the SC019 officers were getting restless. A couple of them were still on the roof of the warehouse, another half-dozen on the buildings opposite, with another group of four in the alleyway adjacent and three squatting on the ground, all with rifles in their hand, and all out of sight from the hostage-takers inside.

The forensic team were erecting a blue tent over the beginning of the trail of blood that had spilled on the ground where Neville had been shot. Banham had requested this as soon as the rain started drizzling down. If there was any speck of evidence there, he was going to make very sure the elements didn't destroy it.

He had been handed a paper cup of coffee. He now stood in the street sipping it, feeling anxious about how long it would be before they could get McCaub to the location, and also wondering if Alison was at the airport yet. He figured she would be sitting sipping champagne on her own. He felt bad. It was now 2.30 pm. He had spoken to Lorraine Cory and she had updated him on the fact they had tracked down McCaub and were interviewing him – but how long before they could get him here, he wondered, as he also wondered how badly shot his colleague was. And was he doing the right thing, risking this McCaub's life to, perhaps, preserve others?

He was fully aware time wasn't on his side. He also had his eyes on PC Byfield, who hadn't obeyed Banham's instructions and gone to sit in a unit car with his partner PC Levington, but was instead sitting at the end of the road, on the pavement, his head in his hands, surrounded by his uniformed colleagues, all incapable of knowing what to do or say to help.

Banham's own thoughts went again to Alison. He had let her down. He had let Diane down too. Perhaps fate had intervened today because he didn't deserve a second chance at happiness by marrying Alison.

In his heart he knew he had moved heaven and earth to find Diane and Elizabeth's killer, but he had failed, and he couldn't undo the past. Seeing Peter Byfield's situation was bringing all his own memories back. Life gives you moments, and you must grab them. His moments with Diane were too brief.

He loved Alison. She was his life. But Elizabeth had had no life. Counsellors had told him it wasn't his fault, and he had to hang on to that. Maybe with Alison he would have another chance at fatherhood. He was pushing forty, but he would dearly love to try. As soon as this hostage situation was sorted, they would be together in Greece, planning another wedding, and maybe he would suggest they try for a child.

He pulled his phone from his pocket, and his floral bow tie which he had been sporting for the nuptials slipped out with it. He picked it up and brushed it with his fingers, looked at it, then replaced it in his pocket. He didn't want to grubby it. It would be worn again. Then he started a text to Alison. He had got as far as *Hope you are celebrating for both of us* when his phone belled. He saw the call was coming from the super. He immediately abandoned the texting and picked up.

'Ma'am,' he said as he pressed green.

'We have McCaub in the back of the car, and are on our way over to you,' Lorraine told him. 'We must play this one very carefully. I won't take any risk on this boy's life. He is married to one of the hostages, apparently. This is a family feud. They want McCaub for marrying into their family. It is a very delicate situation. We can show them McCaub, but I won't let him out of the car. We need Martin Neville out, and then all the other hostages. McCaub is happy to help, but we have to tread as gently as we would on a shoal of bloody jellyfish.'

'Great news,' Banham told her. 'I'll be very pleased to wave Neville safely off to hospital.' Then he hesitated and then said, 'And I can't wait to join Alison.'

But he spoke into an empty space. Lorraine had hung up.

He walked back and stood in front of the warehouse.

'McCaub is minutes away,' he shouted into the hailer. 'That's our side of the bargain done. Now I have to insist you release the wounded hostages.'

Chapter Nine

Farzi's nose was still bleeding. Hannah was squinting as she watched with concern. One of her own eyes had swollen since she had landed on her face after she was thrown across the room. Her vision was hazy but, even with one good eye, she could see it was a bad nosebleed. It would stop, Hannah knew that, if only the girl would put her head forward into the tissue and not lean back. The older woman was with her, telling her to lean her head right back.

'Try putting your head forward,' Hannah said in a raised voice so Farzi could hear.

'I know what I'm doing,' the old woman snapped back. 'Her head should be back.'

'I think you lean forward with a nosebleed,' Hannah argued. 'I've done a first-aid course and that's what I was told.'

Sadiq moved over to her and kneed her in the back. 'Shut the fuck up,' he said.

She decided to say no more. The nosebleed would stop. Her concern was keeping Martin alive. She was also concerned for the welfare of the older man. She knew he owned a confectionery shop because he had come out and argued with the rioters when they broke his window and started to steal his goods. For that, the poor man had received a beating and had found himself a hostage. He needed medication, he kept saying so, but no one took any notice. But how badly did he need it, and what would happen if he didn't get it? She couldn't plead for everyone, and she was going to take care of Martin and worry about the others when he was out of there.

She had half of her blouse left, the other half was completely soaked in Martin's blood, and if she gave some of it to the girl, Farzi, to stop her nose, then she might not have enough to make another tourniquet, which she knew she would need very soon if he wasn't out of here in minutes. His blood was still pumping out. She wasn't sure if she was relieved to see he was still bleeding, because that meant he was alive, or if she was worried, because how much more blood could he safely lose? And now blood had started to bubble from his mouth again and his face looked a pale mauve colour. Things were not good. Hannah knew the new mouth bleeding could be a sign there was internal haemorrhaging. Either way he wasn't getting any better lying here, on a cold concrete floor, fighting to stay conscious.

'McCaub is minutes way. You need to release the hostages.' DCI Banham's voice came through loud and clear, and it was music to her ears. Martin would be on his way to hospital in a very short while. Yes, there was hope, she told herself.

Then Farzi started to sob loudly.

'Shut up,' the woman told her with a hard dig in the girl's ribs. 'Don't make them angry.'

'What's going to happen to Devlin?' Farzi was just understandable through her sobbing and bleeding nose.

'I am going to tear his dick from his body and stuff it in his mouth, that's what's going to happen,' Massafur told her. 'Then we'll squeeze the witch out of you and bury you alive.'

Those words sent a cold shiver down Hannah's back. 'What!'

'Can I go soon?' the old man spoke up.

Now Hannah knew her instincts had been right. This was most definitely about Farzi's involvement with this Devlin McCaub. Farzi was perhaps Massafur's sister, certainly a close relation, and Sadiq too. Farzi had gone off with Devlin McCaub, which was against their so-called rules, and they were intending to kill him for it – and possibly her too, or was that just a threat? Fortunately, Hannah knew Banham's reputation as a skilled negotiator. He wouldn't just hand McCaub over to them. He would use him to negotiate, to get

Martin out and to hospital, and then the rest of the hostages. She wanted to cry with relief. She now felt sure that very soon all this would be over. She just prayed it wouldn't involve a shoot-out. She was the only one capable of caring for the hostages, and at the moment she could only squint with one eye and her body ached. She was badly bruised and swollen. Her arm might even be broken, it hurt like fuck. And she would have to carry Martin when the time came, as no way could he stand. She only hoped she could lift him with her working arm. He could lean against her and they could stagger to the door that way.

She also knew that the building was surrounded by SC019, who might burst in at any time, so she would have to keep them all clear of that. But she was relieved all was moving towards the end of this horrendous situation. The old man was getting delirious. He clearly needed his medication.

'Can I ask your name?' she shouted over to him, turning her back on Nevs, just briefly.

'Buisha,' he said. There was a bit of slurring to his voice, she noticed. 'I . . . don't remember the rest.'

The slurring worried her. 'Is it blood pressure pills you need?' she asked, turning to Massafur who was once again propped by the window, the AK in his hand, watching out, ignoring the sobbing and shouting going on behind him. 'I'm sure if Massafur asked, DCI Banham would get your medication, and get it brought in. But, if you could hang on, I think we will be going soon.'

Massafur turned at this. 'Shut your fucking mouth,' he said.

The man raised his trembling voice, 'I'm on medication,' he said now speaking to the wall. Hannah had to strain to hear what he said. 'I need to have it,' he told the wall. 'If I miss my meds, you know . . .'

'Jesus,' Hannah said, looking back to Massafur, 'at least—' but the jerking of Martin's body took her attention. She turned to him and stared in horror as his body went into spasm. The man's torso was jerking up and down. 'Oh, dear God,' she spoke before she could compose herself. 'Martin,' she pleaded, her voice breaking as she pushed the tourniquet harder into his stomach. She lifted her pain-filled arm and placed it against his cheek. 'Stay with me, please, Nevvy, I need you. The ambulance is outside, we'll have you in it within minutes.'

She looked up and both Sadiq and Massafur were watching. Sadiq then switched his gaze to Massafur.

Chapter Ten

Alison walked back into the CCTV monitoring room. She still wasn't a happy bunny. Banham should not have let their private life mix with their professional one. She should be down there with her colleagues, helping with the hostage situation. She didn't want to go to Greece on her own. She was needed in Henry Street and that was where she wanted to be. This was an emergency. They could get married anytime, if indeed it was a good idea. She certainly was never wearing a frilly dress again. If they did do it, she would wear something very plain and simple.

She leaned over Sergeant Derek Bridge's shoulder to check the goings-on in Henry Street. The street was teeming with officers, forensics doing their job, but other than that nothing much was happening. All were waiting for Devlin McCaub to arrive.

It had started to rain again, but she was confident that wouldn't be a problem for forensic evidence as there was a tent erected, protecting the blood spill. She smiled to herself as she watched Banham check the back of his hair then smooth his hand over the ends. He hated it when his hair got damp, as the ends went curly, something, he once told her, he was teased about as a child in school. She thought it was endearing.

She wondered what he would think if he knew she was watching him from a monitor inside the station, and wasn't at the airport, with her high factor sun cream, headed for Mykonos.

A few uniformed PCs were sitting on the damp pavement just along from the warehouse. They looked exhausted. There were never enough available uniformed police when an emergency like this arose. The government needed to up the police budget, not cut it back, she thought angrily. What was wrong with politicians' priorities? They didn't have a clue what went on in reality, on the streets in London. They should come down and see this situation, then watch some of the footage from the riots. These uniformed police had worked a double shift back to back to keep the public safe.

She looked down the road on the monitor screen and recognised Peter Byfield. His head had been in his hands, but when another PC placed a paper cup of coffee on the pavement beside him, he looked up. The poor man had been out there all night. Her heart went out to him. He was due to marry Hannah Kemp in a few weeks and now he didn't know if he was even going to see her again.

Alison turned her attention back to Banham. He was still standing opposite the warehouse, and seemed to be listening. Something was obviously going on. And he looked worried. He would know now that Devlin McCaub was on his way, and with luck this would all be over soon. So why was he looking so concerned as he watched the warehouse? What was going on in there? She asked PC Ryan Good, who was watching another CCTV screen, if he could get the video to go in closer on Banham, and turn up the sound on Banham's radio monitor.

There was nothing she could hear clearly, just shouting in the warehouse.

She watched Banham pull his phone from his pocket and press buttons. Christ, was he texting her again? She shook her head to think, then she checked her watch. He would be expecting her to be in the pre-take-off area at the airport. And she was right, within seconds her phone bleeped. She read the text. *Thinking of you. Wish I was there. Things moving on here. With luck will be on a plane to you soon. Travel safely, don't forget the sunscreen, and I'll see you at the villa.*

'Can you get a close-up of Banny?' she asked Ryan. He did, then turned and gave her a sympathetic smile. She felt a sudden pang of regret. This was supposed to be their wedding day. She had spent the last week doubting her feelings for him, but watching him there, the ends of his hair curling in the rain, all those doubts were getting washed away. She wasn't pleased with him, in fact she was downright cross with him, but she couldn't doubt her love for him. Marriage didn't matter to her, she wasn't bothered whether they were married or not, and she could most certainly live without a pantomime of a wedding ceremony. But she had loved him enough to agree to it.

He was an old-fashioned lad at heart, and she knew marriage mattered to him. So, for him, she would go through all that circus again. She just needed him to understand that she, too, had to be allowed to be who she was. She would never give up her job. She wanted to be with him, she knew she loved him, but she wasn't willing to give up her work, if she had to choose between them, she knew which way she would go.

She half thought of grabbing her jacket and turning up at Henry Street, and facing him with all this, telling him she was there to assist him on the case. She couldn't though, Lorraine had stuck her neck out for her, by just allowing her on the case from inside the station, and she would be facing a disciplinary if she disobeyed her superintendent's orders. And Lorraine could face a disciplinary too. It was Banham's case, he was the SIO on this one. Alison wasn't about to drop Lorraine in it. The women in the force stuck together. It was an unspoken rule. She looked at the text again, decided not to answer it, and pushed her phone back into her pocket. She then went off to interview, charge, and bail some more of the overflow in the noisy cells.

Banham was becoming concerned. He had been listening to the shouting, and now there was crying coming from inside the warehouse. Then loud sobbing and heated exchanges of words. He signalled to Crowther who was in the alley to the right of the warehouse. 'What's going on in there, do you know?' he asked as Crowther approached. 'Can you hear?'

'There's a barney going on in there, guv. The gunmen are losing it, and a girl is hysterical. But I'm sure it's not Hannah.'

'Where are the refreshments?' Banham asked.

'Over there, guv,' Crowther told him nodding his head in the direction of four paramedics who sat on the pavement next to a tray of water and biscuits.

Crowther called to them. 'Guys, over here, and bring the refreshments,' he told them.

'McCaub is on his way over in a car,' Banham told them as they walked over. 'With luck we'll have our boy out very soon.'

'We're ready,' the ginger-haired paramedic, Patrick, told him. 'Blood is on standby at the hospital. We've already checked Neville's blood type from his medical records. What do you want done with the water and biscuits?'

'Put them outside the door, would you, and tell the SC019 under the window to stand by, but to stay hidden and out of sight.'

'There are refreshments for you, by the front door,' Banham spoke into the hailer. 'And McCaub is only minutes away. Can you please stand by with the hostages.'

'That was quick,' Jim Carter said. He had been standing with Crowther, and had checked each of his team were where he wanted them then walked back to Banham.

Banham nodded. 'I've told the car with McCaub to stop at the end of the road, not to enter Henry Street. They will be able to see McCaub from the window, I should think.'

'If they lean out,' Carter said. 'Which would be good because I can get a close look at the rifle they're using.'

'I will tell them McCaub is here, and they are to release hostages as I go down the road to get McCaub. They will have to bring the hostages to the door—'

'That's when we'll go in,' Carter interrupted.

'Get the hostages well out of harm's way first,' Banham told him. 'And I'd like the hostage-takers alive if we can.'

'I think we should get Byfield out of this road, guv, if I may suggest,' Crowther said.

'I agree, but he refuses to leave. He won't leave Hannah, whatever the cost, and who can blame him.'

'Let's lock him in a patrol car then, guv. Imagine if it gets nasty? Supposing something was to happen to Hannah?'

'Let's not go there.'

'No, but let's be realistic.'

'Lock him in a car, then,' Banham snapped. He lifted the hailer again. 'Please take the refreshments outside the door. McCaub is on the way, you have time. This isn't a trap,' he told the gunmen.

'Stuff your refreshments, just give us McCaub.'

'Perhaps your hostages may like some water. Are they ready for release? As I said, McCaub is on way, and our deal is hostages, wounded first, then you send the others out as I walk McCaub up the road to you,' Banham spoke in a tone a lot calmer than he felt.

'Talk to me again when he's here,' came the reply.

Hannah was kneeling over Martin, his body had stopped convulsing and had become still. Very still. She fell back on her heels and watched and prayed for any sign of movement. After a second she leaned over him again. She could still only see out of one eye; the other had swollen making it impossible to see anything other than a blur.

She was aware the room had gone very quiet, and all eyes were on her. She put two fingers on the side of Neville's neck and then lifted his hand and pressed two fingers onto his pulse. When she got no reaction, all her training on staying calm in a crisis left her, and she became frantic. She leaned over him, her mouth over his, blowing air into him as her flat palms jerked, with as much force as she was able, with one causing agonising pain through her whole being. Up-down, up-down, until exhaustion took her over and she stopped. Another second, and she leaned in and started the frantic process again; she could taste the metallic flavour of blood in her mouth as she tried desperately to breathe the life back into him. Up-down, up-down, her palms again against his chest, like a clockwork doll in overdrive. She gave no concern to the pain in her own shoulder and arm, although she was aware her right arm carried little weight. 'Martin, come on. Come on. Martin, don't give up, we're getting you out of here,' she pleaded, as she worked him again, up-down, up-down, up-down, this time even faster. Then as exhaustion and angst took her over, and his body remained still and unmoving, she leaned back on her heels and stared at his lifeless corpse. A dropped pin would have been heard in the large, hollow space of the warehouse.

She bit hard into her lip, which was already smothered in Martin's blood, as she stared into the face of her dead friend.

Chapter Eleven

The noise had subsided and all seemed quiet inside the warehouse, but Banham was concerned. He put the hailer back to his mouth. 'Everything OK in there?' he asked. 'Nearly over. Your friend Devlin McCaub will be with us any minute. So, would you show good faith and allow the injured officer out? We have paramedics here, they will take care of him, and you can help yourself to the refreshments. There is no trick. You have my word. I have done what you asked. Please understand, I am concerned for the wounded hostage.'

There was silence within the warehouse.

'Did you hear me?' he repeated, 'Devlin McCaub will be here any minute. You will be able to see him. He will be in a car with my officers, but will not be allowed out until I first get my wounded officer, and then the rest of the hostages.'

Still no answer came.

Banham flicked a glance at Crowther, then turned back and lifted the hailer. 'This is as it is. No trick. I have kept my side of this bargain. However, my patience has its limit. You must release that wounded man. As soon as you do, and the other hostages are brought to the door, you will see McCaub.'

'McCaub is on his way, right?'

'Right. Yes,' Banham answered.

'It's an eye for an eye, then,' the voice came back. 'When I get McCaub, you get your man.'

The three paramedics who were standing next to Banham, two

holding a stretcher, one an oxygen mask, and the other the medical bag, looked at each other, all wearing concerned expressions.

'And the other hostages?'

There was a silence which seemed like an eternity, then a voice answered, 'When we get McCaub, then I will talk to you about your other hostages, and what we want in exchange for each of them.'

'No, that isn't how it works,' Banham told them. 'Hostages come out, and then I walk up the road with McCaub. That is the agreement.'

When no answer came, he looked at Crowther, and then nodded to Jim Carter. Carter made a hand signal to his team on the roof, who all immediately went onto their stomachs and wriggled, like alligators approaching water, towards the hatch door. He then nodded to the team in the alley. One gave a thumbs up back to him.

Carter turned and gave a thumbs up to the ones on the roof opposite the building.

Hannah was aware all eyes were watching her. If Massafur or Sadiq came anywhere near her she would kick them so hard, and have no concern for the consequences to herself. Her best friend was dead. She had failed to keep him alive. She forced herself to stay silent. She turned to face Sadiq. He immediately turned his attention to Farzi. She too was watching, her hand to her face, which was covered in the drying blood from her nose.

Hannah flicked a glance at the older hostages. The woman was aware that Neville had just died, she looked very afraid, but said nothing. Buisha was still in a world of his own. He was still talking to the wall, asking the wall to get his medication, and help him.

Hannah became aware Sadiq was walking over to her. She took an intake of breath, unsure what he was about to do. He aimed his cruel eyes at her, then turned them to Martin. He prodded her friend in the shoulder with the butt of his rifle. Hannah would like to have kicked him, but her whole body felt so heavy she had no energy to object. She merely kept her eyes on the unmoving body of her best friend. His blood was all over her hands and around her mouth.

Sadiq poked Neville again with his rifle. Hannah's temper started to burn at this. She took a breath and was about to tell him he would rot in prison for this, and she would make sure he never came out, but the cry from Farzi interrupted her.

'He's dead. You've killed him,' Farzi shouted at Sadiq. Then raised her voice again and shrieked. 'You're a murderer, and you'll kill Devlin and—'

She didn't get to the end of her sentence. Sadiq had charged across the room and grabbed her by her arm. Farzi fell on her knees, but Massafur grabbed her other arm, undid her tied hands, and pulled her to standing, all the while cursing at her in a different language. His fist thudded into her cheek. Sadiq followed this with a hard smack across the top of her head. Farzi screamed, and more blood spurted from her nose.

Hannah knew she should try and calm the situation, but she was numb. She felt past caring about any of them, including herself. Her friend was dead in front of her. She couldn't save him.

The old woman intervened. 'Stop,' she shouted as Massafur repeatedly banged Farzi's head against the brick wall. 'No more,' the woman shouted. 'You will kill her.'

The raised voice of Banham outside, demanding to know what was happening, stopped them all.

Hannah then heard the noise of running water. They all turned in the direction it was coming from. It was Buisha, he had turned to the wall and was urinating. Hannah made a quick decision, she was past caring what they did to her. Buisha had their attention, so she ran to the window and pushed it open further. 'Sir,' she shouted, 'PC Nev—' but a hand again gripped tightly around her face, covering her mouth, and she was dragged back and pushed into the wall.

'Hannah, is that you?' Banham answered, but Hannah could no longer answer him. Sadiq was behind her, leaning into her at the wall. First he ripped into her vest, then tore off her bra. Her bare breasts scraped the wall, as she felt his erection pressing into her buttocks. Then he grabbed the waistband of her black uniform trousers.

'Nooooo!' She kicked out, and was rewarded by another thump to her head as he banged her into the wall. She fought back, but her right arm was in agonising pain, and he was much stronger than her. She was scared and angry, and that made her fight harder. As he pulled at her trousers, she knew he intended to rape her. She ignored the pain she felt in her arm, and kicked and fought back with her whole being. She expected the older woman to intervene on her behalf, but the woman had her attention on Farzi and her bleeding nose.

'Stop.' It was the voice of Massafur shouting to Sadiq. Sadiq released Hannah.

'McCaub is on his way,' Massafur told him. 'First we deal with that. Then you can do as you please with her.'

Sadiq took a few steps away from Hannah, leaving her leaning into the wall, trying to pull her torn clothing around her scraped and bleeding breast. She stayed, facing the wall, breathing heavily, and trembling, listening to Banham shouting her name from outside. She heard Sadiq zip himself up, and then the older woman was beside her, helping her get her bra over her nakedness, and clipping it done-up for her. Hannah was grateful. Her own arm was in agonising pain and she couldn't raise it to reach the clips, but she refused to let them know that.

Then Sadiq leaned in over her, stinking of BO, nearly touching her ear with his mouth. 'You speak only when we tell you,' he whispered, but the threat was clear in his tone. 'I haven't finished with you. I will punish you.'

Out of nowhere his free hand came up and he banged her head into the wall again. She felt the crack as her forehead took the blow. Her head span again and her knees gave way but Farzi's screaming stopped her from losing consciousness.

'She isn't your business,' Farzi shouted. 'Haven't you done enough damage? You've killed that man. Spare Devlin. Kill me if you must, but spare Devlin, please, I beg you.'

Hannah was lying in a heap on the floor. She couldn't move, but she listened.

'Keep quiet and do as they say,' the older woman was saying, 'Don't antagonise them, why are you making them so mad?' but Hannah didn't know if the woman was talking to her, or Farzi, or Buisha.

'I need to know what this shouting is in there. I have McCaub only a street away. I need to know the welfare of your hostages is sound.' The voice of Banham sounded again.

Hannah felt herself being pulled up to standing. Sadiq's pinching grip on her sent yet more pain through her arm. It hit her brain immediately. She now felt sure her arm was broken. It had been throbbing intensely before, but this pain was practically unbearable. She struggled not to pass out. If she did get out of here, alive, then, with her wedding just weeks away, the beautiful dress she had searched for for months, and endured four fittings for so it would look perfect on the day, was now not going to get worn. Her arm would be in a sling, her face probably still bruised and swollen, she would look the last thing from a beautiful bride. But then she wouldn't want the big wedding they had planned, scrimped, and saved so hard for without Martin Neville there. He was going to be their best man. Her wedding was now not going to happen, she decided.

'Answer him,' Sadiq commanded, dragging her to the window.

She somehow managed to find her voice, and stood, out of sight of the window, as she knew her face was stained with Neville's blood, and one side of her face swollen badly. 'Everything's fine,' she shouted, as bravely as she could manage.

'Louder,' Sadiq commanded to her.

'Everything is fine in here. No problem,' she repeated.

Sadiq then dragged her across to where Martin lay, growing cold, on the filthy ground. He threw her down. As she landed, he narrowed his cruel eyes. 'You are a whore,' he said, 'and soon you will be treated like one.'

An icy shiver ran through her. Being raped was the worst thing she could think of. She still had her camisole vest over her, but only just, it was torn and covered in dirt and Martin's blood. Her arm was throbbing and increasing in agony. She knew she wouldn't have the energy to fight Sadiq off. She had to hope Banham would get them out first. She told herself to be strong. That bastard had killed her best friend, and she was determined he wouldn't get the better of her. She had to live to make sure he got put away for life. She was an officer of the law, and a fighter, and now was the time to prove it. Her thoughts went to her lovely hubby-to-be, and the bridal underwear she had bought to please him, and their plans for their future lives together. Would she ever make it out of this place to see Peter again? Or would it be her fate too to die here, with her friend, in this dirty, cold building, then lie waiting for her body to be released, only to break her Peter's heart?

She had to fight. Peter needed her, and it was down to her now to keep the other hostages alive. Wasn't that what she had signed up for when she became an officer of the law? Martin had taught her not to show fear, and to fight for what was right. She was going to do just that. She owed it to him and his widow, Edna, to get justice for Martin's life.

She swallowed down her fear and turned to face Sadiq. She even found a tone of authority as she spoke.

'They are getting Devlin McCaub for you,' she said quietly, and evenly. 'You heard the man outside. He is on his way. That was DCI Banham outside. I know him, and I know he will not trick you or lie to you. Soon all this will be over. You will have what you want, but you have now killed an officer, and if you rape me, you will never see the light of day outside prison.'

With her one working eye she held his evil stare.

'They would have to catch me first,' Sadiq answered with a knowing laugh. His eyes then moved from her face to where her bosom was protruding. By his tone she knew he intended to carry through his threats.

Chapter Twelve

Peter Byfield jumped away from the patrol car he was about to get into. The PCs with him also turned. All had recognised Hannah's voice, and then heard the screaming that followed.

'That's her,' Byfield shouted.

Banham looked at Crowther and rolled his eyes to heaven. 'I thought we agreed to keep him out of the way of all this,' Banham snapped.

Crowther nodded. 'He needs to go, guv. Not just from the end of the road, but back to the station. He needs to be a long way away from all this. He could cock the whole thing up. Shall I get rid of him? We can't wet nurse him.'

Banham nodded. His attention was on the warehouse.

Before Crowther had time to tell PC Shaun Levington to get Byfield out of Henry Street, Byfield had started running towards the warehouse, shouting, 'Hannah, Hannah, I'm here.'

Crowther moved in and grabbed him as he neared where they were standing. Banham then stepped in, blocking his way. His free hand was in the air. 'Whoa, hold up there, matey. This isn't helping anyone.'

'I told you to put him in a squad car and lock the fucking door,' Crowther snapped at Levington and John Piper, the two PCs who had run after Byfield. 'I won't have an irrational and unbalanced officer on duty here. No matter what the circumstances. Get him out of my sight.'

'Sir—' one of them went to protest.

'Just do it,' Crowther commanded throwing a hand in the air to indicate he wasn't interested in histrionics or emotions.

Byfield struggled as Piper and Levington dragged him way, 'That was Hannah,' he was protesting, but was calmed and coaxed and eventually taken down the road to a waiting car.

Crowther shouted after them, 'I am holding you two responsible for him. You do *not* let him back, or you will all be on a disciplinary.'

After a minute, Banham followed after them. He opened the opposite door as Byfield was put in the back, and the door about to be locked.

He leaned in. 'I'm sorry, mate. We are doing this for both you and Hannah's good. We'll get her out of there, I give you my word, if it's the last bloody thing I do. But you have to stay out of it.'

Byfield tried to argue, but Banham spoke over him.

'We do understand, mate, we truly do. This is for your good as well as Hannah's. You're understandably emotionally involved, and you can't help in that state.'

Crowther meanwhile had walked over and was on the other side of the car.

'Now get the hell out of here,' he snapped at PC Levington, who was in the driver's seat. And do not obstruct a police inquiry. Or so help me . . .'

'You think I give a fuck about your threats?' Byfield argued.

At the same time Levington and Piper turned to each other, both looking very displeased at Crowther's tone.

Banham knew Crowther was doing the right thing, but as usual, the detective was wading in with size eleven feet and no sensitivity, while Banham more than understood how Byfield was feeling.

Banham tapped Byfield on the shoulder. 'Trust me, you are best out of the way,' he told him.

As Banham walked back to the warehouse, his thoughts turned again to Alison. His doubts had now completely gone. Marrying her was the right thing to do. The past had to be the past and the future was going to be Alison. Unlike Hannah Kemp, she was safely away from all this, he had made sure of that. She would be boarding a plane about now, and soon so would he. He intended getting his mate Martin, along with Hannah and the other hostages, out first, and then he could hardly wait to join Alison and start their life together. He pulled his phone from his pocket and pressed Lorraine Cory's number.

'How far away are you? he asked.

'Another few minutes,' she told him. 'Traffic's bad. McCaub is beside me in the back. We are in one of the fleet cars, the black Volvo.'

'Keep him in the car. Don't let him out. Park at the end of Henry Street. They need to release Neville, and we need to get him safely into an ambulance, before we go any further.' He paused, rubbing his hand thoughtfully down over his mouth. 'And then I need to see the hostages. We know for sure we have PC Kemp in there. Byfield has confirmed it was her voice shouting to me out the window. That lad is in a bad way, so Crowther has sent him away. As I'm not one hundred per cent sure how many others are in there, we need to take this one careful step at a time. Hannah Kemp has only been with the force a short time, so I'm very concerned for her safety. Can you make sure you are a good distance away, but in sight of the warehouse?'

'Will do. Your op, Banny. I'm following you on this one. We'll be turning into Henry Street in just a few minutes.'

Banham quickly sent Alison another text. *Not long to go,* he texted, *and then I will be on a plane on my way to you, and our life together.*

He walked up Henry Street, signalled to Carter to keep SC019 in their positions, then stood in front of the warehouse, waiting.

Alison heard the beep of the text. She pulled her phone from her pocket, read it, and then looked at the CCTV screen in front of Derek Bridge. She shook her head and pushed her phone back in her pocket.

A few minutes later, Banham recognised the black Volvo carrying the super and McCaub. It had turned into the end of the road where it pulled up just behind the cordon, out of sight of the warehouse.

He nodded to Carter, then nodded sideways again to indicate McCaub was here. Carter immediately signalled to his team to stand by.

Banham then put the hailer to his mouth.

'I have good news, I have your friend McCaub arriving.' He waited for an answer. When one didn't come, he carried on. 'So listen up. You now must follow my instructions, if you want McCaub. Are you clear with this?'

There was a few seconds of silence from inside the warehouse. Banham and Carter held eye contact. Then Massafur's voice came out loud and clear.

'Where is he?'

'First release the wounded hostage.' Banham nodded to the three paramedics who all moved nearer the door.

'Where is he?'

'First, you release my wounded officer.'

'How do I know he's there? This could be a trick.'

'You will still have your other hostages.'

'I don't trust you. Till we see him, no one goes nowhere.'

'There is a black Volvo two minutes away. Your friend is in the back. There are three paramedics standing here, waiting. So let's be clear on this. McCaub will not leave that car until the wounded hostage is brought out and safely in the hands of these paramedics. We will then talk about the other hostages. This was the deal. I now need that wounded hostage.'

Again, there was no answer.

SCO19 had their rifles out in front of their chests, they were all edgy and wanting to move, their eyes on Jim Carter, ready to charge in on just a wave of his arm. Three of them were silently moving like alert snakes after their prey, sliding silently, on their bellies, on the side of roof towards the back of the building.

Everyone hardly dared breathe. The tension was sharper than the newly broken glass shards.

'I'm waiting,' Banham said after a few minutes.

'I told you, when you give me McCaub, then you can have your man.'

Banham's clasped hands pressed against his mouth, then slid across his lower face as he tried to think.

It was very clear these gunmen weren't going to give way, and they had the upper hand. They had the hostages. Banham's job was to get Neville to hospital, get the other hostages to safety, then arrest the gunmen, keeping everyone alive in the process. No easy feat. However, the safety of the hostages came before that of the hostage-takers to him. He also didn't know what condition Neville was in.

He beckoned to Jim Carter. Carter immediately came and stood beside him. 'We may need the boys on the roof to take our friends by surprise from the back. Looks like they aren't going to play ball,' Banham told him.

'They're ready, guv, they've been ready for two hours, and so is the team at the front. However, it'll take a few seconds to break in from the back. That door is heavy and well secured from inside. So when we go in, we go in from the front.'

Banham nodded. 'Nothing happens until I give you the go-ahead, is that clear?'

Carter shrugged. 'Your call, mate, but as I've said all along, I don't see this ending any other way. And how long can our boy in there cope? We don't know how bad that wound of his is. I still think the sooner we get in there, the better.'

'There are innocent people in there, and my job is to get them all out alive and safe.'

'Here's hoping,' Carter said, with a little shrug and little sincerity.

'My friend is in there, and the fiancée of one of my officers,' Banham reminded him sharply. 'I won't take chances with their lives. Or any others for that matter.'

Carter nodded. 'Which is why . . .' but Banham wasn't listening. He walked down to the end of the road. He was anxious. He walked past the car with the super and McCaub sitting in the back. He had to make a decision: did he send in SC019 in? Or did he allow them to see McCaub? The only way he could do that was to get the man to stand in the street. That was risking his life. So, that was out of the question. So what was for the best, he wondered?

'They won't release Neville until they see McCaub,' he said as Lorraine Cory wound down the window.

McCaub leaned over. 'Let me out of here. I'll go talk to them,' he said to Banham.

'He's not getting out of the car,' Lorraine told Banham. 'That's not happening. We will not let them hold all the cards. And I won't risk this boy's life.'

'Then it's over to SC019,' Banham told her.

'If that's to be, then let's get on with it.'

'One minute,' Banham said as he looked over at the unit car that Peter Byfield sat in. He walked down the road to the car and knocked on the window. It was immediately lowered by the young PC Levington.

Banham leaned in the window towards the back where Byfield sat next to PC Piper. 'Hopefully not much longer, mate,' he told him, speaking in a comforting voice. 'If you hear gunshots coming from up there, I don't want you to be alarmed.' He turned to Levington. 'Take a drive, will you, please? I'm not asking you to go far away. I understand Hannah's in there. But take a drive a street or two away. SC019 may go in, but all is safely in hand, and then we'll call you back.'

He didn't give Byfield a chance to answer. He looked at Levington, 'So take a little drive round the corner,' he told him.

As he pulled his head back out of the window Banham was wishing he could believe his own words, that all was in hand. Truth was, it was far from it. And his heart bled for Byfield. All three constables looked pale, tired, and drawn. They had all been out in this street now for nigh on twenty-four hours . No one understood just how hard they worked, least of all the sodding Home Office.

He turned and walked back to the warehouse, taking in the empty street. His eyes skimmed over the burned out vehicles, and the overturned dustbins, abandoned sticks, and broken furniture which had been used as weapons to fight the police and were now abandoned over the pavements. Thank goodness for CCTV, he thought. It would take time, but the station would get every one of the rabble who attacked any police officers and they would all be charged. He would make sure of that.

He checked around, he was looking for any sly journalists or photographers who might have sneaked back in, desperate for a story and a bit of fame, but who would surely get in the way and could mess up this extremely sensitive operation. He was satisfied the street was clear, apart from the uniformed presence who had been told to be there, plus the three waiting ambulances and the paramedics who stood, agitated and concerned, awaiting their patient. SC019 were in place, by the side of the front door, on their stomachs on the side of the roof, and now behind the building, as well as on the roofs of the houses opposite, still as frozen figures on an icy day. The forensics officers, who had been busying themselves around the scene in their bluebell plastic outfits, were now unzipping the outfits with matching plastic over-shoes and pulling off their white masks, and packing everything away in their oversized van, after being told by Crowther to finish up and clear the scene as swiftly as they could.

All was ready. Banham had decided there was no other way, it had to be a SC019 operation. He wanted the hostage-takers alive, but more than that, he wanted Martin Neville alive. As long as he got Neville to hospital, and Hannah Kemp out safe and sound, as well as the other innocent hostages, Banham told himself that the fate of the gunmen was now out of his hands. They had been given their chance. If you played with fire then you could well get burned.

'McCaub is here and waiting,' he spoke into his hailer. 'You must release the wounded man. I will then show you McCaub, and you will then release the other hostages. That is the way it will be, otherwise our bargain is over.'

'How do we know he's here? We only got your word. Show him to us, and then we'll talk about giving you that hostage.'

Banham sighed. He didn't see this ending well. They weren't

giving an inch. He now reckoned Carter had been right all along and the only way was to go in with SC019. It was all about to go up. He wanted Alison to know he had intended to spend his life with her, even if things ended badly and he didn't get the chance.

He pulled his phone from his pocket and texted her, *I love you, I truly and deeply do, and I want to spend my life with you.*

Chapter Thirteen

Alison read the text and sighed loudly. She then tapped a speedy reply and pressed *send*. She had brought up two youths from the riots, charged and bailed them. She knew she should be questioning more of them and freeing up the cells, but she kept going in and out of the CCTV operations room. She wanted to see Banham use McCaub to free the hostages. Then, she knew, he would find out she was still there, and working on the case, against his orders. She wondered if he would still love her and want to spend his life with her then. She would have to prepare for a real dressing-down. After that, at least they would start off on a better footing. Banham should know she wasn't the kind to be told what to do just because she was his wife. He had to respect her position as an officer, even if she was also his wife – but then that status was up for discussion.

She was watching Banham on the CCTV now. She could feel the tension. McCaub and Lorraine were in the car and Banham was waiting for the release of Neville. She turned to Derek Bridge, who was watching the CCTV that had the best view of Banham and the street. 'That was me Banny was just texting,' she told him. 'He thinks I'm at the airport on my way to Mykonos. He has no idea I'm watching him from here. Good start to a marriage, isn't it?' she mumbled, speaking half to herself.

'You're not married, though,' Bridge reminded her, turning around from the CCTV unit, to give her a grin and a wink. 'I am, and I tell porkies to the wife all the time. You have to, sometimes, to keep a marriage going. So what did you say to him?'

'I told him I was at the airport waiting to board a plane to Mykonos.'

Bridge raised his eyebrows. 'Well, you might be soon.' He pointed to the screen. 'This could all be over in a minute. Look over on CCTV, E unit. Banham was negotiating release of the hostages only minutes ago.'

'He told me,' she nodded. 'He said all was coming to a head, and he would be joining me in Mykonos soon. He keeps apologising for not marrying me, and has just said he loves me again.' She sighed, and lowered her eyelids, shaking her head. 'And I do too, Derek, I do love him.' She shook her head again. 'But marriage. It's too binding. It's just not for me. I'm actually glad I didn't have to go through with it, isn't that just awful?'

'No. But why are you afraid of marriage?'

'Big commitment. It makes it so final. And Banny's bossy too.'

Bridge frowned, then he smiled and seemed a little amused. 'Marriage isn't any different from living with someone really, you can still walk away you know. It doesn't come with a ball and chain these days,' he teased. 'Banny's bossy because he has to be, to be good at the job he does. You two are good together, you argue all the time, and that is the healthiest way to have a relationship. You need to sort your head out and be ready to jump,' he told her. 'But it's our luck that you didn't marry him today, because we need you here. We need all the manpower we can get. Everyone is on their knees with tiredness, but no one will go home until our Martin Neville is safe and our young Hannah Kemp too. So I, for one, am glad you are not at the airport. You can blame me if you want, when the shit hits the fan. I'll say I asked you to stay, and I made you lie.'

Alison took a of breath. 'Thanks, but I wouldn't do that.'

'Seriously, at the moment we all need to stay focused,' he told her. 'And you must do what you do best – detecting. You have been left in charge here. You know that though, you don't need me to remind you.' He turned back to the screen he had been watching. 'Look, Banny is talking to Peter Byfield. Can you imagine how that lad feels at the moment? He's less than a month away from marrying Hannah. Childhood sweethearts. They went to the same school, and ended up on this force together. He must be out of his mind with worry.'

Alison rubbed her head. It still itched where the twinkly tiara had been pinned into her hair. Had all this not happened, the marriage ceremony would all have been over with by now, and she and Banham would be in their comfy jeans, on their way to Mykonos as Mr and Mrs. She still didn't know if she was pleased it hadn't happened, or not.

'Don't let anyone take their eyes off any of those screens until the hostages are out,' she told Bridge. 'Any sign of the black Volvo moving into the street?'

'Can't see it,' Bridge said, just missing where the Volvo would park, as the edge of this screen had cut it off. 'It will be on full on CCTV screen B, though.'

'Let me know when it moves into Henry Street,' she said turning to the officer manning screen B, and then addressing the room of about a dozen uniformed police all behind various CCTV screens, all with different angles on Henry Street and the surrounding roads. 'And if anyone needs a pee, someone has got to replace them in their seat. We can't miss anything here. The super will want to see all the tapes when this is all over. So we want close-ups, or as close as we can get of anyone who has been involved in any form of violence out there. Anyone wandering around the back streets, hone in on them and get photos. We also need to try to follow the hostages' steps up to the shooting, so go back on those CCTV moments and get all you can, blow it up and print it out. National press are on this. We have to be seen to be handling it with utter confidence and professionalism, and charging everyone who committed a crime out there. The Home Secretary has just OK'd the hoses, how do you like that? More than a few hours too late. He probably had other things to do first,' she added sarcastically.

'Lunch at some fancy restaurant, I expect,' PC Adam Kent turned from his CCTV monitor and joked.

Alison nodded. 'Anyway, all that is over, we hope, so hoses won't be needed. Just the SC019 unit by the looks of things.'

'We keep them on standby though?' he asked. 'Just in case of another fire?'

Alison nodded. 'Yes, for sure.'

Bridge looked at Alison. 'Talking of burning, aren't you a bit of a redhead?' Before she had time to answer, he carried on. 'You know you'll need extra factor when you do get to Mykonos, to stop you burning in that Greek sun.'

'I'm not going though, am I,' she said, swallowing down the urge to tell him how many times a man had nagged her about what SP factor she should need in the last hour. Now she knew why she didn't want to be married.

Banham slipped his phone back into his pocket after reading the text. At least Alison was safe. She would be sipping champagne just before boarding, he felt sure.

Then his phone rang.

'What are we waiting here for?' Lorraine Cory asked him. 'Where is Neville?'

'They need to see McCaub. Until they see him, they say they won't release the hostages. Is he safe in the back of the car?'

'Yes, he's sitting in the back handcuffed to PC Stewart, and the car is central-locked. He can't get out.'

Banham could hear McCaub arguing that he wanted to get out and meet Massafur one to one. He wanted Farzi out of there.

'Shut it,' Lorraine shouted.' 'Sorry, Banny, not you,' she turned back to the phone and said. 'Drive the car up and park a few yards down on the other side of the road, so McCaub's side of the car is facing the warehouse. Then they can see him, but he'll be safe.'

'Will do.'

'If they don't release Neville when they see McCaub, and then the other hostages. I am handing the operation over to Carter.'

'Your call.'

Banham then walked the few steps and stood directly opposite the warehouse. Crowther joined him.

'They aren't going to let Neville out until they see McCaub,'

Banham repeated to Crowther. 'They've made that clear. So we're letting them see McCaub. He stays in the car though. Then the car can drive further down and round the corner. If they don't then release Neville it's over to Jim Carter.'

'Guv.'

Banham watched the three paramedics who were still standing near the door. They all looked nervous and very concerned.

'If this goes to plan and they give us Neville, make sure the exhibits officer has the longest lens he can get,' he told Crowther.

'I'm on it.'

'Tell him to get shots inside the warehouse as the door opens to let Neville out. It will be vital for SC019 to see the inside. They will have no reason to keep the other hostages, but if they then use them to barter their way to escape, it'll give the team a big advantage if we know exactly what we're facing inside.'

'Guv.' Crowther hurried off to talk to the exhibits officer.

Banham looked back down the street. 'Christ, here we go,' he said half to himself, as the black Volvo drove at a funeral procession pace, passing the warehouse, with McCaub sitting in the back. The Volvo then came to a stop, parking just a hundred yards up from the warehouse, as he had been instructed, but with McCaub in clear view.

Hannah had started to shake again, badly. At first it was her hands trembling, but now her legs were at it too. She just couldn't get a grip. She sat on the damp, cold, dirty floor, staring at her dead partner, her arm and heart both screaming in pain. No one else in the room seemed to care, and for that she felt even worse. And if those animals felt like that, when they were standing just a few feet from the police officer who they had murdered in cold blood, then there was no doubt they were capable of killing again. She felt she would be next, and then it would be the rest of these innocent hostages.

She could hear Banham shouting his instructions, asking for Neville to be released. She was trained to ease tension in a situation, but right now she was capable of nothing, she felt like a soggy rag. She wanted to cry out, but stopped herself; they would hurt her again if she did. As it was she couldn't see straight, and she was in agonising pain. The worst though was the pain in her heart. She felt she had let her best friend down. He had died in this dirty, terrifying place without his wife to hold his hand. She stretched her good hand out and gently touched his face, then she moved it down and held his lifeless hand. What a way to go. How would she tell Edna how he'd died? That was if she got out of the hellhole herself.

Massafur and Sadiq were both standing by the window, far enough back not to be seen, but near enough to get a good eyeball of McCaub as he arrived.

'It's him,' Hannah heard Sadiq say, followed by a confident nod. She then watched, as best she could, as they turned to each other, shook hands, and lifted their rifles.

Another shudder, like a volt of electricity, shot through her being. What did that mean?

Alison had been half-heartedly looking through the list of prisoners. She stopped abruptly as she spotted a prisoner with the name Kevin McCaub on the list. This couldn't be a coincidence, it had to be a relation. She told Sgt Bridge to call her if anything started happening in Henry Street. Meanwhile she hurried down to interview room B, where she summoned the young Trainee DC Hank Peacock to help her interview, and called for Kevin McCaub to be brought up to be interview room C.

After the usual introduction of officers present and the explanation he was being videoed and recorded, Alison said to Kevin McCaub. 'You have been charged with theft and causing an affray.' She was studying him very closely as she spoke. He certainly resembled Devlin. He had the same black hair and the piercing blue eyes, and he too wore a gold ring in his left ear. He also spoke with a soft Irish lilt. He looked older though, and she noted his age: twenty-six. She was sure they were related.

When he merely nodded by way of, 'I couldn't give a shit,' she continued.

'So who were you fighting with?'

He shrugged, making it clear that he wasn't going to be cooperative, and if she wanted to charge him, it wasn't going to bother him one iota.

She leaned forward. 'See, I have a situation here, and it involves a Devlin McCaub. And I believe you know him?'

He immediately sat up in his chair. She had his attention.

'Why do you believe that?' he asked.

'Are you related?'

When he answered with another of his arrogant shrugs, she changed her attitude and became sharper. 'Listen, we both know I can look your details up in a minute on our computer, and I'll even know what size underpants you wear, but I thought you might want to be known as helping in an inquiry . . .'

'I'm not a grass.'

'I certainly know that. But I think you know Devlin McCaub.'

He showed no reaction. But he was listening.

'If he was in trouble, which he is, and you were related, I feel sure you would want to help him. Am I right?

Still no reaction.

'I also think if I get the CCTV evidence, which we have, of you fighting and breaking into a shop window, I will find you were with this Devlin, and were fighting a family headed by a Massafur Khan. I am right, aren't I?'

His eyes bored into hers. He had taken in what she said, and was obviously weighing up what to say.

'You can talk to me. Devlin has already told us everything.'

Kevin said nothing. Alison pushed again.

'He is going with Massafur Khan's sister, right?'

His eyebrows went up but he didn't say a word.

'She has been taken hostage,' Alison told him. 'Which I think you also know. And Devlin is helping the situation by accompanying our officers, as we speak, and helping to negotiate her release. Khan has also taken other hostages into the warehouse there, one of which is a badly wounded police officer. Now this—'

'No, for Christ's sake . . .' Now his attitude changed. His hands flew up in the air. 'OK, OK. Devlin is my brother. And yes, he is with Farzi. She is his wife, for the love of God. He married her in secret. That Khan family are fucking unbalanced killers. Oh, but you know everything, as you just said.' He leaned towards her. 'Well, did you know they have murdered five people already?'

This took Alison by surprise. 'Who?' she asked.

'Do you remember the bodies that were found in that park near Beckenham, three years back, when no killer was ever found? Two male bodies, the men were shot through the head. They were wrapped in rubbish sacks, and buried under piles of leaves, over by the woods beyond the golf course there. They had been tortured, burns all over them, and the fingers on their left hands cut off.'

'Go on.'

'And shortly after that, a woman's body was found in the same park. A Muslim woman. Stab wounds and a multitude of burns to her body, third finger missing on her left hand. And then another one. Her genitals mutilated, then burned. She was in a shallow grave, in another park in Catford.'

'What are you telling me?'

'I'm telling you there is another woman. Her name is Nounia Ashraf. No one reported her missing. Everyone was told she went back to Pakistan. Her body has never been found. When, and if, it is, it will be in the same butchered mess as the other women's. Nounia and Farzila were cousins. Another cousin is a man called Sadiq Ashraf. Massafur Khan and Sadiq Ashraf murdered those men, and then the two women, who were also their cousins, Aisha and Priya Ashraf. They had married their English boyfriends in secret, and because the husbands weren't a family choice for the women, the *family*, that's those bastards Sadiq Ashraf and Massafur Khan, tortured and killed them. Nounia too.'

Alison's mind went into overdrive. 'How do you know all this is the truth?'

He leaned forward towards Alison. She could see he was worried and worked up.

'Believe me, or don't believe me, but why would I tell you? And, yes, Devlin is my brother, and he married Farzi to keep her safe from those butchers. If you've put him anywhere near that family, then his life is in grave fucking danger.'

'What happened in Henry Street before you were arrested? Tell me everything that happened, right up until you were arrested,' Alison asked, ignoring his remark, although her mind was now in overdrive for Devlin's safety. 'We know you were there when the gun went off. Who fired it?'

'It all happened so quickly. I was accompanying Farzi and Devlin, guarding them if you like. We were going to meet Massafur, or so they thought. Devlin asked me to come, to help keep an eye on Farzi. He hadn't wanted to go at all, but Farzi had. Massafur had said he was OK with her, just wanted to see her. It was the family, not him, that were against Devlin. Devlin and I suspected trouble, tried to persuade her it was a trap, but she wouldn't have it. She wanted to believe him, wanted to see her brother, so we agreed to take her.

'Riots had broken out as we walked into the area. Sadiq and Massafur must have spread the word, posted info to rival gangs, so trouble would break out in that street, which it did, and he would be free to get to Farzi and Devlin.

'As we walked down the street, we were jumped on, I don't know who they were. Maybe Massafur's family. But there were more of them than us. Devlin and I broke the window in the shop we were next to.'

Alison raised her eyebrows.

'We needed weapons, and quick. The shop was there, and we went for it. We came out with TVs for arming ourselves. I remember hearing a bang, I wasn't worried, fireworks were going off all the time. It could have been anything. It was mayhem out there. There were people everywhere, fighting and scrapping, and feds were there, with horses and dogs. It was way out of hand. So I didn't think the bang was from a gun.'

Alison watched him, very carefully. When she made no comment he continued.

'There were home-made petrol bombs getting thrown at the feds. It was bedlam. Cars had been set on fire, bits of them exploding in the air. I'm telling you, fucking bedlam. Sorry, sorry for swearing.'

'OK. And then what happened?'

'It was a set-up for sure, the word had been sent round that there was a party happening and rival gangs would be there. Everyone wanted a bit of the action. If you hear a bang in a situation like that, you don't think of it as a gun going off.'

'Tell me what happened to you and Farzi and Devlin.'

'I had my head turned, eyes on the men that jumped our lot. I hadn't recognised them, but as they came for us, I hit out with the TV I'd pulled from the shop. That's when the shot happened. I didn't see Devlin as I turned back, but I saw Farzi, she was being dragged—'

'Who by? Who was dragging Farzi?'

'Massafur, definitely Massafur, and a few others, I didn't see who. I didn't see that Sadiq Ashraf, not at that second.'

'Who else? Can you give me names. I need names.'

'No I can't, I only know Massafur and Sadiq Ashraf. I don't know the others well enough. They had things over their heads. Don't you have CCTV?' He leaned into Alison. 'Listen, I need to know that my brother is not being put at risk. They will kill him given the slightest chance, that's what all that riot was set up for. And then they'll kill her, without a doubt, but they'll really hurt her first. You don't need to be here giving me the . . .' He lifted his hand and put his fingers towards her, then touched them over the thumb several times, imitating a person talking too much. 'You need to let me out of here. I need to go and help him.'

Alison believed him, yet she couldn't phone and warn Banham. Lorraine was with Devlin McCaub at this moment. She would have to be careful if she rang and relayed all this to her. McCaub might overhear. But she had to convey all this, somehow, and warn them all.

They already knew that Farzila Khan was one of the hostages. Devlin had been so keen to get to his new wife and help her, understandably, that he hadn't said anything about the fact that the hostage-takers were known to him as cold-blooded killers.

'Does Devlin know what his wife's family are like, and the risk he's taking? she asked.

'He loves her. That says it all, doesn't it,' Kevin said sincerely.

Alison nodded. 'Thank you,' she said, then leaned in to the tape, 'DI Alison Grainger leaving the room. Two fifty-seven pm.' She then nodded to Hank Peacock to keep an eye on the prisoner. She clicked the video and the running tape to *off* and left the room.

She rang Lorraine Cory's mobile, but it went to voicemail.

Chapter Fourteen

Banham watched as the black Volvo drove slowly past the warehouse and stopped a good few yards up the street, but within seeing distance from the window of the building. He could hear McCaub from where he stood, ranting and shouting like a madman from inside the car. He knew the man was handcuffed to Stan Stewart in the back, so couldn't jump out.

No sound came from inside the warehouse, no more hysterics. All was silent. Banham knew both the hostage-takers would have their eyes fixed on that car.

SC019 were back in their position, on the side of the warehouse roof, across the road, and in the alleyway at the side, all with rifles at the ready. The only sounds came from McCaub inside the black Volvo.

Carter and Crowther both were stood by Banham, also in nervous silence.

The three paramedics stood together, at the side of the building, oxygen and a stretcher beside them, all anxiously awaiting their patient.

It was Banham's move. His eyes took in the scene around him, then he lifted the hailer to his mouth.

'If you open the front door you will see Devlin McCaub. He is in the black Volvo a few yards up the street, on the left. But I think you know that. I have brought him to you. Now you must bring the wounded hostage to the front door, then get the others ready to follow. You will then get your friend.'

No answer came.

★

Hannah was still holding Martin's hand, but she had sat up and was listening. Sadiq and Massafur were either side of the window. They made eye contact at Banham's words.

Hannah glanced over at Farzi, who was looking terrified, and then at Massafur, who was pressed against the wall by the window, Sadiq next to him, both watching and whispering to each other. They knew they couldn't release Nevs, Hannah thought anxiously. She also knew if they didn't open the front door, there was no doubt the gun team would burst in and start shooting.

Hannah remembered there was water outside the front door. If she asked for it again, and in the slim chance Massafur agreed, then they would have to open the door, and that would give the team an upper hand. It was worth a try.

'Please,' she asked. 'I need a drink. There is water outside the front door, may I have some?'

Neither Massafur or Sadiq answered her. They were still whispering to each other in a language she didn't understand. The older woman seemed to be listening. The older man had his back to everyone, and Farzi now had her head down sobbing.

Then she saw Sadiq pull his handgun from his belt and march purposefully over to the three hostages, who sat a little apart from each other against the far wall. She held her breath, were they going to release them, or kill them?

Sadiq grabbed Farzi by the hair, as Massafur speedily untied her hands from the radiator she was attached to. Sadiq then dragged her to her feet and held both her hands behind her back with one of his. He then pushed his pistol into the side of her temple. She shrieked in terror, and then tried to spit at him. He quickly moved his hand from hers and hit her across the back of the head, then grabbed her hands again as she attempted to fight him back. 'If you move, I will blow her head off,' he announced, looking straight at Hannah.

While Farzi wriggled agitatedly, and kicked out, at the same time licking the blood that had dripped from her nose and onto her lips, Buisha turned and spoke with much distress in his voice. 'I will have a stroke soon,' he shouted. 'Let me out of here, I want to go now. I need my pills. Mariam!'

The older woman, who Hannah realised was Mariam, turned to him. 'Hush your noise. We are getting out of here in a few minutes.' She then turned and spoke sharply to Farzi, 'Quiet down. Don't make things worse. Just do as they say.'

Massafur flicked a glance in her direction, but made no comment. He turned back to Sadiq and in a whispered tone, Hannah heard him say, 'Do it.'

The thought jumped into her mind that he was going to shoot Farzi. She wished she had the strength and energy to intervene, but she didn't. She was in too much pain, both emotionally and physically. Her partner was dead and the pain in her arm was so bad, she was losing the ability to think straight. Staring at Nevvy's lifeless body had drained any energy she had. Her fighting spirit had died along with him. He had been her best friend and close colleague. She suspected Banham was near to finishing this. She would leave it to him. Martin wasn't being freed, so Banham would most certainly send in the armed response team, and there would be a shoot-out. She would keep herself together for that. It would be down to her to try to keep the other three hostages safe if that happened, and then get them out. And Martin's body would be her priority. She didn't want him getting trampled on, or his dead body shot again. She was determined to stop that happening, at all costs, for his widow's sake.

'You will keep your word, won't you?' she spoke again before she could stop herself. 'At least release Martin's body to them, so they can take him away and bury him.'

Sadiq still had a gun to Farzi's head. She hadn't heeded Mariam's words. She was still wriggling and kicking out at Sadiq, and spitting where she could.

'If you don't stop your whinging, there will be two dead bodies,' he snapped back at Hannah.

'He can go when we have McCaub,' Massafur told Hannah.

Farzi bit Sadiq at that moment. At the same time she lifted her leg and kneed him in the balls. He pulled his hands back and bent over with pain and shock.

'Don't trust him. This is a trap for Devlin. They are lying,' Farzi shouted to Hannah.

Massafur immediately grabbed her while Sadiq got his breath. Massafur then smacked her hard in the head again. 'You want me to take your eyes out, so you can't see him?' he threatened, smacking her across the head again. 'You dirty whore.'

Hannah opened her mouth to try to calm the situation but was stopped in her tracks by Mariam, who butted in. 'I told you, you need to shut your mouth,' she told Farzi sternly.

Sadiq then hit Farzi in the face with the butt of his gun. Blood immediately spurted from her nose.

As Farzi cried out in anger and pain, the older woman continued. 'You are your own worst enemy. If you make them angry, they will kill you.' She too was getting hysterical.

Then the old man started again. He was addressing no one in particular. 'I need my pills, please let me go.'

Farzi didn't heed the woman, she screamed loudly, 'Help. Someone he-elp!'

Sadiq was now seething. He was in pain from being kicked and all the screaming had obviously got to him. Hannah watched, in horror, as he pulled his pistol from his sock, still holding Farzi's two hands with his other hand.

Hannah jumped up. 'Don't, please,' she shouted, using her good arm to reach over and try to pull Sadiq from Farzi.

Massafur grabbed her by her bad arm and threw her back on the floor. She landed on the already damaged arm and heard another crack. Agonising pain went through her. She became immediately quiet.

'Next time, I'll knock you out,' Massafur spat at her.

Both the older hostages had become silent. Hannah realised they were terrified.

She too became silent.

Sadiq then cocked the pistol and, quick as a flash, he aimed it in the air and pulled the trigger.

Everyone froze except Farzi. She screamed so loudly, you would have heard the noise on the other side of London.

Banham was standing opposite the door watching, and waiting for it to open when the shot went off.

Then everything seemed to happen at once.

Jim Carter, having heard the shot being fired, hurried across the road and was standing in the alleyway, out of view from the warehouse, but in front of his team. He quickly gave signalled orders to the men on the roof of the warehouse, to move to the back, as the shot had soared upwards through the roof.

Then the front door of the warehouse opened and a hostage-taker stood in the doorway. It was Sadiq. He held a young woman – Farzi – as a human shield, a gun to the side of her head. Blood was dripping from her nose and had dried around her face, which Banham could see was red and swollen.

Banham put his hailer on the floor without taking his eyes off Sadiq. He outstretched both his hands, palms facing out, as a way of telling the man to take it easy. The SC019 team were within eyeball, and to his right. Banham signalled to them to move back. He could see how difficult it would be to take the hostage-taker out without any risk of the girl getting shot by either SC019, or even the hostage-taker if he saw all the rifles aimed at him and panicked. And Banham wasn't taking any risks.

Carter stood in the alleyway, a pistol in his hand, diagonally facing the hostage and captor from the back.

Everyone was still. All eyes were pinned to Sadiq and Farzi.

All had taken their eyes off the Volvo carrying the super and Devlin McCaub.

'I have McCaub right here,' Banham said, speaking slowly and calmly. 'And, as agreed, we get all the hostages in return, so let the girl go.'

Sadiq pulled the tearful, shaking, bleeding girl tighter into himself, but said nothing.

'What was that gunshot just now?'

'None of your business,' Sadiq answered.

'I need to know no one else is hurt,' Banham argued. 'And I am waiting for the release of my officer.'

Sadiq stood, but said nothing.

Banham pushed on. 'Do you want to tell me what's going on?' He flicked his eyes to Carter, who now had the back of Sadiq's head in range of his pointed pistol.

Carter nodded to Banham.

Banham's eyes went back to Sadiq. His attention was on the gun pressed into the girl's head. Then his eyes went from the man to Carter. He wanted to tell Carter to put the pistol down, but he couldn't risk the hostage-taker seeing it.

The next moment the passenger door of the Volvo opened. Banham's eyes were so fixed on the scene in front of him, he didn't notice. Nor did he see Massafur creep to the window, his AK47 out in front of himself.

As Lorraine left the car and hurried over to Banham, no one realised she had released the central locking on the car, or that the back window had slid down and Devlin McCaub's head was through it.

Banham heard the warning from both the SC019 team on the roof of the building opposite the warehouse, who shouted, 'Sir, the car!' at the same time as Stan Stewart also shouted, 'Get back!' But the words were muffled, as it was the exact same time that Farzi shrieked to Devlin.

'It's OK, darling, I'm—' Devlin shouted back from the open window.

But they were the only words he got out. Massafur's shot had hit him square between the eyes.

Banham and Lorraine both swung round to see McCaub's head bump down, hitting the outside of the back door of the car. Blood and mucus had burst through the young man's brain and shot like a party popper into the air. The side of the car was slowly dribbling dark blood and mucus into the road.

'Jesus!' Lorraine shouted.

Banham lifted his hand to give the go ahead to SC019 to take a shot at the hostage-taker, but Sadiq wasn't there. He had pulled the screaming, hysterical Farzi back inside the warehouse.

The door was locked and Farzi was pushed back onto the floor. She was still screaming and spitting as they dragged, and then tied her back to the radiator. 'Murderers! Murderers!' she yelled in tearful hysteria. She kicked and fought, receiving heavy blows to her head in retaliation. Then she became silent – then the screaming started again.

Hannah had sat up. She was both terrified and horrified. She had seen Massafur take a shot out the window.

'My God,' she said. 'What's happened?'

'Just shut the fuck up,' came the reply from Sadiq.

Lorraine Cory, Banham, Crowther, and Carter had hurried back to the blood-spattered car. There was now just a trickle of blood from the young man's head. McCaub had died instantly.

'It all happened so quickly,' Stan Stewart said to Lorraine. 'I shouted and we were about to pull the window up, but in that second, he was gone.' The poor constable had gone white. Even he, who had served in the Met for more than twenty years, had seen nothing like this before.

Banham put a hand to his face as Lorraine told Stan Stewart, who was still handcuffed to the dead McCaub, and Les the driver that neither could move, they had to stay exactly as they were. Forensics had been called.

Chapter Fifteen

Farzi couldn't keep quiet, no matter what they threatened. The sobbing had now become blood-curdling screams again, and could be heard all the way down the street.

Hannah sat, perfectly still, looking from Farzi to Sadiq, then to Massafur. She knew they wouldn't take much more, and was now terrified for the fate of the young woman.

A few seconds prior, when Massafur fired the rifle, she had thought he had shot Farzi. Now, as Farzi was dragged back in, she was slowly realising that it was McCaub he had killed, the man they had been saying they would free the hostages in exchange for. And if Massafur had killed him, in cold blood, what would the fate of the hostages be now? It was their lives he had been bartering with.

She shivered as she thought how Martin Neville had just died, in her arms, in front of them, and, despite how she had pleaded, they had shown no interest or compassion to save him. She now doubted any of them would get out alive. There was no intervention from SC019, despite someone having been shot, and as far as she could hear — even though with Farzi's hysterical screaming, it was hard to hear anything — no one outside was asking questions.

If only she could let DCI Banham know that Martin was dead, then SC019 would storm in, and end it. They must be planning something, she was sure of that, as sure as she knew they were treading very carefully because they believed Nevs was still alive and injured.

There were now three hostages, as well as herself. She really had

117

to stay alert. Massafur and Sadiq, and the woman Mariam, were all around the hysterical Farzi and the older man, Buisha. The window was free, and if she could get to it, there was a possibility of calling out to Banham to tell him Martin was dead. But it was just too chancy. They would definitely hurt her badly if she did, and the threat of rape from Sadiq was too much to risk. Her arm, she believed, was broken, her face so swollen she could barely see. And she had to look out for these hostages, because something could happen any minute, and she wanted to be in a position to help them. She was dealing with killers. If she wanted to see her Peter again, she told herself, she had to stay quiet, but very alert.

'Murderers!' Farzi screamed again, at the top of her voice, with Mariam trying desperately to shut her up.

'Shut up, or they will kill you too, here and now!' But it was all in vain. 'I will kill you myself!'

Farzi screamed even louder, even with her hands tied. She was acting like a wild animal, spitting and trying to bite them.

Massafur lost his temper. He lifted his rifle and, turning it round, butted Farzi hard across the head with the end of it. She dropped, unconscious, to the floor. As she did, he kicked her stomach. 'You wait till you see what we will do to you,' he spat at her. 'Burn your dirty soul free, then we will cut you up, and bury you, but not your head. We will let the rats eat you.'

That sent a shiver through Hannah. Was there no end to their brutality? She was half glad Farzi was unconscious and couldn't hear.

'After they have eaten your eyes, we will choke the witch out of you,' he added.

Hannah sat in silence by her dead best friend, starting to feel terrified as the pieces were coming together. This had been a set-up all along, but it had gone wrong. McCaub should have been there with Farzi when they were all dragged into the warehouse, but he had got away because the police had swooped so quickly when the shooting happened, and he had been arrested, and dragged into a meat van to get locked in a police cell. Hence how Banham had found him so quickly. McCaub too had now been shot, but how badly, she didn't know, yet, unless Farzi's screams were accurate and he was really dead.

And there were the other innocent hostages. Hannah remembered she had seen Buisha during the riots, when he had wandered into the middle of it all. He had possibly been on his way home, or closing up his shop, poor man. He seemed to be in a different world to everyone else. Maybe that was better, she thought, as she listened to his mumbling. It was clear he needed his medication. He needed to be freed. She knew they wouldn't free her, she was a fed, and a valuable commodity for negotiating with, especially once the DCI found out Martin was dead. She knew the force would be very concerned for her safety, and that these murderers would use that for their advantage. They could release the older hostages, they had others. As for Farzi, this was all about her, so Hannah knew the poor woman was going nowhere. She was the big concern. Keeping her safe when the shit hit the fan, which could be any second now. Farzi had been beaten a lot, and she was unconscious, so Hannah would have to carry her. But in a way that was better: the girl was very highly strung; unconscious, at least she was quiet. Hannah's priority was Martin Neville's body. But she couldn't carry Farzi as well, only one of her arms worked, and she could see only through one eye.

It had all happened so quickly. They had been working the riots together, her and Nevs, talking about the wedding. They had moved to the wrong place at the wrong time. It could have been any of that on-duty team in their place. A fight had broken out near where they were, and both of them had ploughed in to break it up. She now knew it had all been a set-up to get to Farzi and McCaub. And Martin had lost his life because of it. And now she might lose hers. And then what would her Peter do? He was always saying that she was his world and he couldn't live without her. Maybe he would have to. They might not even see each other again. Would she live to walk down the aisle with her Peter, she wondered? And would she ever get to wear that beautiful hand-made dress, even if the arm of it had to be altered yet again, to accompany a sling?

Chapter Sixteen

The local and national press, as well as TV cameras and all radio stations in the area, were only a road or two away when the shooting happened, all waiting for their headline of the day. After the gun went off, they were all on the move, hovering as near as they could to Henry Street, their long-lens cameras out trying to get a picture. The already exhausted uniformed team were keeping them at bay at the cordons.

'Get Forensics back here,' Banham told Crowther. 'Tell them to turn round and come straight back, we urgently need a tent over that car. And get uniform to cordon the area even further out. And any press that sets foot in the road, or the surrounding roads, confiscate their cameras and arrest them.'

'Guv.'

An ambulance screamed its way into the road as Banham spoke. Lorraine Cory moved from the car and hurried over to Banham.

'Jesus,' she said quietly. 'What a complete mess.'

Les, the driver of the police Volvo, sat unmoving, knowing if he opened his driver's door, he might interfere with evidence. Stan Stewart also hadn't moved, he just sat, his hand joined to the one of the dead man, palm up and facing outwards, as if stopping traffic.

'Let the ambulance through,' Crowther roared at the crowd of press who had now gathered around the new cordon into Henry Street. 'Do not cross the cordon. Back, all of you, no one can enter this street. It is a crime scene.'

'What's happened? What's the latest?'

He ignored them. He had his mobile at his ear and was urgently calling the forensic team back.

'Clear this area. Now,' Banham barked loudly from his place further up in Henry Street. He could see a couple of other press mounting a wall, cameras around their necks, hoping not to be noticed.

'If I see or hear a camera flash, I will confiscate your cameras and have you up for obstructing a crime scene,' Crowther barked at them. 'Now take the order, and back off.'

At the same time, the paramedics Ainsley and Mary moved towards the dead man slumped at the window with a bullet in his head. Blood had bubbled and formed on McCaub's lips. His head, which had briefly twitched as the bullet went into his skull, was now still. All knew he was dead, but Mary reached out, and placed her finger on the vein in his neck, nodding the confirmation.

'We need to get this car covered, and then lifted,' Banham said to Lorraine.

Lorraine had a cigarette lit and was inhaling like an asthmatic on much-needed oxygen. 'This is my fault,' she muttered quietly.

Banham shook his head. 'Don't say that,' he said.

Jim Carter still had his team held on standby. He walked over to join Banham at the car. At the same time, the van carrying the forensic team sped in and pulled up parallel to the car, blocking any view to it from the warehouse. Banham, Crowther, Carter, and Lorraine then moved a few feet away to give them space.

'But it is my fault,' Lorraine said, lowering her voice and speaking directly to Banham. 'We were locked in, I released the locks as I jumped out when the shots went off. The lock should have gone back on as I closed the door, but he obviously had his finger on the window button by that time. It just happened so quickly. It *is* my fault.'

Banham shook his head. 'We'll talk about it later,' he told her. 'We need to concern ourselves with the other hostages in there. We are dealing with cold blooded killers.' He turned to see Peter Byfield hurrying up Henry Street towards him.

'Oh shit,' Crowther said, hurrying over to stop him.

How he had been allowed to get out of the Panda car, Banham couldn't guess, but Byfield was the last thing he needed right now.

'What's going on? I need to know,' Byfield shouted out.

Banham kept calm as he said to Crowther, 'Get that man off this street. Now,' speaking in an even tone.

'Tell me what's going on,' came the reply from Byfield.

'I won't tell you again,' Banham raised his voice. 'Get off the street now, or we will lock you up.'

Byfield took a step closer, but Crowther stepped in to block his path to Banham.

He put his outstretched hands firmly against the man's chest. 'You've been asked to go home three times, mate,' he said. 'Even when it became an order, you refused. My patience is running out. So,' he raised his tone to loud and authoritative, 'back off, this minute, or you are facing jail, and a misconduct charge. I'm not kidding. Make your mind up, you either wait in the car in the next road or back at the station in a cell. I said move!'

Byfield held his ground and stood in front of Crowther. 'I will not leave Hannah,' he barked back.

Banham walked over to him. 'There is no reason to believe that Hannah is not safe, Peter,' he spoke in a gentle but firm tone. 'We're doing everything we can to get her out. We have a crisis on our hands here. You are not helping – in fact you're causing problems. Best way to help Hannah is to leave this to us and wait in the car. We understand how hard this is for you.'

'How the fuck can you understand?'

'OK.' Crowther swung around and grabbed Byfield's arm. 'That's enough. You are obstructing a police investigation. You have two minutes to get off this crime scene, otherwise I will have you arrested.' His voice grew louder yet again. 'And don't think I won't. Along with that, your so-called mates will also be done too, for letting you out of that car' He moved into Byfield and pushed him in the shoulder. 'If you don't want to get your mates locked up too, do it. Now. Get off this street.'

'Please, don't make me leave Hannah,' Byfield started pleading.

Crowther showed no sympathy. He signalled to two PCs standing on the corner of the road. 'Baker, Spiers,' he shouted, rolling his forefinger inwards for them to hurry over. 'Get this man home. If he won't go, or won't stay locked in the back of that car, arrest him and lock him in a cell.' Before either had time to argue, Crowther spoke again. 'That's a direct order, break it, and you'll both be sleeping in the same jail cell tonight.'

Banham had turned his back to them and walked back to Lorraine. Crowther knew the DCI was thinking that he was cold-hearted, but then someone had to be. Crowther knew about Banham's first wife, and of course he sympathised, which was why he knew he had to take the strong line. They had hostages to get out, and a police witness slumped over the window of a police car with a bullet in his head. A massive cock-up, with the surrounding streets buzzing with press. Nonetheless Crowther then softened his tone to Byfield.

'We'll keep you in touch and up to date with everything that happens, Peter,' he added quietly. Then putting the authority back in his voice he said, 'Now get the fuck out of here.'

Jim Carter crossed back from the side of the warehouse to Banham. He was less than happy. 'I hope you agree now,' he said to the DCI, 'when I say the only chance of getting those hostages out is for us to go in and get them. What have you got to barter with now? Nothing. Hand the operation over to me. I'll take the flak. You know I'm right.'

Banham rubbed his hand over his mouth, then said calmly, 'They've just murdered someone in broad daylight. There are innocent civilians in there as well as police officers. You can't guarantee any of those their safety. The answer's no, I won't chance anyone else getting shot.'

Lorraine's phone trilled at that moment. She noticed Alison's name on the screen, and quickly turned her back on Banham, walking speedily out of his hearing range to pick up the call.

Alison told the super she was back in the CCTV room. She had seen what had happened. Then she updated her on Kevin McCaub interview.

'Under no circumstances is Kevin McCaub to know that his brother has been shot,' Lorraine told Alison. 'Get photos of Sadiq Ashraf and Massafur Khan and show them to him. If he can confirm they are the same two men that murdered those people who were buried in the parks in Beckenham and Catford, then get a written statement saying so. Get as many details on them as he can give you. Full names, addresses etc, then run it through HOLMES, and get back to me, ASAP.'

'Will do, ma'am. Would it be a good idea to let DCI Banham know I'm here, now? I could come down and help.'

'No, definitely not a good idea.' Lorraine quickly cut the call then walked back to Banham. She relayed the news.

Carter was listening. 'With respect, ma'am,' he said, 'I don't think we should wait a second longer, if they are guilty of previous murders and have just shot someone in broad daylight.'

'My priority is to get the hostages out alive,' Banham told him sharply.

'We need to find out the full names of who exactly is in there,' Lorraine said. 'I have the names of the two cold case female bodies with missing left fingers, and Kevin McCaub, Devlin's brother, has told us they are the same family as these two, Sadiq and Massafur. If I can confirm these bastards' full names, then I can piece this together, and we can move on charging them for those park murders, the four confirmed, as well as this cold-blooded killing. Plus another, if we can find the other woman's body.'

'And another, if Martin Neville dies,' Carter added.

'So let's ask them who they are.'

'I know this is your operation, mate,' Jim Carter said to Banham. 'But you should listen to my expertise. You are dealing with pure killers here. My advice all along has been to get in there and finish this. We might have avoided this death if we had.'

Banham was furious at that remark. He swung round to Carter. 'And we might have caused more than just this one,' he argued back.

'And you are right on one thing, this is my operation. So *I* will make the decisions. Keep your men on standby. I will tell you when to go in.'

'On your head be it,' Carter snapped back. 'I've told you what I think. You didn't listen before. Now one man is dead. So who's going to take the rap for any other murders? My team are trained—'

Banham's hand flew up. 'I've already told you. I'll take the flak, but I won't take chances.'

'A thinking man,' Carter said sarcastically. 'Is that what you were doing, thinking, when you left Alison Grainger at the altar?'

'Get out of my way,' Banham said to him, feeling his temper rise. He walked past him and stood behind the line that the police had cordoned off around by the car. He spoke to the PCs, Stan and Les, who were still in the car. 'How are you doing in there?' he called out.

'We're OK, sir.'

'Sorry you have to stay there for a bit longer,' Banham said. 'Forensics will be finished here in a while, and we'll be lifting the car and sending it to the pound. You can both go home then.'

Stan nodded. 'Thanks, sir. We're OK. Our mates are in the warehouse, we'll be staying around until they are safely out.'

The word *safely* echoed in Banham's ear. He was a cautious man, but Carter's constant advice was making him doubt his own decisions. Could he have prevented McCaub's death? The boy was twenty-two years old and newly married. His wife was inside the warehouse breaking her heart right now, just like he had over Diane all those years ago. His heart went out to Byfield too, for the woman he was marrying in a matter of weeks was also in there. He wasn't prepared to take a risk and inflict the pain he himself had suffered all those years, and still did, just because the armed police unit thought they knew best. But perhaps they did. And there again, perhaps they didn't. He wouldn't take that risk with those lives at stake.

He turned to Lorraine. 'I'm going to talk to them, see how things stand now,' he said.

She shrugged. 'Your call,' she said. 'You are SIO. On your shoulders.'

He knew from that remark that she agreed with Carter.

'You think I should have let SCO19 go in?' he said.

She shrugged. 'You're SIO. You decide. I take responsibility for McCaub being shot.'

Banham put his hand on her shoulder. 'We're really not infallible, none of us,' he told her.

He walked the few yards to stand in front of the warehouse. Then, lifting the hailer to his mouth, he spoke, coldly, but with much authority.

'I brought you Devlin McCaub, as we agreed. Now you must open the door and let the wounded police hostage out. Then the other hostages must follow. That was the deal. I will keep my word. If you keep yours, no one will try and shoot or enter.'

There was silence.

'We had a deal. You have just killed one man, and we know one of the hostages is shot. Don't let him die because we couldn't get him to hospital in time. I also need to know there are no other casualties in there.'

'No one else is hurt in here,' Massafur shouted back.

'Good,' Banham said.

'So, open the door please, and release first the wounded man, as agreed,' Banham continued. 'And then the—'

'I'm thinking about it. Things have changed now, see.'

'No, I don't see. Nothing's changed, inasmuch as we had a bargain.'

'And now, we don't.'

Banham took an intake of breath. 'I kept my side of it.'

No answer.

Carter was looking at Banham. There was anger in his eyes. Banham ignored him.

'How many other hostages have you got?' he asked Massafur.

'You ask a lot of questions.'

'There is an ambulance out here, waiting to help. You have other hostages in there with you, so you are in a strong position. Nothing will change that, if you release the wounded officer. I believe you have a PC in there too, is that right?'

'Yeah, that's right.'

'Can you confirm her name is Hannah Kemp?'

'Never asked her name.'

'Well, would you mind doing it now. We would like to know. By the way, my name is Paul, what is yours?'

'What, you think I'm stupid? Mind your business.'

'What can I call you? You can call me Paul.'

A pause, then Massafur spoke again. 'Call me MussyMan.'

'Is that a nickname?'

'Sort of.'

Banham turned to Crowther, who had joined him. 'Get onto the station, get them to run it through, see if anyone with the street name MussyMan comes up linked with Massafur, or all the Massafurs they can find on file. And, tell them to try linking him with Devlin McCaub.'

Lorraine Cory had been standing on the other side of the road listening. She crossed over to Banham. 'He is the brother of Devlin McCaub's wife,' she told Banham. 'At least that is what Kevin McCaub, Devlin's brother told—' She stopped just before saying the word Alison.

Banham was so involved in his conversation with Massafur, it went over his head.

'Tell them we need everything they can find about him, and any associations he has,' Banham told Crowther. 'We know there is one other man in there with him holding the hostages. See what you can get up.'

Carter moved in to Banham. 'Some of my team are on the roof of the building next door, at the edge. They could quietly open that hatch, pulling attention to it, while the rest of the team go in from the back.

'I'll give them a little longer to let Neville out,' Banham told him. 'But keep them there, in position.'

Banham lifted the hailer back to his mouth. 'We're getting impatient out here,' he had raised his voice. 'The paramedics are here. The refreshments are still here, by the door. You can open the door safely. Give us our wounded officer, as agreed, and take the refreshments. I have given you my word no one will try anything, and then you can retreat inside, and we'll talk again.

No answer.

'Guv, come on. He's not playing ball,' Carter pushed. 'He's making a mockery of us.'

'I'm not risking lives,' Banham said.

'But you are,' Carter argued. 'That's exactly what you are doing!'

Banham shook his head. Lorraine lifted her eyebrows at Carter but made no comment.

'How many hostages did you say you had in there?' Banham asked.

'I didn't.'

'I'm waiting for my wounded officer,' Banham pushed.

'I'm thinking about it.'

Banham took an intake of breath, then turned to Lorraine. She screwed her face up, shook her head, then flicked her gaze to Carter.

Banham stayed calm. 'If anything happens to him, you will go to prison and never see the light of day. Murdering an officer carries a non-negotiable life sentence. Don't be a fool. The man is shot. He is bleeding and has now been in there for a good few hours. We both know he needs urgent medical attention. And, if he doesn't get it, I am very concerned what will happen to him, and to you. And I certainly can't say you did all you could to help him.'

'If that's a threat, I'm shaking in my boots.'

Banham's calm negotiating expertise was beginning to crumble. His temper was beginning to boil. He pulled the hailer from his mouth and took a deep breath. He was aware more and more journalists and TV cameras were arriving, awaiting a story, behind the cordon. Forensics had by now covered the car with the dead man still in it with a tent, and no one could see in. Also, Banham was relieved there were so many vans, ambulances, and police vehicles by the cordon that blocked the view for the press.

Again the hailer went to his mouth. 'This is a warning, if the injured man isn't released, we are coming in.'

There was no answer.

A second later, the door to the warehouse opened and the body of Martin Neville was rolled out the door. It tumbled and turned a few times, and then became deadly still.

At first Banham thought it was a dummy. Blood had soaked and stained the police uniform that it was dressed in. He then noticed the half of the female police uniform shirt that was tied around his middle, and he knew it wasn't a dummy.

Banham stood stock still. Crowther and Lorraine ran up to where the body lay.

The paramedics hurriedly followed. All knelt down by the dead Martin Neville. No one needed to lift his wrist to check his pulse.

Chapter Seventeen

At that same moment, the black coroner's car turned into the street and drove up, parking parallel to the tent covering the Volvo with the dead Devlin McCaub leaning over the rear window. Another van full with another forensic team followed behind.

The paramedics were on their knees by the body of Martin Neville. The tiny medic, Mary, had her red hair pulled back and tied in a ponytail. She shook her head. 'He's dead,' she confirmed.

Banham turned his head to the coroner's van. 'Over here, please. Change of plan. Can we have a body bag over here,' he called out, then noticed a lone journalist who was sitting on a wall at the end of the street, holding a camera up. Banham turned to Crowther. 'Take that camera from him, and get every available uniform to police the surrounding streets. Keep them away from here. Jesus fucking Christ.'

As Crowther turned to obey, Banham added, 'And tell everyone that under no circumstances is PC Byfield to know about this yet.'

'Quickly as you can,' Banham said to the coroner's assistant.

'We can take both bodies together,' Charles, the coroner's driver, offered to Banham as he walked back after safely placing Martin Neville in the back of the long black car.

'Not this one,' Max, the head of the forensics team that had just arrived, told the coroner. 'I'm arranging to get this whole car lifted, leaving the cadaver in situ.'

'How soon can you get that done?' Banham asked Max.

'A couple of hours,' Max told him. 'But we'll leave the tent cover meanwhile, keep the elements out, as well as prying eyes.' He jerked his head in the direction of another photographer who was balancing his upper body on a wall, snapping the whole scene. Crowther hurried over to him. He grabbed the journalist's camera, lifting it roughly from around the man's neck. The journalist fought back.

'Not the camera,' the journalist argued. 'I'm just doing my job.'

Banham wasn't in the mood. 'Confiscate it,' he said. 'You were warned. You can get your camera from the station in a couple of days. I will be destroying all the film.'

'You can't . . .'

'Shut it,' came the voice of Lorraine Cory. 'Next time I'll lock you up for trespassing. Now get the fuck out of here.'

The man fled.

Banham was looking to see if anyone from inside the warehouse was watching through the window. No one was in sight. All had gone quiet.

He turned to Jim Carter and nodded. Immediately Carter lifted a hand and a half a dozen visored, vested, and armed SC019 officers started moving. All had been watching the warehouse from the roof opposite, and beside, and seeing his hand-signal hurriedly climbed down and across the street, ducking and then lying, stomach down, on the pavement, rifles in hands, aiming at the side of the warehouse.

Then the voice of Massafur boomed out again. 'One step closer with those boys and I'll kill the woman fed here.'

That silenced everyone.

'Don't think we won't. We got nothing to lose now. And then it'll be the other hostages, one by one,' he shouted. 'You got that?'

Banham heard a scuffle from inside the building, then a woman's fearful cry.

'Just one more move, and your fed gets a bullet.' The crack of a hard slap followed by a cry followed. 'Tell them to back off, away from this building.'

'We heard you,' Banham shouted, turning to Jim Carter with a sharp jerk of his head to tell him to stop. Carter immediately told his men to retreat.

Banham took two seconds before he spoke again. 'You can't stay in there for ever, and if you shoot my other officer, we will come straight in. That's a promise.'

'We don't want to stay in here for ever. Nor does your fed. She is quite distressed as it happens. Her bleating is getting on my wick. So I'm willing to barter with you.'

'You already have done. You broke your side of it, and you have killed a police officer.'

'But you want the female fed, right?'

Carter was shaking his head, but Banham ignored him. Lorraine stood stony-faced, one hand to her nose as she listened, but said nothing.

'Yes,' Banham said calmly.

'Then here's the deal. We want a helicopter, with a pilot, and a hundred grand. Deliver that, and you can have your fed, alive, and we'll even throw in the other hostages. But if you don't find that within, say, an hour or so, your other fed will die.'

Banham and Lorraine Cory made eye contact. Just then Lorraine's phone then rang. She read *ALISON* across the screen. Again she walked away, turning her back on Banham as she took the call.

'That doesn't sound sensible,' Banham made himself say. 'If we say no, and you kill our other officer, and then the other hostages, what will you have to barter with? You still won't get away, and we will come in and you won't stand a chance. Best way is if you open the door and release them, and then we can talk this over.'

'If there is no helicopter, we will kill your pretty fed, then the others, then ourselves,' came the reply. 'You can't win this, Mr Policeman. Get us what we want, or everyone in here will die. Maybe even you too. Have a think about it. We will wait a little longer.'

Lorraine Cory walked back to Banham at that moment. 'I've just spoken to the station,' she said. 'Their full names are Massafur Khan and Sadiq Ashraf, no street names on the system. So not part of any gangs. Al—' She was about to say Alison again, but stopped herself in time. – 'says Kevin McCaub can prove they murdered four people.

He also told us that they know where that missing woman, Nounia Ashraf, is buried.'

Jim Carter turned to Banham. 'You have no choice,' he said. 'We ain't gonna get a helicopter, or a hundred grand, so now we have to go in and try and get those hostages out alive.'

'Be honest,' Banham said to him. 'What's the chance of no one else getting killed?'

'I'm ninety per cent sure we could get all the hostages out alive,' Carter told him.

Banham rubbed two hands down his face again. 'Ninety per cent,' he said with a shake of his head. 'It's not enough. I gave Byfield my word I would get her out safely. The odds are not good enough.'

'You don't have a choice, mate. Unless you want to kow-tow to their every demand,' he said condescendingly. 'After they've killed two people in cold blood, one an officer, they won't keep their word, you know that. Think logically.'

Before Banham could answer Carter spoke again, 'And where are we going to get a helicopter from?' he added. 'Not to mention a hundred grand in cash.'

'We could request they bring in the police copter from Epping,' Lorraine Cory told him. 'Filled with armed SAS officers.' She looked at Carter, who didn't look amused. 'A crack SAS team to back your team up,' she added. 'Would that make the ninety per cent any nearer a hundred?'

Chapter Eighteen

Alison had been on the HOLMES computer and brought up the reports on the unsolved cases of the four burned, mutilated, and shot bodies. The reports had identified the females as belonging to a family by the name of Ashraf, exactly as Kevin McCaub had told her. No one had been charged for their murders. Inquiries on the case had led them to believe that Sadiq Ashraf, a cousin, who was wanted for questioning, had left the country. The file had been left open, but the budget closed, as no one knew which country Sadiq was now living in. Kevin McCaub had also told them there was another body buried, a little way away in the Catford park, also with genital mutilation and the third finger on her left hand missing. Nounia Ashraf. Alison intended to bring in a request, in light of this new evidence, to re-open the cases. Although Ashraf was a common surname, Kevin had given her a signed statement, which would give her evidence and ammunition to request they open the case and send a digging team into the park.

Kevin had now been released on bail. Alison wasn't happy letting him out after his brother had been murdered, but she had given him her word that if he helped them with their inquiries, he would be released. She honoured that, on the condition he went nowhere near the hostage situation. If he did, she told him he would be rearrested and charged with obstructing a murder inquiry. He agreed. She told him he was on bail to appear in court, but would talk to her supervisors and request that the charges against him were dropped, on account of his help furthering the cold case.

She walked back into the CCTV room and stood, once again, watching the tragedy that had unfolded in Henry Street. When she saw Martin Neville's body thrown out on the street, a shudder went through her. The young PC in there, Hannah Kemp, was someone Alison had become friendly with, having had numerous conversations with her about weddings. Hannah was due to get married a month after Alison, and Alison feared for her. She was also aware that the fiancé, Peter Byfield, was down there at the scene, and couldn't begin to imagine how he must be feeling. His whole world would be crumbling in front of him.

She watched Banham again on the CCTV. She knew she loved him, with all his faults. And his hair that curled up at the back when it rained, and made him bad-tempered, she adored that curl. If anything happened to him, her world would be over. She felt another strong urge to be there right now, helping him. He looked so tired and he needed her strength and intelligence. She knew he relied on that. She had worked with him for years and years, even back when he was just a DI and she a DS. He needed her, even if only to straighten out the curl he so hated at the back of his collar.

Yet he wanted her to be lying in the sun, away from the dangers that police work brought. That wasn't her, she wouldn't be that stay-at-home wife, no matter how much she loved him. So their relationship couldn't work.

Why couldn't he love her for who she was, not the wife he wanted her to be?

Hannah was shivering again. She had been listening to Massafur's demands. A helicopter and a hundred grand! That wasn't going to happen. So now that meant the hostages were in immediate danger of getting shot. If they were going to survive, it was down to her. She had to make something happen. Yet she was in too much pain to think. Deep down, she knew their chances of survival were shrinking fast. She had to pull herself together and do something. She attempted to rub her shaking hands together, but that unbearable pain shot through to her shoulder and stopped her. She knew her arm was broken and, sadly, her spirit was going the same way. What had she to lose now?

'There's no way there's a helicopter out there to give you,' she said to Massafur.

When Massafur ignored her, she persisted. 'Can I make a suggestion?'

'Why don't you shut up?' Mariam shouted across at her. 'You make this worse for everybody.'

Hannah ignored her. 'Why don't you say, you will let us go if they let you go?' she pushed. 'You don't get done for murder then, and you're free to live your lives, and us ours.'

When neither of the men answered, and the only sound came from the mumbling Buisha, who still sat facing the wall, talking nonsense, she persisted. 'You have what you want. Wasn't this about Devlin McCaub? You got him. Isn't that the end then, of all this for you?' Hannah asked them.

She looked at Farzi. The woman was conscious again, but barely. Her eyes flickered and then closed. Hannah could see she was fighting to wake up. She was young and beautiful, and still had her life before her. As Hannah did. Hannah knew it was down to her to fight for both of them to have that life.

When neither man answered her, or even glanced in her direction, she felt her insides churning at the thought of how this could end. So what had she to lose? She persevered.

'It's your best option,' she said, keeping her voice calm. 'And in everyone's best interest.' How she wished Martin was here, alive and guiding her. She felt guilty. She should have been able to keep him alive. A pain like an electric current hit her heart and she had to fight with herself not to crumble. If she could get her hands on a knife right now, she would not be responsible for her actions. Those murdering bastards. She took a deep breath and pushed on.

'You must see that makes sense?'

'Why don't you shut up? the older woman shouted again. 'You are making them mad.'

'This is to help you,' Hannah told her politely. Then turning to

Sadiq, she said, 'At least let those two older hostages go. If you show willing by doing that, our guys are much more likely to get that helicopter and money for you.'

When it looked as if Sadiq and Massafur were listening to that suggestion, she pushed on. 'You will still have Farzi. We know this is about her, and you will also have me. I am an officer of the law. I will be a very valuable asset if they threaten you in any way.'

Massafur looked at Sadiq, who lowered his mean eyes and shook his head.

'She has a point,' Massafur said, looking at the older woman, who had her eyes on Farzi. Farzi was bent forward, she was once again conscious but moaning in pain and crying.

'We can't stay in here for ever,' Massafur said to Sadiq. 'If we say we let the oldens go, when we get the 'copter, with a pilot. We can get the pilot to fly us out of the country.' He indicated with his head to the old man and woman. 'There isn't room for everyone and we need the fed.'

Hannah was suddenly dizzy. Her arm was racked with pain, and her face was throbbing. She was afraid she was going to pass out. She wanted to do something to help the older couple while she had any strength. She pushed on.

'The police don't have spare helicopters, so getting one for you would be a big coup. But I'm sure if you showed willing by letting the older hostages go, then they would move heaven and earth to get one for you,' she lied. 'And you're right, you can't stay in here for ever. If you don't negotiate, there is a real possibility the firearms team will shoot their way in, and then you'll never get away. Letting the older hostages go will be your ticket out of here, I am sure of that.' She paused, aware that Sadiq was now listening, and dare she even hope, considering the rubbish she was telling them. Then she said, in a tone as genuine as she could muster, when deep down she wanted to shoot both of these monsters herself, and watch them dying as they pleaded for their lives as she had done to them for her friend Martin, 'And I will speak for you, and I will tell them you were reasonable.' She watched Sadiq's lizard-like black eyes narrow, and quickly corrected herself. 'That's if it came to anything, although I am sure, on those terms, it wouldn't be necessary. But it certainly would count for a lot if I spoke up for you. Which I would,' she said again. 'So please, let the older hostages go. That man is very unwell.'

Sadiq then walked over to her, pulling his pistol from his back pocket as he marched and cocking it in her direction. Fear burned through her body when she saw that, like another volt of electricity. She felt the cold metal of the weapon as it was pushed into the side of her head. He then pulled her up to standing by her wounded arm. The shock and pain of it all made her feel she was going to urinate. Try as she did to concentrate and clench hard, she failed to stop herself. The warm liquid trickled down her leg. It dripped from her trouser legs and flooded the floor, so she stunk like a street tramp. She swayed back and forth, forcing herself not to pass out.

Sadiq looked down at the trickling urine, but made no comment.

'As you can't shut your mouth. I am taking you to the door, and you will tell them that if they don't get us a helicopter that we are going to kill you. But if they do, plus a hundred thousand pounds, then you tell them they can have you back.'

'And the older hostages too?' she managed to ask.

'Yes. But you tell them what I tell you to say. Or else we will hang you up in the window and shoot you, while they watch. Or take you with us on our journey out of here and cut you up.'

Her whole inside seemed to freeze up and shake at the thought that if a helicopter did miraculously appear, and they did get her into it as a hostage, she would be driven off to a foreign country, where she would surely be killed, and never see Peter again. She pushed the thought from her mind, assuring herself that it was just fearful thinking. No helicopter would be coming anyway.

'Just do it,' he said, watching Massafur go to the window and shout to the many detectives, forensic teams, and uniformed police who were busy outside, dealing with lifting the car with the dead McCaub.

'Listen up!' Massafur shouted through the open window as Sadiq opened the door holding Hannah in front of him. Her arms were pulled behind her back with one of his hands, his other held the pistol which he pressed hard into the side of her head. Her now greasy and matted, shoulder-length fair hair had fallen over her face, obstructing the swelling on the right side of her forehead and her half-closed eye. She knew if he wasn't holding her up, the pain that burned through her would have made her fall to the ground.

Chapter Nineteen

The hailer flew to Banham's mouth. Jim Carter, Crowther and Lorraine Cory moved in beside Banham. Carter held his hand up to stop any of his team taking a shot.

Lorraine had been a few yards away, talking to Alison on the phone. She was back beside Banham in a heartbeat. All stood staring in horror at the trembling young PC with the gun to her head.

'Jesus fucking Christ,' Lorraine muttered quietly. Then she turned to Crowther. 'Make sure there are no press with long lenses within a mile of this, and for fuck's sake, check Byfield is nowhere near.'

'I'm listening,' Banham said calmly.

'Let's talk about that 'copter,' Massafur's voice bellowed from inside the window.

Banham stayed very calm and kept his voice steady. 'As I have told you, we are on it. It's a big ask, so it won't happen in minutes, but rest assured, we are on it.'

'And the money?'

Banham's eyes were on Hannah. He felt a stabbing pain in his gut, he couldn't help but think of Diane.

'The money is being dealt with too. Would you like some water and biscuits? It looks like my young officer could do with something. The refreshments are right there by your feet. I'm sure the water, at least, would be welcome by your hostages.' His eyes flicked to Carter as he spoke. Carter got the message.

Sadiq kicked Hannah in the foot to speak.

'If you don't get the helicopter soon, and the money they want,' she told Banham, speaking in monosyllabic, flat tone, 'I am told to tell you they will kill me.'

'Shit,' Carter said quietly. He leaned in to Banham. 'For fuck's sake, what are you waiting for? Let my boys take him out, now.'

'No. I'm taking no risks,' Banham answered, without taking his eyes off her.

'They won't miss. That young girl will die of fear in a minute. You can't let them get away with this.'

'He's right,' Lorraine's voice was sharp as she turned to Carter. 'We've made enough mistakes already. I will not risk that officer's safety. We already have a media circus with all this.'

'No need for the gun. Can you take it away from my officer's head?' Banham said, still keeping his calm tone. 'We are on the case for a helicopter. Please bear with us. I won't ask for your word that the hostages will then be freed, as you and I both know you don't keep it. So, I'll make this clear. You want a helicopter and money, and I want my officer and the other hostages safely handed over.' He was watching Hannah, her body was trying to bend forward as it swayed unsteadily. Sadiq was holding her upright. Banham could see she was in pain. 'Should anything happen to that officer,' he said, 'or any more of the hostages, there will be no helicopter and no further negotiating. This team of armed police will be coming in.'

Massafur's voice was cold and clipped as he spoke. 'When we see the helicopter, we will talk again. If nothing happens soon, you'll have another dead fed.'

'For the love of Christ,' Carter turned to Lorraine. 'Ma'am?' but Lorraine put her hand up to stop him speaking. She shook her head.

'No,' she said quietly.

'We are trained for this,' Carter argued. 'Someone tell me, why? We won't miss the target.'

'You can't say that for sure,' Lorraine told him.

Banham turned to him, and lowered his voice. 'If you take this one out, the one inside would shoot Hannah for sure. It's frustrating to say the least, but no chances, for now this is a waiting game.'

'You're the boss,' he said, but the sarcasm in his tone wasn't missed by Banham.

'I have requested a police helicopter, it's on standby,' Lorraine assured Carter. 'I've given instructions at the station to ask the minister for an SAS team to come with the 'copter. The six-man team will be out of sight, down on the floor. Not taking your job,' she said gently. 'They'll be giving you assistance. No way we won't take them by surprise then. They will be there to back you up.'

Carter nodded grimly.

Banham spoke again, through the hailer. 'It will take another hour at least, maybe more, to locate and bring you a helicopter,' he told him. 'But I need you to release one of the hostages, before we go any further. To show good faith.'

'Well done, keep him sweet,' Lorraine said quietly. 'Hannah Kemp looks terrified. We have to get her out of there. And not because the world's press is in the next street. They don't know the full story yet, of the two murdered already. Either way, I agree, we take no risks.' She turned to Carter. 'Imagine how you'd feel if that was your wife.' She then turned to Banham, realising what she had said. 'Sorry, Banny.'

Banham ignored her remark. He lifted the hailer again. 'Is that a deal?' he asked.

Hannah was fighting to stay upright. The pain was excruciating as her body bent forward, desperate to fall and pass out. She was swaying like foliage in the wind, Sadiq pulled her upright by her wounded arm. The cold metal that was digging into the side of her already throbbing head stopped it lolling. She felt like throwing up. The feeling, so near her, of his sweaty finger on a trigger that held her life in its grip, was terrifying. She spoke quietly to Sadiq. 'The police will keep their word. I know they will. You will get your helicopter, but you'll have to agree to something. This is your chance to get away,' she whispered. 'Agree to free the older hostages. What harm can that do? You'll have me, and Farzi.'

At first there was silence. She expected Sadiq to hit her for speaking, but he shouted to Banham. 'We will show willing, as you say, and release two hostages. But if you do not deliver us a helicopter, as agreed, plus a hundred thousand pounds in cash, within two hours, then we will kill the remaining two.'

There was another silence from the other side of the road, as Banham turned to Lorraine and Carter. Crowther had come back from the end of the road and had heard the conversation.

'He won't kill the other two,' Crowther said to Banham. 'He would have nothing to barter with if he did. He's bluffing. Play him at his own game. Make sure he releases Hannah in the two he frees.'

'We agreed, we are taking no chances,' Lorraine said. 'I'll check to see how soon before we can get the copter.' She walked a few steps and got her phone out and started stabbing in numbers.

Banham lifted the hailer again after a few silent seconds. 'We are, at this minute, checking that we can get the 'copter within two hours. You must understand, a helicopter has to be serviced and then checked for safety, and then filled with fuel. It all takes time.' He glanced nervously at Lorraine, who had her back to him, talking on her phone. 'But I can assure you it will be with you as soon as humanly possible. So, now, you release two hostages, one being my officer, and I will give you my word the copter will be on its way.

'Not your fed. She stays. We will give you the older two,' Massafur shouted out the window. 'If we get no helicopter within two hours, then we will kill your little fed, slowly and painfully.'

Banham looked at Hannah. It was all he could do not to grab a gun and shoot the bastards himself. He thought of Diane again, and wondered how she felt as her killer lifted the axe to their baby, before splitting both their heads open. He turned to see Lorraine still talking nine to the dozen into her phone.

'Look to your right,' he told Sadiq. 'Our chief is sorting it out as we speak. There is no need for threats. We have kept our word all along. You will get your helicopter, as soon as humanly possible. If you kill your hostages, you will have nothing to barter with.' He was watching Hannah as Sadiq held her upright and her legs fought to give way. He took an intake of breath. 'Let two hostages go, and your helicopter will be here as quickly as we can humanly get it.'

'If it doesn't, we will kill everyone here, and then we kill ourselves,' Sadiq told him. 'We have explosives in here with us, powerful ones, so everyone in the area will go with us. Just in case you were thinking of sending your armed team in here, one foot inside and we blow everyone to cinders.'

Hannah suddenly got a rush of adrenaline and anger. Even with the gun pressed into her head, her anger bubbled. She opened her mouth and shouted to Banham, 'I haven't seen any explosives. Don't—' She was stopped in her tracks as Sadiq speedily pulled the gun from her head and fired a shot into her foot. Her screams echoed around the road and beyond as she collapsed and folded at the waist.

Carter gave a signal, and one shot was fired, but Sadiq was fast. He had pulled Hannah back into the warehouse before the signal was taken.

Alison was back in the murder unit room. She was reading up on Massafur and Sadiq, and the four bodies found. The photos she had found of the corpses were horrific. The bodies had been burned, tortured, and mutilated. There were close-up shots of the two women's genitalia, which had undergone savage mutilation, and the left ring fingers were missing on all of the victims. So Kevin McCaub had been absolutely right. Alison now knew she was on to something. Kevin had said there was another woman, Nounia Ashraf, buried in another park near Catford, or another part of that park. As he was right about these three victims and the torture they had undergone, she believed him. A body was buried in the Catford park, not too far from the others. The next stage would be to dig up the area, and hope to discover the remains of a cadaver with similar wounds. That would be the proof that it was part of the same inquiry, and Forensics would prove it was the woman that supposedly had left the country. And if she could persuade Kevin to stand witness, then she would have solved five murders, and all on her own. A big help for her next promotion board. First she had to get permission to excavate the grounds in the park and find the missing corpse.

To dig up the park she would need permission from the Home Office. That would have to wait for this hostage situation to be over, too few manpower to spare at the moment. Also, a valuable witness was currently a hostage: Farzila, the wife of Devlin McCaub and sister to Massafur Khan. She felt a rush of adrenaline. This would make being grounded in the station all worthwhile, and would make Banham realise her value. Greece would have to wait for her. She had found all this evidence, and once they got permission, it would be her case, she would be running this one. Banham would learn she was never going to give up on her career. When the hostage situation was over, which she knew would be soon, as she had just had an OK from the Home Office on the police helicopter and team of SAS soldiers, then she would tell Banham *he* could go to Greece alone, and take the right sun cream to protect his tiny bald patch, which she had to admit she found sexy. She would take her evidence to Lorraine, and ask for the job of senior investigating officer.

She nearly jumped out of her skin when her mobile began to ring. Now what did he want? Where should she be now? Her mind wasn't on her honeymoon. What time was it there, her scrambled brain tried to think. Three something? Or more? Would the plane have landed yet? Would she have arrived at the hotel? There was a time distance between London and Mykonos, but what was it? Her mind wouldn't focus quickly enough. Best not to answer the call. As she pulled her phone from her back pocket to reject the call, she noticed *Lorraine* written across her screen.

She immediately picked up. 'Ma'am.'

'Told you, call me Lorraine, or better still Lorry, unless there are other officers present,' came the reply. 'Anyway, get on to the Home Office again and tell them the helicopter they have on standby, and the SAS backup, is needed, and ASAP. We have just seen Hannah Kemp take a bullet. Are you watching the CCTV?'

'No, I'm checking out Sadiq Ashraf and Massafur Khan.'

'Go and look at the CCTV. Jesus, she's in a bad way. Time is at a premium here.'

'Will do.'

'Tell them the hostage-takers have said they will release two of their hostages on the condition they see a helicopter within two hours. If they don't, everyone gets killed. They now say they have explosives in there, powerful enough to blow the street up.'

'I'm on it. And I've got very interesting news on those hostage-takers for you, but it can wait.'

'What?'

'Massafur Khan and Sadiq Ashraf are wanted for handling firearms and drugs, and, according to a well-informed witness – Kevin McCaub – they are responsible for the park bodies murders. Computer has Sadiq Ashraf as having left the country, so somehow he must have got back in. Ashraf was also suspected of murdering a trader from East Lane market. But no one could prove it, or would speak out, so he was never charged. He then, apparently, fled the country. But it looks likely the evidence that Kevin McCaub has given us could put him away for another five murders. Carl Ihrim and Brian Taylor, two missing men, secretly married two cousins of Sadiq's. Those are the four mutilated bodies that were discovered, and there is one still to be found: Nounia Ashraf, she's a cousin to both Sadiq and Massafur. Kevin McCaub is sure that her body is either buried in the Catford park, or possibly another park one mile away. He says that she too will be minus the third finger on her left hand. Can I, when this hostage situ is done, request permission to send a digging team into the park?'

'The press will have a field day with all this. Sorry, excuse the pun. Yes, but it'll have to wait until this is all sorted. Get on to the Home Office, and get the helicopter on its way immediately or sooner. Hannah's life depends on this. Ah, got to go,' she said suddenly and cut off.

Alison clicked her phone shut. She didn't feel quite so excluded now. She had always been ambitious, and Banham excluding her on this big case had really rubbed salt in the wound, but now fate seemed to have handed her a trump card. She picked up an internal phone. 'Put me through to the Home Office,' she said. 'I'm calling on behalf of Superintendent Lorraine Cory, and it is an emergency,' she told the receptionist.

Lorraine walked back to Banham. 'We don't have a time or a positive yet, but the request has gone in and they know it is top priority. They'll know they have to get it within two hours, and we'll get our Hannah and the other hostages.'

'So now we have to keep them calm,' Banham said.

'He's just shot young Hannah in the foot, that bastard,' Carter said. 'You call that calm.' He shook his head and took a noisy breath. 'And we are doing fuck all.'

'Let's get the two hostages out that they promised us,' Lorraine told him.

'We're letting them dictate everything. They've killed two men, and shot another one of our officers in front of us,' Carter said. 'Are you really going to stand by and let them walk all over us?'

'I can't and won't take a chance that they haven't got explosives in there,' Banham told him at the same time as Lorraine Cory said to Carter, 'What part of no don't you understand?'

Banham then noticed a few journalists edging in closer around the cordons at the end of the road, and also a television news camera with its light whirring red, which meant it was recording. 'Get rid of them,' he snapped at Crowther. 'Now. And confiscate the camera.'

While Crowther hurried down the road, Banham quickly pressed Alison's number. It went to message.

'Love you,' he said after the bleep. 'It's a little more complicated here than we thought. I'll keep you informed, and as soon as it's all sorted, I'll be on the plane to you. Don't forget to smother yourself in sunscreen, wear a hat, and miss me.'

Hannah was lying on the floor by Martin's dried blood. Her foot was stinging like a hive of bees had been at her. Her arm was in agony, and she could now see nothing out of one eye due to the mass of swelling in her cheekbone and forehead. She wanted to cry with terror and exhaustion. She also knew that whatever happened now, she couldn't help the other hostages: she could no longer stand, she could hardly see, and her right arm hung limp from her shoulder. She stank of urine, and she honestly felt she was past caring whether she perished there or ever saw the light of day again. She found the most comfortable position and lay still and unmoving, breathing deeply to help the all-consuming pain.

Alison was back in the CCTV room, waiting for more information from the Home Office. The helicopter was at Epping, she had been told. It was the force's only one. First, it had to be checked and fuelled up, then the SAS team had to get there, have a quick meeting, and get on board, then it had to get to the warehouse. They said they would be lucky to get all that done in a couple of hours. Alison told them that every moment mattered if they were to save the hostages' lives, including a female police officer, and get the hostage-takers out alive. She told them they had threatened to blow up the building and street around it.

She moved in behind Derek Bridge's CCTV, asking him to rewind the tape of the hostage bringing Hannah out. She peered closer as she watched Hannah trembling at the door of the warehouse, the pistol pressed into her temple. Alison couldn't hear clearly the dialogue that went on, as the audible video cameras were belted to Banham and Lorraine and Carter, so she could only hear Banham's speech. She could see, clearly, the gun being moved from Hannah's head, and being turned and fired into Hannah's foot.

Alison's heart went out to Peter Byfield. She knew he was down there somewhere, in another street, not being allowed to know that the woman he was about to marry had been shot, and beaten, and was in infinite danger of being killed. She immediately felt responsible for Hannah's life. She had to stay on the Home Office's case and keep pushing them. If they didn't deliver that helicopter within two hours, Peter might never see his fiancée again.

She pressed *messages* on her phone, and listened to the voicemail from Banham as she watched him standing talking to Crowther. He was again rubbing his hand across his mouth in his habitual manner. Alison's heart went out to him too. What a situation he was in. She loved him, very much. She knew that as clearly as she now realised she wasn't the marrying kind. She felt so confused. She loved him and loved being with him, being in his bed, making love, eating Chinese food after a case and drinking too much beer. But, *Don't forget to smother yourself in sunscreen and wear a hat,* was the message she had just listened to. He also irritated the life out of her. What did he think she was, a four-year-old? Hardly a respected colleague, a detective inspector in the same murder department. It was a good thing they hadn't gone through with the marriage. Why were emotions so complicated? Poor Peter Byfield was desperate to marry Hannah, and Alison was desperate not to marry Banham. She shrugged, and turned back to the screen, and her love for him welled up again. She wanted to be beside him, helping him. Then she began to get angry. Why couldn't she just *not* love him?

Either way, he had no right to forbid her to come back on duty and help with this major police crisis, when they had called out for every available officer to help. And if he had no right, why was she obeying the order? A call had gone out for all available help. She was available. She had made a major breakthrough with the hostage-takers, and their past records. She might be on the way to solving a minimum of four old murder cases. She had the right to see this through.

The internal phone rang and she realised the number was for the Home Office. They were on schedule for the two hours requested. She phoned the news through to Lorraine Cory.

She watched Lorraine on the screen as she passed it onto Banham.

Alison stood in the corner of the room, pondering.

Banham's hailer went to his mouth again.

'We have good news for you. The helicopter is being prepared for you,' he told them. 'It will be here, soon. So now you must free two hostages, and I have to know how my young officer is.'

No reply came.

Banham persisted, keeping his calm. 'Are you there? You must let two hostages leave the building. And we are insisting that one of the hostages is the PC that you have just shot in the foot. She needs medical treatment. As you know, I have paramedics here waiting.' His voice became authoritative. 'I want my young officer released, along with one other hostage. When the helicopter arrives, you then will release the rest of the hostages. You will have the money too. It will be in the helicopter. You will be free,' he lied. 'But you must first release two hostages, one being the PC. You can take the pilot, or you can fly it yourself. Is that clear?' he lied again.

'Yeah, yeah. That's clear. We'll do it,' came the voice of Massafur.

'Good. So, I am waiting,' Banham said after another couple of seconds.

'So are we,' Massafur shouted back. 'For the helicopter.'

Banham then moved in to Jim Carter and spoke in a low voice. 'Do you think it could land on the roof? Lorraine has clearance that it is being fuelled and the SAS team are being prepared. Could you liaise with the captain, and take over the operation as it lands?'

Carter nodded, and pulled his phone from his pocket. 'Yes, but I'm not sure that roof would be safe to land a 'copter on. It isn't that solid.' He stabbed numbers into his phone. 'They'll have to release the last hostages before they come out themselves, and before it lands. Then we can be sure no harm will come to the hostages. Are we confident we are getting the helicopter with an SAS team within the two hours?'

'I'm told so,' Banham told him, 'but at the moment, everything is a waiting and hoping game,'

'Let's get the first two first hostages out,' Lorraine said.

The hailer went to Banham's mouth again. 'All is in hand our end. We agreed two hostages, once the helicopter was on its way. The 'copter is on its way. We are waiting,' he said again.

There was silence.

'That will be our officer and one more, of the three,' he paused. 'I believe it is three others, isn't it, that you have in there?'

When no answer came back, he said again. 'We are being very patient here. You are getting a helicopter to leave London in, but it can easily turn back. If it did, it wouldn't be my doing, but because you haven't released two hostages, as you agreed.'

When no one answered, he said firmly. 'My patience is wearing thin. The helicopter will be cancelled if—'

'You'll have them in a few minutes,' Massafur's voice bellowed back. 'We are getting them ready. Not your fed though. She stays.'

'He's not going to let Farzila Khan go either,' Lorraine Cory said. 'This whole thing is about her. They'll want to take her with them. They've killed McCaub. There is no doubt they intend to kill her too. We absolutely can't have another murder on our hands.'

'They won't even get inside the helicopter,' Carter said reassuringly. 'They'll be taken out before they get that far. You've got a crack SAS team backing my team.' He looked at Banham and added, 'Once you hand this over to us, we'll finish it in a minute.'

Banham turned away and put the hailer back to his mouth. 'We are insisting one of them is our officer,' Banham spoke calmly. 'One choice to us, the other to you.'

'They won't give her up, guv,' Crowther said quietly with a shake of his head. 'They know she's their ticket out of here.'

'It would still be possible to storm in from the back and surprise them as they bring the two hostages out the front,' Carter said. 'That would be the last thing that they expect, one of them would bring the hostages out, so they'd only be one in there with Hannah and the girl. We could take him down and get both the girls out.'

'Too risky,' Banham told him. 'There would still be the other gunman.'

'We move quickly. We'll take him down as soon as he turns round.'

'Hannah has been shot in the foot,' Lorraine snapped. 'She can't run. You saw her, she can hardly stand, let alone get out speedily.'

'If you surprise them, as you put it, she could get shot again,' Banham told him. 'How many times? I will not risk that officer's life.'

'She's in a bad way,' Lorraine said to Carter. 'Banham's right. We've got the helicopter and SAS backup coming. Two hours. Let's try and keep calm until then.'

Carter was adamant. 'She's wearing her uniform,' he argued. 'That'll be their first call for her safety. Trust my boys, they'll get her out safely.'

'Not her full uniform,' Crowther said.

Banham put his hand firmly in the air. 'It's a no,' he said. 'End of.' His heart was with Peter Byfield at this moment. He thought of him, in the next road, locked in a unit car. Banham hoped word hadn't got back to him that Hannah had been shot. He knew it didn't matter how many times they told Byfield to go home, or how much they threatened him with a disciplinary, the man wasn't going to leave his fiancée alone, a hostage to cold-blooded killers. And Banham admired him for it. He intended to keep his word and was going to do everything in his power to keep Hannah safe.

'The whole country's media are now on this story. It will be all over national news. We already have two deaths we have to account for. If we want to salvage public confidence in us, then we need to get the remaining hostages out safely. That means not taking any risks on their lives,' Lorraine Cory told Carter. 'Let's wait for the helicopter and the SAS team, and push to free the two hostages first.'

'Where are the hostages?' Banham spoke impatiently through his hailer.

'You'll have them,' Massafur's voice boomed out. 'Very soon.'

'What's the hold-up?' Banham replied.

Massafur didn't answer.

Carter scratched the back of his bald head, but said nothing. A second later he turned back to Banham and said, 'Ask them who is being freed.'

'No,' was all Banham said.

'I agree,' Lorraine said quietly to Banham. 'Let's just hope there is no hold-up and we have a helicopter in the allocated time. Until then, you're right, let them think they have the upper hand.'

'Trouble is,' Carter turned back, 'they *do* have it, and can we turn that round in the next two hours?'

Chapter Twenty

Alison was standing at the end of the corridor, by the door that led to the car park. Her green parka was on and her car keys dangled in her hands. She would be disobeying orders from the SIO, and would be facing a disciplinary by going down to the location. Worse still, she could be putting Lorraine in front of a disciplinary too, for allowing Alison on the case in the first place. Lorraine wasn't the senior investigating officer on this case, she had passed that baton to Banham, and he had said a firm 'no' to Alison being there. But as Alison knew, it was nothing to do with her professional standing, his decision was completely personal, emotional and unbalanced, and she would argue she was needed down there. Which she was. He would have to get over it. She had already done some very good work by finding a lot of information about the hostage-takers and the bodies in the park – plus the info about Nounia Ashraf, which would probably never have been found out had she not interviewed Kevin McCaub.

As she stood, in her jeans and over-sized man's jumper, her olive green coat over her, and keys jangling in her hand, deciding whether she should just turn up and tell Banham she was there whether he liked it or not, Derek Bridge walked along the corridor.

'Are you off?' he asked. His head inquisitively tipped a fraction to the side. 'I thought you were staying on this situation with us.' He tilted his head a little more and looked at her. 'We need all the help we can get with our Hannah still a hostage.'

'I'm not abandoning you. I'm going down to the location. I'll be more help there.'

'You are kidding me?' He studied her, trying to read her thoughts, then his tone changed to one of a friend offering advice. 'Don't be bloody stupid. You would be disobeying the super, too. We have had this conversation. We've got a young, inexperienced PC in trouble. She's just been shot. She needs all of us working together right now to get her out. That's what this is about. If you go down there, you know the DCI and the super will lock horns. We don't need you to do that to us. We've just lost one officer. We have to save Hannah. And you are needed here to help do that. Please, Alison, don't be stupid.'

'I should be down there with my team.'

'Why? What can you do, that isn't already being done?'

'I should be on the scene.'

'Why? Because Paul Banham says you can't?' His attitude changed. 'This is what this about, let's face it. Well, you need to get rid of your personal issues, and get professional. We have a very serious situation ongoing here and we need you to guide this operation. We need your experience in the CCTV ops room. No one else in the station right now has your experience.'

'They need me there. It's Banham that has made this personal, not me.'

'Who do you think you are, Superwoman? There's a crack SC019 team down there, an SAS team en route, as well as that team of first-class uniformed officers. Being here, you have possibly solved five murders and a missing persons case. That is a very big coup in my book, and the missing woman's loved ones will never stop thanking you for it, if we find her. Which I think we will, now. There are cells full to bursting with youths that need questioning and arresting from the rioting down there last night. Who knows what more you can bring to light from them.'

When she didn't answer, he persisted. 'Get a grip, Alison, and grow up. This is about Hannah Kemp now, not you and Banham. Her life is hanging by a thread. This isn't about Banham telling you what to do. If you feel like that, then, quite frankly, you shouldn't be a police officer.'

She looked at the ground and rubbed her lips over each other. He was right. She was thinking only of not letting Banham boss her about and not what really mattered, which was the job in hand. And Derek was right, she was needed here. What was she thinking of, upsetting the DSI and putting her and Banham at loggerheads? She had no right to disobey Lorraine when the woman had been good enough to let her on the case, if only from the station. She immediately felt ashamed.

'You're right,' she said quietly, as she put her keys back in her pocket, and took her coat off. She then turned and walked back along the corridor.

Banham, Lorraine, Crowther, and Carter were still standing in the road in front of the warehouse. They had turned their attention to the crane that had arrived. They watched as the forensic officers, supervised by the coroner, carefully lifted the body of Devlin McCaub away from the car and into a black body bag. Then, very carefully, the police officers were told to step out of the car on the opposite side to the window where Devlin had been shot. The crane then moved in and lifted the black Volvo, placing the car in its rear space so it could be driven to the police car pound where it would be protected as it awaited further forensic examination.

Lorraine flicked the bleached stripes at the front of her thick hair, back over the top of her head, and rubbed her forehead. 'Jesus,' she said. 'I released that central lock when I jumped out of the car. If I hadn't . . .'

Banham put his hand on her shoulder. 'We've all got regrets,' he said. 'Let's not go there.' He was interrupted by Massafur's voice coming from the window of the warehouse.

'Your two hostages coming out,' he shouted.

The four officers quickly turned their attention back to the warehouse. The front door opened and the old man walked out first. He looked confused and frightened. The older lady followed behind. She walked unsteadily through the door.

Immediately the waiting paramedics rushed to them, covered

them both with silver-foil blankets and guided them into to the waiting ambulances.

Banham nodded to Crowther, who hurriedly followed the paramedics to catch a brief chat with the two, before they were taken off to be checked at the hospital. He then instructed two female PCs to accompany them in the ambulance and take their statements, if possible.

'We kept our word,' Massafur shouted. 'Where's our helicopter?'

'How is my officer?' Banham replied sharply. 'We know she needs medical attention.' He raised his voice. 'You disappoint me. I asked for her release, as one of the two to be freed. She has a bullet wound in her foot. We both know she needs medical attention.'

'It's only a graze, nothing to worry about, it barely touched her. She's as fine as rain. So, now how long for my helicopter?'

Banham would like to have shot the man himself at that second, with his carefree attitude. Hannah should have been able to walk up the aisle in a few weeks, not limp. She clearly wasn't fine as rain. He could only hope that she was nursing a graze, but if there was a bullet lodged in her foot, then it needed to come out.

Lorraine sensed his anger and moved in beside him. 'Keep your cool,' she told him, speaking quietly.

His thoughts were with Peter Byfield once again. He took a second to compose himself and kept his temper.

'Helicopter is on its way,' he told them. 'Won't be long now. They said two hours, so just over an hour or so to go. Put the other hostages on standby. There is medical help here, waiting. You won't get in the helicopter until the hostages are safely released.' He turned to Lorraine and raised his eyebrows. 'What now?' he said. 'Have we got an update?'

'I'll ring through and check,' she said walking away.

'And ask one of the forensic team to look for the bullet that apparently missed Hannah's foot,' he said.

'Not to go too near the front of the warehouse though,' Carter butted in. And if they can't see it, then it's in her foot still.'

'Bastards,' Banham muttered under his breath as he turned his back and walked over to the ambulance that was loading in the older man and woman.

Hannah was still lying on the floor. The bullet was lodged in the base of her big toe and the toe had swelled to the size of a small orange, and was adding to the agonising pain in her arm. She knew the bullet needed to come out. It wasn't an emergency, the bleeding was minimal, but her foot throbbed, her arm was agonising, and her head was thumping like a warrior's drumbeat. She knew her walking was hindered, as well as her arm movement. She thought about her wedding, just weeks away, then dismissed the thought. With her swollen face, only one foot working, and a broken arm, she might as well cancel the ceremony now anyway. Then it crossed her mind she might not even be alive in four weeks. Like Martin Neville, was her fate too to die here in this dirty, paraffin-smelling warehouse, with strangers around her, not caring a hoot? She wrapped the bloodied, grubby half of her shirt around the wound in her foot, trying not to cry as fear took its hold.

She was sitting in a pool of her own urine, and was aware she stank. She inched a little back, wincing with the pain at the effort her arm needed to do it. She knew Sadiq was watching her, a cynical smirk on his cruel mouth. She believed he would like to have shot her in the head a few minutes ago, and that only the knowledge of being blown to pieces by the volley of bullets that would have followed stopped him. Instead he shot her in the foot. But there was no doubt in her mind. He had showed not a hoot of compassion as Martin had slowly died in front of his eyes. He could have saved his life, but didn't.

She avoided making eye contact. Her emotions were frazzled and it wouldn't take very much for her to lose it and tell him exactly what she thought of him. He would shoot her again, and she didn't want to end her life where she was. For Peter's sake she had to try to survive this unbearable ordeal. She had to help Farzi too, to do the same. The girl was incapable of helping herself.

She peered through her hazy vision at Farzi. The woman had

been placed on the far side of the warehouse, in a sitting position, next to the radiator, leaning her back against the cold wall. Her head had lolled to one side. She kept opening and then closing her eyes, as she fell in and out of consciousness.

Hannah was concerned for her. The hostage-takers had agreed with the DCI that when the helicopter arrived they would release her and Farzi. Hannah believed they wouldn't, so her worry was, would they take them somewhere and then kill them both? That's if the helicopter arrived. And if it didn't, would they kill them anyway? If they did that, they would never get out themselves. But did they care? She thought not. Hannah might have been fairly new to policing but she felt pretty sure a helicopter wasn't going to arrive at the click of their fingers, certainly not in the two hours that the hostage-takers had said. So what was her fate and Farzi's to be? She looked around as much as she could, but her swollen face and blurry vision were making it difficult to focus. Still, she was pretty sure she couldn't see any explosives. But how would she really know? Was her fate to get blown up with the other three, while stinking like a tramp that had lived on the streets for years? She shivered again, then pulled herself together.

She had just watched the older woman and the old man walk through the door to freedom. The old man still mumbling. She was relieved for them, it was nothing to do with them, they had just been in the wrong place at the wrong time. Although the woman Mariam was pretty terrifying. If they had got out alive, then she and Farzi could too.

Hannah had always wanted to be an officer of the law, although she knew that it brought many risks as well as rewards. So here was the worst side of it. If she got out alive, nothing would ever be this bad again. Then she pulled herself sharply up and told herself it was when she got out, and not if.

She looked at the now drying blood that stained the floor from her colleague, and a volcano of emotion rose from her heart, threatening to erupt and cry itself free or choke her.

She told herself to get a grip, she was braver than this. It was down to her alone now, to help Farzi and get them both out of here alive. However, with a swollen face, blurred vision, a bullet in her foot, and an arm that was agony if she shifted it either way, she didn't know how she would manage the job. She felt alone and frightened. She prayed that someone would come in and get them. The reality was, they didn't stand a chance against two unbalanced men holding guns and sharp knives.

She assured herself that the DCI would have a plan. There was a crack gun team right outside. They were never going to allow these killers to take off into the air in the one police helicopter that ran London. So if the helicopter was just a bluff, and not going to arrive, what then was their plan? They must have one. Or did they?

Again, she was aware she was shaking, and that Sadiq was watching. She willed herself to stillness. She was a police officer for goodness' sake, someone who looked out for the vulnerable public, and here she was crying and shaking. The team outside would get her out. The murderers were threatening they had bombs, but she hadn't seen any. So that was a lie. But then she wasn't that sure what a bomb looked like, she had only seen pictures of them in the training school at Hendon. She then assured herself they wouldn't kill her, they would want to keep her alive as a means to barter with, for now. They had killed Devlin McCaub. Hannah would have taken a bet they would have preferred to take him alive, with Farzi, and have tortured him before they killed him, like they'd threatened. They were sadists, and sadists liked to kill slowly, but they'd taken the opportunity they had and shot him. So, if these two madmen lost their tempers, then neither she nor Farzi were safe from being killed. It was all down to waiting for the helicopter which Hannah wasn't sure was going to come. That's when they would lose their tempers and kill them all. The DCI had said two hours, so for those two hours, they were safe. But she still had to plan how she would to get them both to safety if the armed response team burst in.

In the meantime she had to stay strong for Peter.

★

PC Shaun Levington had been given the task of keeping Peter Byfield calm and still, and away from the crime scene. The car they were in was not to be parked within yards of the end of the street, he had been told. It had to be out of sight of where the hostage situation was taking place. He had been warned that he too would be up on a disciplinary if Byfield got out of the car. The paramedics had given Byfield a light sedative in his tea, and he was currently calm, although a little drowsy.

'Mate,' Levington said, speaking quietly to Byfield, who had been sitting half awake and half asleep, for the last half hour. 'Mate,' he said again. 'I'm listening in to the in-house radio here on my headphones. They have released two of the hostages.'

Byfield sat up quickly.

'Not Hannah, as yet,' Levington continued. 'They have been told they're getting a helicopter apparently and have agreed to release Hannah and the last hostage when it arrives. They were told to release the first two hostages to show willing. And they have. So things are looking good for Hannah.' He pointed to an ambulance that blue-lighted its hurried way past them on its way to the hospital. 'That was the ambulance taking the two hostages away to get checked out. Those hostages are safe and free. It'll be Hannah next. It's going to be OK, mate.'

Byfield blinked himself awake. He dragged his hands down his face. His face was white and drawn. Levington thought he looked at least ninety years old. His heart went out to his partner. Both watched as the ambulance got smaller and smaller as it sped out of sight, whirring its lights and shrieking its siren. A stream of photographers and men with TV cameras on their shoulders ran down the road after the ambulance, filming, and trying to keep pace and photograph the happenings as the ambulance sped from the end of Henry Street and out onto the main road.

The PCs guarding the cordon had undone the plastic crime scene tape and the entrance to Henry Street was open.

'The police tape is down,' Byfield said, 'can we get any nearer?'

'No can do,' Levington told him. 'They'll send us home if we try.'

'That's if they see us,' Byfield argued. 'Come on, mate, I'd do it for you.'

Levington shook his head. 'They'd see us all right, then we'd be sent home.' He shook his head. 'Not worth risking. Tell you what, though. I could drive down Burton Street and turn into that cul-de-sac behind the warehouse, and you could get a blinding view of the back of it. No one said we couldn't go down there, they just said no way can we pass the cordon and go into Henry Street.'

He fired the engine, reversing quickly and turning the car before Peter argued. 'There are no SC019 on the roof. They were made to withdraw when those bastards released the hostages. They're around, but not on the roof, so no one should see us. And if anything is happening, like SC019 going in at the back, we would have a great view. We might even catch a glance of Hannah that way.'

'Go for it.'

'You know, I'm taking a huge risk of a disciplinary for both of us, by doing this, so you can't leave the car.'

When Byfield didn't answer, Levington said again, 'Just promise me, mate, that whatever happens you won't leave this car.'

'Yeah, I promise,' Byfield said flatly. 'Although, I don't give a shit about a fucking disciplinary, myself. This is about Hannah, not me.'

'I get that,' his partner told him, turning into Burton Street.

Alison was back in the control CCTV room. She had again been watching, from all angles, all the comings and goings. She moved to another camera and clicked a new angle of the warehouse, just as Sam, one of the uniformed police working the CCTV operation, came in with coffees on a tray and offered her one. At first she didn't notice, she was glued to a frame on a CCTV machine.

'Sorry,' she said, and accepting the coffee he had brought her. 'I was miles away.' She looked at her notebook, frowning thoughtfully as she read her notes and sipped her coffee. She had scribbled in her book to remind herself of the location, and of the comings and goings on every CCTV camera she had studied from the time during the riots right up to the time Martin Neville was shot. She pressed replay on the machine she was on, then paused it, then replayed it again, then did the same over and over again.

'Can I go back further on this shot that I am holding?' she asked PC Larry Becks, the CCTV operator beside her. 'And can you widen the shot as much as you can?'

'Yes. Can do,' he muttered as he pressed a few buttons.

The filming she was asking for was a crowd scene during the riots, in the street, near the warehouse. She leaned in closer. Right at the back she could see Devlin McCaub. 'Close in on this man, that's Devlin McCaub,' she said to Larry.

He did. McCaub was walking along, beside the shops at the end of Henry Street. There was a girl beside him. They weren't holding hands, but they were clearly together, he was shoulder to shoulder with her. 'Freeze there,' Alison said, moving in to study the shot. The girl was strikingly pretty, and was just as McCaub had described. Long dark hair and petite in height and build. This had to be his wife, Farzila. There were other hoodie types walking around the two of them, like security. And then she spotted Kevin McCaub.

'Can you blow up this picture?' she asked Larry. 'I'll need single shots of all these faces, every single one in this crowd.' She pointed and made a ring with her finger where Devlin and the crowd were.

She then moved to another CCTV station, which was being manned by PC Alan. This was the same crowd, only from the angle as they turned into the main street from the corner of Henry Street, where the riots were in full swing.

'Get these all blown up too,' she said to Alan. 'Freeze that shot, and make sure you miss no one out, in, or around this group.' As he nodded, and made a pencil note in a pad, she sipped her coffee and said, 'Carry the film on, would you please?'

He pressed the button to continue the CCTV film. There was smashing of windows and brawling going on. The street was so busy with action it was hard to see anything too clearly. An older man came out of his shop and seemed to be shouting at Devlin, and as the picture moved on, she could see that Devlin had his arm wrapped awkwardly around a television as he walked into frame. 'Freeze that too, and enlarge it, as much as you can,' she told Alan. She leaned in again, nodding her approval as he froze the shot and then enlarged the screen.

In the distance, but still quite clear, were two men, standing side by side, both had arms folded. Neither were involving themselves with the looting going on around them, but both were looking in the direction of Devlin and Farzila. 'I'll bet that's Massafur and Sadiq,' she said half to herself. She had looked at their photos earlier on the police computer when she ran their names through, and knew what they looked like. They were older here than the pictures she had seen earlier, one had his hair drawn back in a ponytail, the other had a beard. Annoyingly, they were quite far in the background of this picture, but she felt confident it was them.

She then walked around the many screens in the observation room, studying each CCTV until she found a reel that showed the street from the opposite side. This was from the back view of Devlin and Farzila but facing where the men she felt sure were Massafur and Sadiq were standing, watching. As the film moved on those two men moved in towards the couple. Now she could see Hannah Kemp and Martin Neville hurrying into the frame, towards Devlin, who was holding the television in front of himself, ready to hit out at someone. There were other people walking in between them, so the film was busy and hard to follow. An older man and a woman were coming in and out of shot, and that got in the way of what she was trying to see. These two were much older than the rioters, likely they were shop owners shouting about their shops that were currently being looted, or locals fed up with the noise and fighting and hurling of objects around their houses. It was clearly noisy, too, there were explosions, and shouting and screaming coming from various gangs. Smoke from the fires was slowly filling the street. It was bedlam. So it was impossible to pick up any dialogue, even if lip-reading experts were brought in. But then all heads seemed to turn in the direction of this fight. The men that she believed were Sadiq and Massafur were now in the front of the frame, but had turned so she could only see them from the back view, and Devlin

McCaub had thrown the television at the men. And the crowds seemed to be retreating from the fight. The next thing, Martin Neville came into view, as he fell backwards. Blood was pumping through the hand he held against his stomach. He then fell forward, face down, onto the road. Hannah Kemp immediately masked his view from the CCTV as she leaned in to help him, so all Alison could now see was the back of Hannah. Then Massafur leaned into the shot. The back of his head, and bits of Hannah, now masked everything that was going on with Martin.

'Freeze that,' she said urgently to Alan. He immediately stopped the action and Alison leaned in, studying the frame very closely. She was looking to the side from where Martin had rushed in, with Hannah behind him. Massafur and Sadiq had been on the opposite side of the screen, both were shouting as they attacked Devlin and Kevin McCaub. Kevin held a television above his head. He was thrashing out at Massafur with the television in front of Farzila, to keep her back. Devlin was holding her back. Farzila then ran to one side, she was screaming. She had a hand to her face. Alison could see Massafur and Sadiq's hands clearly, as they pushed up to defend themselves and kicked out. Sadiq was holding a knife, and Massafur a chair leg, but neither seemed to be holding a gun. They were also on the opposite side from where the shot was fired. There was no way they could have been in the position to fire the shot that hit Martin Neville, Alison felt sure of that.

'Can you roll it on?' she asked Alan.

'It stops a few seconds after,' he told her.

'Show me that next few seconds,' she asked.

'It's on here,' Larry told her, pointing to his screen.

She moved to his screen. It showed the same, just more of the fight.

'Have we got more of this?' she asked looking around the control room. 'From the opposite angle? I want to see from where the fight is happening and Martin and Hannah come in.' She looked around the control room. 'I need this CCTV from this opposite side of the street. Where is that?'

'We've been through everything,' Sam called across. 'We were all looking, too. That's the only angle we have on that fight. And we've all looked at it,' he told her. 'Someone pulled or broke all the CCTV at that point, or whatever, but there isn't any other angle.'

'Shit. Shit.' She blinked thoughtfully. 'OK. Here, let's look at what we have here. This picture.' As she pointed at the frozen screen, the team all got up and gathered around the CCTV machine. 'We have that good close-up of the men we now know to be Massafur and Sadiq,' she told them, pointing to the two men. 'We know these two are them. I have their pictures on the computer. And we also know, without doubt, that these other two are Devlin and Kevin McCaub. So blow that shot up, as big as you can. She turned to Larry and Alan. 'Correct me, if I am missing something, but Massafur or Sadiq couldn't possibly have fired that shot, could they? That gunshot came from . . .' she pointed to right of the CCTV. 'It has to have come from over there. Massafur and Sadiq were here.' She now pointed back to the left of the screen. 'We know that is them, and we have seen them since, at the window and door of the warehouse, holding the hostages, and holding guns.' Again she pointed to the opposite side of the screen and at the warehouse. 'They couldn't possibly have shot Martin Neville from where they are. Here is Martin falling forward into the shot. Unless he was shot in the back, which we know he wasn't, someone else shot him. That shot came from this angle. She pointed off screen. Someone else shot him. Oh my God.'

The room fell into silence.

Kevin McCaub was beside himself. He was angrier than he'd ever been. He and Devlin had been the closest brothers ever, and now he had learned that those fuckers had killed him. Well sure as hell, they were going to pay. Within minutes of hearing that news, he had been on his phone, and had pulled together a gang of family and friends from the travellers around the area, all boiling up with anger and ready for retribution. They were all tooled up, pickaxes, guns, machetes, knives, and a variety of other weapons, and were planning to shoot their way in to the warehouse, to kill Sadiq and Massafur and get Farzi out.

They were careful as they walked up the surrounding streets, avoiding the places where the police presence lurked. All had balaclavas in their pockets, watching carefully for the CCTV and ducking around, or under, each camera. They turned, unseen by any feds, into one street, and then into another, and then into Burton Street. There was one camera at the end of that road, they noticed it immediately. Kevin climbed up on his mate's shoulder and blacked the screen with the spray he carried in his pocket. Then they moved on towards the back of the warehouse.

Shaun Levington and Peter Byfield had found a spot where their car would be unseen by the CCTV, which they believed to be in working order, and had parked up. All was quiet. They knew the SCO19 were all gathered in Henry Street awaiting news on the helicopter. The two had a good view of the back of the building, and both settled down in their seats to wait on any happenings.

Within minutes Kevin McCaub and his thirty-strong gang marched into the street. Levington caught sight of them in his mirror, along with the weapons which they carried as they marched purposefully to the back of the warehouse.

'What the . . . ?' he said urgently, sitting quickly up in his seat. 'Look at this, mate. We need to get out of here and call the guv'nor,' he said urgently to Byfield.

Byfield leaned forward in his seat, watching. 'Wait, see what they do,' he told his friend.

'There are no SCO19 on the roof,' Levington reminded him. 'They are all waiting for the helicopter. No, mate, this is trouble about to happen, I ought to call it in. Hannah's in there, remember?'

As Kevin McCaub marched nearer to the police car, and Shaun noticed the weapons which they were all speedily concealing under their clothes on spotting the unit car, he wound the window down.

'What's going on here?' he said to Kevin, keeping his attitude friendly and calm. 'You're not thinking of doing anything stupid are you, mate? You need to leave this to the police.'

'He's got my sister in there,' Kevin told them sharply, speaking in his thick Irish brogue. He seemed very het up and full of adrenaline. 'So fuck your lot. Your lot stood by while they killed my brother.'

'Calm down, mate,' Levington told him, immediately realising the man was a McCaub. 'You need to back off . . . the police have—' He was quickly interrupted, by Kevin's Irish temper.

'You fucking back off. Where were you lot when my brother got shot? Fucking watching, that was what you were fucking doing. Well, you'll have to kill me too, to get me to back off.'

His gang then started jeering at Levington and Byfield, and then kicking out, and rocking the car.

'Time to get out of here,' Levington said, firing the ignition and starting to reverse the car, so the gang at the back of the car had to jump clear. They all turned and hurried up the road, gathering again near the back of the warehouse.

'Hannah's in there. This is going to be trouble. I'm getting out to help her,' Byfield argued, pulling at the door handle. He didn't have time to finish his sentence, Levington was doing the fastest U-turn in police history.

'The door's locked,' Levington told him. 'It's for your own good.' He then sped back down the road.

Kevin McCaub rapped hard on the steel back door of the warehouse. 'Get your fucking face here, Khan,' he shouted. 'And give me my sister, or we'll be in there and we'll take the lot of you out. You murdering bastard.' He then started kicking at the metal door, and his gang moved in with their pickaxes and joined in, hacking with their weapons.

Shaun Levington stopped the car as he got to the end of the road. He was shaking as he rang Crowther's mobile and reported the goings-on.

As he was speaking, with Peter Byfield arguing from behind him, a television crew and a crowd of journalists ran up Burton Street, microphones, boom stands, and red lights all turned on and ready to record.

'It's all going to happen,' Levington told Crowther. 'You need to get some armed police round here.'

Chapter Twenty-one

Crowther had been aware of a noise coming from the back of the warehouse. He had been walking towards the alley when Levington rang. Carter and Banham, having heard the rumpus, sent Crowther over to see what was happening, and were about to put some SC019 back on the roof.

'Jesus, that's all we need,' Banham said as he listened to Crowther and then relayed the information to Lorraine Cory.

'Get rid of them,' she told Crowther and Carter. 'Arrest them; if they resist, get SC019 to fire warning shots. DO NOT let anyone get hurt. Crowther, you sort the press. If they go into Burton Street, arrest them. Get a dozen uniforms from around to help you, and Carter, get your men back on the roof, as backup. Don't let this get out of hand.'

Banham nodded his agreement. He had walked to the alley and was listening to Kevin's gang shouting and making threats. 'And I thought this couldn't get worse,' he said half to himself.

'I'll chase the 'copter,' Lorraine said. 'See what the latest is.' She flicked the bleached hair back from her face as she mumbled, 'Christ, I need a cigarette.' She then walked a few paces away to call Alison.

Banham turned to Jim Carter. 'Just warning shots, and only if necessary. Do not shoot anyone. If trouble starts, those women could get hurt.' He turned back to Crowther. 'And for the love of Christ, make sure Peter Byfield is well way from all this.'

Crowther decided not to tell him that the news came from the PC in the car with Byfield.

★

As soon as Massafur recognised Kevin McCaub's voice, he turned to Sadiq. 'Trouble,' he said quietly, picking up his rifle.

He moved over to look out the tiny window at the side of the warehouse's back door and then turned back to Sadiq.

Sadiq had his revolver in his hand. He cocked the gun and moved nearer to Hannah.

Hannah's heart skipped a beat. What was coming now? She couldn't see as far as the back of the warehouse, but she heard all the rumpus very clearly. Would this nightmare ever end? And if it did, how? She looked over at Farzi. The girl wasn't even conscious. Probably for the best, Hannah thought. It looked like a battle with guns was about to start and either she, or Farzi, or both, could lose their lives any minute.

She turned her head in Sadiq's direction. 'What's happening,' she asked him. 'I can't—'

'Shut the fuck up,' came the reply.

Alison took the call from Lorraine, and then followed it up with another call to the Home Office, and then the helicopter port, who put her through to the SAS captain, Vernon White. He assured her everything was being done as quickly as they could safely manage. Once in the air, and with luck, they could cross London in twenty minutes. His team would be on board, and once the hostage-takers came out with the hostages, the whole thing would be over in seconds.

She reported back to Lorraine, then walked down the corridor to the coffee machine. She put coins in and got herself a black coffee. She wanted thinking time. She was pretty sure she had the CCTV proof that the shot which had hit Martin Neville was fired from a different direction to where Massafur and Sadiq were. They were certainly responsible for not getting him medical attention, which led to him losing his life, and they would get a life sentence for that. But if they didn't actually shoot him, next question was – who did? Which posed another problem: would it be possible to free the hostages without killing the hostage-takers? They would be a great help in finding out the truth.

Now she felt involved, really involved with the case. There was nothing like the adrenaline fix she got from being a murder detective, when she actually found the bad guys and then physically caught them. And, by being in the station, she seemed to have brought this case on leaps and bounds. It made her question, yet again, a marriage to Paul Banham. How hard and confusing it was to love him. She wanted to be with him, and yet she knew he would ultimately, make her choose between the job and him. It wasn't that he was a bully or a chauvinist, it was that the murders of Diane and Elizabeth had left him so desperately frightened of losing her.

At this moment, if she had to, she knew she would choose her job, but then when she was with him, in bed, feeling his tender lovemaking, and his breath in her ear, telling her how much she meant to him, and making her feel like no one in her life had ever done, she felt she would give up everything to keep his love. She felt so confused.

She swallowed the last of her coffee, threw the cup in the bin, and walked down the corridor to the interview rooms. She needed to talk to more of the rioters: someone must have seen the incident, and maybe the key witness she was looking for.

Massafur opened the rear window of the warehouse just enough to push the rifle through and see over it. 'Are you looking to get your head blown off?' he shouted. 'Get the fuck out of here.'

Kevin McCaub moved nearer in to the open window, showing no fear. 'I'll go, just as soon as you give me my sister, you murdering bastard.'

'*Your* fucking sister? Forty seconds,' Massafur shouted. 'Fuck off, or you're a dead man.'

Kevin stood his ground. 'We're coming in if you don't give us Farzila McCaub,' he shouted back. 'She belongs with my family, not yours. Hand her over or we'll break the fucking door down. And if you shoot me, my family'll have the door down and they'll be in. Either way she's coming out.'

When Massafur didn't answer, Kevin raised his already angry

voice. 'You are well outnumbered. We've guns here too, and you know the saying, an eye for an eye. You shot my brother, you fucking scumbags, so you'll give me my sister, or you are looking at a lot of trouble.'

Hannah could hear the conversation. She guessed his identity from his Irish brogue: the brother of the boy that had been killed, Devlin McCaub.

It now fully sank in. If this guy was saying Farzila was a McCaub, then Farzila had definitely married Devlin, and not just gone off with him. That meant big trouble, and the poor, unconscious Farzila was in the midst of it.

'Your brother took her under force,' Massafur shouted, provoking the Irish man further. 'Her words. She said she's glad he's dead. So fuck off, or I will blow your fucking head off too, have you got that?'

Hannah then heard a scuffling on the roof. She felt a lot of relief, assured that SC019 were about to sort this. If she was able stand up she could run to the window and shout a warning to Banham, tell him who was at the back. Sadiq now had his back to her. He had picked up his rifle, and moved nearer to the back door. He was whispering with Massafur. It was a chance she had to take. She used her good arm to push herself up, and was just about to put her second foot on the ground when she caught Sadiq's eye. He had turned from Massafur and was looking in her direction. Her heart missed a beat. She watched, terrified, as he put his shotgun down, and then his revolver back in his ankle-holder, and then drew a knife from the leather holder around his waist. It was a small but very sharp-looking knife. She nearly urinated again. 'Sorry, I . . .' she started to stutter, but he ignored her and walked purposefully over to the unconscious Farzila.

With his free hand he pulled the unconscious Farzila by the arm and threw her against the wall. Her head lulled to one side, then her eyes blinked to open, slowly closing again. He lifted her left hand, pinning it back against the wall, and pulled the third finger forward, and then lifted the knife.

'No,' Hannah shrieked out, quickly realising what he was going to do. Then, speaking again before she thought, she shrieked, 'Please. Don't! NO!'

'Shut your mouth,' Sadiq turned his head and commanded. Hannah desperately tried to stand and walk to Farzila before the knife cut her. She failed. Her throbbing foot stopped her, it wouldn't take her weight and she fell to the ground.

'Nooooo!' she screamed loudly.

The noise woke Farzila. Her terrified eyes stared as Sadiq's knife dug into her third finger, and the finger came away in his hand.

'Tell them to fire, but into the air,' Banham shouted to Jim Carter.

Carter quickly spoke through his radio to the SC019 team on the roof. He relayed back to Banham that there were about thirty youths in Burton Street, arguing at the back of the warehouse, but no fighting had erupted. All were now listening to the screaming inside.

'Why are the women screaming?' Banham shouted into the hailer, but his voice went unheard, as at the same time, SC019 fired shots in the air. He turned to Crowther. 'Clear that street, before war breaks out,' he told him. Then to Jim Carter. 'No shooting into the mob, is that clear?'

'Your call, guv. You are the boss.'

'Why is that woman screaming?' Banham shouted again to the warehouse.

When no one answered, his voice became a lot firmer. 'You need to assure me the hostages in there are OK. Can you answer me, please? Our gun team will shoot on order. I need to know what is going on.'

'We are going to give you a present,' Massafur told McCaub, before shutting and locking the back window.

Massafur then marched up to Hannah, who was screaming at Sadiq. 'If you don't keep it shut, you'll be the next body on the pavement outside. Got it?'

She became immediately silent, but kept her eyes on Farzi. The woman had fallen to the floor, and blood was leaking dangerously from her missing finger. The wound reminded Hannah of her childhood rabbit when a fox caught it and carved its hungry teeth into the poor rabbit's stomach. Blood spurted out and up from the wound as the rabbit's eyes rolled into the back of its head. It was dead. Farzila's eyes had done the same. They had briefly opened then rolled to the back of her head as she fell to the floor, unconscious, the blood spurting and dripping from her finger.

Hannah lost her composure again. Her loud and desperate cry of 'Help!' shook the air, and stopped everyone in their tracks.

The hailer flew to Banham's mouth.

'I asked what's happening in there?' he shouted urgently. 'What is happening? I need to know.' He nodded to Carter.

The SC019 fired their guns into the air again.

No one inside answered, but more screaming from Hannah followed.

'What is happening in there?' Banham shouted again. 'Answer me, or there will be no helicopter and we will come in with the gun team.'

'We'll blow the women up before you take one step in here,' Sadiq shouted back. 'Your friend is getting impatient, that's all. Just get that 'copter here now.'

Two uniformed police officers ran up the road at this moment. 'Sir,' one of them said to Crowther, 'we haven't got enough manpower to cope with the mob back there. They are threatening us and rioting has started again. They have weapons, knives, crowbars, meat cleavers, and there are too many of them. We need extra men, or we'll have to back off. The mob are trying to get into the back of that building. Press have got through and are filming. I'm telling you, we can't cope. We need more officers and more vehicles.'

'Calling all available units. All units around the area. Emergency backup to clear Burton Street,' Crowther urgently spoke into his radio.

Banham turned again to Jim Carter. 'Tell your men to fire another round into the air,' he ordered.

Carter sent the order, and the team fired once more.

The hailer went to Banham's mouth. 'Listen up,' he shouted into the warehouse. 'We will deal with the street outside. No one will get in. In return, you need to all keep calm in there. The helicopter will be here as soon as it possibly can. Tell the ladies they will be out soon.'

No one answered.

Chapter Twenty-two

Hannah had managed to crawl onto her knees but as she attempted to stand up, her foot gave way and she tumbled to the floor again. She was desperate to reach Farzila. She had to stop the bleeding, or she knew Farzila would meet the same fate as Martin Neville.

Banham was anxious as no one had answered. He turned to Lorraine. 'They have stopped talking to us. Check on the 'copter again.' Then he radioed to Crowther. 'How is that brawl?'

'We've got more police coming to help,' came the answer. 'It's McCaub's brother, apparently. The SC019 are keeping it under control, by firing in the air. The crowd are backing off, and getting arrested as they leave the street.'

Banham put the hailer back to his mouth. 'Your helicopter is coming soon. We just checked. Now tell me, why did I hear the hostages screaming? I need your assurance she is not being hurt.'

'Nothing happening to her,' Sadiq shouted out the window. 'It's spiders see, she don't like them.' He turned to Hannah, his tone changed. 'One more scream and I will rape you.'

Hannah immediately became silent. She half sat and half fell onto the floor, the thought of the monster raping her making her immediately still.

Sadiq held Farzila's thin brown finger up in the air. He wiped his own bloodied hand on his combat trousers, then he handed the finger to Massafur.

As they both walked to the back window, Hannah half-crawled

and half-slid over to Farzila. With her left hand, she pulled the grubby, blood-stained remains of her own blouse which she had wrapped around her foot, and bound it very tightly over the remaining quarter of Farzi's finger, from which dark blood was pumping. She held the cloth over the finger and squeezed as tightly as her strength would allow. She blurrily turned to watch Massafur marching over to the back door holding the finger. Blood and a white mucus-like substance was dripping down his hand. With his other hand, he pulled the bolt back and opened the back window. She could hear the mob outside arguing and fighting with the police. Then firing from the roof.

Then McCaub's voice from the window, shouting and kicking at the door.

Hannah felt her heart vibrate like an electric shock as she realised what Massafur was going to do.

'There's no wedding ring, here's your proof,' Massafur shouted, throwing the amputated finger at Kevin. 'Now fuck off.' He banged the window shut and then pulled the bolt across.

Kevin McCaub took a second to register the finger, which was lying on the ground by his foot. Then his temper exploded and he lifted his machete, hacking angrily into the steel door. 'I'm going to kill you, you cunts,' he screamed.

The members of his gang who were not being arm-wrestled by police and were free of cuffs, and had seen the finger being thrown out, hurried to join him with their weapons of cricket bats and pickaxes or cleavers.

'Stop now, or we will shoot,' came the voice of Jim Carter.

Kevin ignored the warning. He was past caring. His temper had taken over and he carried on angrily swinging the machete, hit after hit as he pounded at the locked door.

The SC019 police on the roof took their signal from Carter, and fired warning shots, hitting the ground, and missing Kevin by inches.

'Drop your weapons,' Carter roared at them. 'Now. This is your last warning.'

As he spoke, more flashing blue lights and screeching sirens and tyres roared up the street. As uniformed PCs jumped out, Carter shouted again.

'My officers will shoot anyone with a weapon in the next three seconds. Drop the weapons and hands in the air,' he repeated.

The gang all dropped their weapons, and put their hands in the air.

Kevin ignored the warning. A second later, a shot hit him in the side of his arm. He dropped his machete.

Before he was led into the waiting meat van, he bent down to pick up the finger, and then used the same hand to nurse the wound in his arm. He was told he was under arrest for carrying weapons and threatening bodily harm and causing affray. He then started sobbing.

'Will she die?' he said quietly as Crowther walked up to him, pulling on forensic gloves and an evidence bag from his pocket, and gently took the finger from him, placing it in an evidence bag.

'We are doing everything we can to make sure she doesn't,' Crowther told him.

Kevin allowed himself to be arrested and taken away in the meat van.

A news cameraman who had stood at the end of the street, hiding in a doorway, was managing to film it all. He now stood in front of his live camera, a red light signalling its use, and told the story so far. He was pointing to the ongoing arrests, the obvious gang warfare taking place, and telling the nation that the police still hadn't managed to free the hostages, that a young British Pakistani woman and a young, inexperienced police officer were still being held in the warehouse at gunpoint, both believed to be hurt and in grave danger.

Kevin started weeping like a child as he was escorted into the van. Crowther put a hand on his shoulder. 'We'll get her out,' Crowther said to him. 'The finger will be put on ice and we'll get her to hospital pronto. The finger can be reattached. I give you my word we will do everything possible to get her out.'

'Alive or dead?' Kevin said as pathetically as a young child might ask if he was in trouble. 'I've just lost my brother, and she is pregnant with a McCaub baby.'

'I will keep you informed, I promise,' Crowther told him, with more compassion than anyone in the force had ever seen him show before.

Carter had moved back to report to Banham. Banham had stayed in front of the warehouse, to keep watch on the happenings from that side.

'I gave you my word that a helicopter is coming,' he said trying to stay calm as he spoke through the hailer. 'Your part was not to hurt those women, which you have broken. I need that woman out here, and NOW. She needs emergency treatment. Her life is in grave danger.'

'Where's our fucking helicopter?'

'I am no longer going to mess around. You have broken our deal. So now, if you don't release that woman, I will cancel the helicopter and we will come in and get her.'

'First sign of any you coming in and your fed gets a bullet in her head.'

Banham turned to Lorraine.

'Helicopter is on its way,' she said.

'And we've got a bomb, and we will light it.'

'You do nothing to risk Hannah's life. Got it?' Lorraine told Banham.

It was a few seconds before Banham spoke into the hailer again. 'I have told you, in a short while the helicopter will be here, with a pilot to take you where you want. But you have to allow that woman medical attention. If you won't let her out, then you must allow one of our paramedics in, to stem the blood. That woman could die if you don't.'

'Funnily enough it ain't too bad. Your own fed is *stemming* it with her shirt,' Sadiq shouted out. 'She's taken her shirt off, and sitting here in her undies. English girls are such sluts. So no need for panic. Oh, yeah, thank you for getting rid of that scum outside at the back.

You should lock them up. It was their fault she lost her finger. How long before we get this 'copter?'

'How is my officer?' Banham asked ignoring the comment, then turning to Lorraine he whispered, 'Do we have an update on the helicopter?'

Sadiq's voice came again. 'Your officer has great tits, but she's getting on my nerves, so hurry up with the 'copter, would you.'

Crowther arrived back at this moment. He updated Banham, letting him know everything that had happened at the back of the warehouse.

'Any press around, were there?' Banham asked.

'Yes, guv,' he nodded. 'I confiscated their cameras or it would be all over every news desk within minutes.'

Jim Carter butted in at this point. 'Sir, I am giving you my professional opinion here. We don't have time to wait for backup, or the helicopter, that woman may be bleeding to death. Look what happened with Neville. I have a crack team. We are ready to go in. This is getting out of hand. I am asking again, let us go in and finish this.'

'No,' Banham almost shouted at him, but at the thought of the hostage-takers hearing he kept himself in check. 'I will not take a chance with those women's lives.'

'You already are,' Carter argued. 'Their lives are in the balance as we speak.'

Lorraine Cory walked up to Banham. 'Sh—' Lorraine stopped herself and quickly corrected the *she*, to avoid mentioning Alison. 'They are in touch with the pilot now. They assure us it is all going to plan, but needs a little more time to brief the officers and load the plane.'

'Time we really don't have now,' Carter said. 'As I am deeply concerned for the welfare of the woman who has lost that finger.'

'Paramedics have it on ice,' Crowther told them.

'Let's go in and get them out,' Carter said to Lorraine.

'I said no. They said they have explosives,' Banham said again.

'I have just come off the phone from the office. Listen to this,' Lorraine said. 'There is reason to believe, from going through all the

CCTV evidence, that the shot that killed Martin Neville didn't come from where these murdering bastards were standing. And we may well be looking at another killer.' She held eye contact with Banham, then shook her head. 'We still have all our cells full of the rioters, so they are being interviewed to see if anyone can throw light on that one.' She looked at Banham. 'Mother of Christ, I need a fag. I was supposed to be giving them up.'

Banham dragged a hand down his face. He was in two minds now. Jim Carter had a point, how long could they wait? Suppose the helicopter didn't materialise. But then, if they sent the armed police in, and anything happened to Hannah, he would never forgive himself. He could only hope he was doing the right thing by not allowing SC019 to take this on. He didn't know if he was making the right or wrong choices. How many hostage situations did an officer meet in their career? He was an experienced negotiator, but this was now out of hand. He wouldn't risk anything happening to Hannah, and he was concerned about the time the helicopter would take, and how much longer these madmen would wait. Did they have a bomb? Neville was dead, Hannah was wounded, and Farzila McCaub had just lost her finger. And now, with the news that they could be looking at another killer? Why and how? And if so, he had let that killer go when earlier he had told Crowther to clear the streets. Was Martin Neville's killer locked in a cell at the station? Or was he out walking the streets, free to kill again?

He turned to Lorraine. 'Have we got an experienced and trusted team at HQ trawling through video footage?' he asked.

Lorraine nodded her head. 'Extremely experienced head of the unit there,' she told him. If only he knew who was running it, she thought to herself.

'Tell them not to release any of the arrested rioters. I will look through the CCTV myself later.'

He walked a few steps away and texted another, *I love you so much*, message to Alison. Then he added, *Hope you're missing me. This is a complicated case, sort of wish you were here.*

Chapter Twenty-three

Alison was again studying the CCTV screens. Her concern was growing as she watched the comings and goings at the front of the warehouse. Her personal video/radio was attached to her waist and through Lorraine's own personal video, she could hear and see all the noise of the riots at the back. She couldn't actually see the action as the CCTV wasn't showing far enough down the road. The uniformed team out there were in close touch with the station though, by radio, so she was getting the updates from them.

'Ma'am, the station phones are going crazy with press trying to get updates, and outside is packed with them,' PC Hayden told her.

'Tell them we will give a news conference later on, and if they don't go away and stop blocking the outside of the building we will arrest them,' she snapped back at Hayden.

Her phone bleeped its text signal. She saw it was from Banham and ignored it.

She then turned to one of the videos in the corner of the room from an adjacent street, and saw the backs of some of the gang running up the road.

'Why wasn't the CCTV in Burton Street working?' she asked Sam.

'Someone blocked it,' he told her. 'The team are on their way in,' he told her, then paused, shaking his head slightly before adding, 'with sixteen more arrests. Have we got room for them? No, we haven't. They are a load of out-of-control travellers, who apparently threatened the hostage-takers. They told our boys that the woman hostage is pregnant, and she has just lost her finger. One Irish bloke called her his sister. Personally I would give those boys a medal. Shall I send them on to another station? We could only take ten at the most.'

Alison's ears pricked up. 'Irish?' She threw her eyes to heaven, 'That's Kevin McCaub's lot. I warned him to stay away. He's just been freed on bail. It's his brother that Massafur or Sadiq shot earlier. No, I want him here, locked up, and on no condition freed until this is all over.'

She walked back to the video screen that was showing the front of the building. Banham was in full frame. He looked worn out and worried. The hailer was against his face as he spoke to the hostage-takers. She then rang the police helicopter station, checking on the helicopter. She was told it was being loaded as they spoke and everything was going to plan. She asked them to hurry it up. The plan was to get the hostage-takers with their hostages out of the warehouse, and onto the roof, where the helicopter intended landing. The SAS team would surprise them as they boarded. If there was the slightest sign of an attempt on a life, SAS would take them down, or SC019 would. The helicopter team knew a young and inexperienced female PC and a young woman were the hostages.

'Who is now minus a finger, and pregnant, we have just heard,' Alison told them, before hanging up.

She then pulled her own phone from her back pocket. She read Banham's message, then dialled Lorraine's number again and updated her on the helicopter.

'How's Banny?' she asked.

'Looking worried,' came the reply.

'He needs me there. I think he would be pleased to see me.'

'What part of *no* don't you understand?' Lorraine said with a lot of irritation in her voice. 'I've enough to deal with at the moment, so just do as you're told, hard as that is for you, Miss Best Detective in my rank.'

Alison felt her stomach turn over. If anything happened to Banham... And why had all this happened, today of all days? She now half-wished they had got married, and were in a Greek taverna sipping ouzo right now, safely planning the rest of their lives.

She didn't answer Lorraine. She hung up.

Hannah was watching Farzila. The girl was unconscious again, face down on the floor, and blood had seeped out from the material at the base of her finger. The bandage that Hannah had tied over where three-quarters of the finger should have been was soaked in blood, as was the floor around her. Hannah's own vision was now even more blurred. She feared she had concussion. From where she sat, and with her half-closed eye and swollen face, she was unable to establish whether blood was still seeping from the wound, or if the thing she dreaded most had happened, that Farzila had died. She knew if the woman had lost more than three pints, then she would have lost her life with them.

Massafur and Sadiq were both sitting on wooden boxes at the other end of the warehouse, holding their guns, and talking quietly to each other. They were concentrating on their conversation. All was now quiet in the streets both behind and in front of the building they were in.

The fact that Massafur and Sadiq showed no interest or compassion in the decline of Farzila frightened Hannah even more. She was family. These men were monsters, and her own heart felt heavy, now believing she too would never see the light of day.

She slithered, very slowly and carefully on her bottom, nearer to Farzila. She flicked her gaze, every few seconds, in the direction of Massafur and Sadiq, terrified if they saw her moving she would endure another beating, or worse still be raped. But they seemed to ignore her.

As she leaned into Farzila, about to stroke her hair and whisper in her ear to see if she got any reaction, knowing that the hearing is more than likely still working when a person is unconscious, Hannah realised her worst fear had come to pass. The girl had a chilling stillness about her. She wasn't cold, but she was unstirring, with no sign of breathing. Hannah put her own fingers to the side of Farzi's neck to feel for a pulse. She got nothing. She then clipped two fingers around her wrist, praying for the feel of a pulse. There was nothing. She urgently tapped the side of Farzi's face. Still nothing. A terrifying chill then vibrated through her own being and made her want to cry out, but she swallowed it back. Farzila was dead and Hannah was now completely alone. Her chances of getting out of this place alive were hardly worth the odds. Before she could stop herself she let out an ear-piercing scream.

Massafur and Sadiq jumped up and rushed over.

Hannah couldn't control her hysteria. 'She's dead, she's dead,' she screamed even louder. 'She's dead, you've killed her.'

Sadiq clapped his dirty and sweaty hand over Hannah's mouth and with his other hand wrenched back her two arms in an agonising fashion. The pain in her already throbbing arm shot through to the top of her head and she almost passed out. Then he kneed her hard in the back. 'Shut the fuck up,' he said as his knee struck into her again, and then again, and the pain from her arm that threatened to knock her unconscious, seemed minimal as she fought to breathe. With his hand over her nose and his knee punching into her back, between her lungs, the pain was totally unbearable. She prayed for unconsciousness.

Alison had been in touch with the arresting officers. She had checked all the new detainees had been thoroughly searched, and who had been handling what, so she knew which of them had been carrying firearms, and was up to speed with the arrests. She was glad that Kevin, although in deep trouble again, was not facing a firearms charge. She was ready when twenty or more of his gang were brought in, all under arrest.

She had been on to the helicopter pilot again, and was told the police helicopter was now loaded, the SAS were in it, and they would be airborne any minute, which meant they would reach Henry Street in less than twenty minutes. She passed this message on to Lorraine, then walked into interview room A and took her place next to Trainee DC Hank Peacock opposite Kevin McCaub.

She was wound up. She should be there, with Banham, when that helicopter arrived and the showdown happened. She was also angry with Kevin. She had bailed him as he had given her his word he wouldn't go near Henry Street. But he had gone straight there and caused bedlam.

'So, what have you got to say for yourself,' she said as she turned on the tape and video camera and introduced both herself and Trainee Detective Constable Peacock as taking the interview.

Banham, Lorraine, Carter, and Crowther had been standing together. They couldn't mistake recognising the scream that came from Hannah.

Banham turned to Lorraine. 'Did I hear right, did she say, *she's dead.*' His voice was now full of distress. 'That was Hannah's voice, wasn't it?' He turned to Crowther.

'It was definitely Hannah, guv,' Crowther confirmed. 'So it could only be Farzila. She must have bled out.'

'Jesus fucking Christ.' Lorraine said, opening the buckle of her tatty brown leather shoulder bag, and speedily pulling her cigarettes from it and raising one to her mouth.

Jim Carter shook his head. 'We should have gone in a few hours ago,' he said. 'Now we have three murders on our hands.'

'I will not risk Hannah's life,' Banham snapped back. 'We have PC Byfield at the end of the road, in pieces. I can't, and I won't, do anything that will risk Hannah Kemp's life.

'You've risked the other girl's.'

'She was murdered,' Lorraine told him sharply. 'DCI Banham is the senior investigating officer on this hostage situation. He knows he will have to make a full report, and take responsibility for his actions. We are grateful for your advice, but keep your jibes to yourself. I am told our helicopter has lift-off. We have less than half an hour until this is finished. So let's hold this together, and work together.'

'And if they've killed their hostage, and they've shot PC Neville, and they've shot Devlin McCaub, don't you think they'll kill that young PC without giving it a second thought,' Carter argued. 'Even if the helicopter is on its way. I think this has gone far enough. They are laughing at us.' He turned to Banham. 'You say you won't risk her life, but you are already risking it. Right now that woman is in serious danger. We can get her out.'

'You can't guarantee her safety if you go in there,' Banham argued. 'You don't know they don't have a bomb.'

'And,' Crowther butted in, 'with respect, we don't know for sure that Farzila is dead. Hannah is clearly frightened. She is an inexperienced, young PC. Everything is probably getting on top of her.'

'All the more reason to go in and get her,' Carter spoke up again in a louder tone.

Lorraine stubbed out her Marlboro and turned to Carter, her own tone hardened. 'I'm giving you fair warning,' she said. 'If you carry on throwing negative and unhelpful remarks at my SIO, I will have you on a misconduct charge.'

Carter stared at her for one second, but unable to hold her defiant gaze he looked away.

Banham lifted the hailer to his mouth. 'You need to talk to me,' he said.

No one answered.

'What's going on in there? Are the women OK? We are concerned out here. Why is one of them screaming?'

'Can you tell me when this helicopter is arriving?' Sadiq shouted back. 'We are all getting pretty fucking tense waiting here.'

'We are too,' Banham replied. 'You have cut one of your hostages. How is she?'

'Where's the fucking 'copter?'

'On its way. Minutes away, I'm told. I can give you my word on that, as I can also stop the plane coming. We had a deal. We have a helicopter for you, and a hundred grand, and in return you give us the hostages, unharmed. You have now cut one of those women. If you don't want me to halt the helicopter, then you need to let our paramedics in to stop the bleeding. I also have a doctor waiting on standby. And I need you to give me your word that you will not harm either of those women further.'

'Why are you asking for his word?' Carter said angrily. 'He isn't capable of keeping it. The man is mad.' He pointed his finger to his skull. 'You can't reason with a madman.'

'I'll give you nothing,' Sadiq shouted in a raging temper. 'I'll tell you though, that if we don't get our helicopter, and very soon, then I will hurt your so-called *officer*. I'll break every fucking bone in her body and then shoot her in the head. Her whining is getting on my nerves.' His voice raised to a shout. 'So get that 'copter on the roof here, now or sooner, or you'll get her back, all right. 'Cos I'll sling her out, limb by fucking limb.'

'And you don't think we should have gone in there, and taken them out,' Carter said, his eyes blazing with anger.

Banham turned to look at Lorraine, but her phone had just rung. She was combing her hair with her fingers, in an agitated manner, as her other hand held her phone to her ear. She was talking to Alison. Then noticing Banham looking at her, she walked away to finish the call.

'That officer,' Banham said calmly to Sadiq, although he was breaking up inside, 'is new to the force, she's frightened, and understandably so.'

'I don't actually give a fuck,' came the reply. 'Maybe I should have chopped her too, her ear perhaps.'

'OK, that's enough,' Banham told him. 'A helicopter is on its way, not far off. Will you release that hostage or let my doctor in there?'

'Show me the 'copter first.'

'I must have your assurance you will not harm those hostages further.'

'Told you. If that 'copter ain't coming soon we will blow the whole fucking place up, and everyone around here. The bomb we have here will get the whole fucking street. You included, fed, that's my word.'

Banham was now beginning to doubt his own decisions. Maybe

Carter was right? Maybe they should have bulldozed their way in. They might have got them out by now, but then on the other hand, it might have got every one of them killed. He had made the decision to play it safe. He was determined not to risk any more lives. He already had Martin Neville and Devlin McCaub's deaths on his hands. At least he had also got the older, innocent hostages out, and to hospital and safety.

Banham's stomach churned as, again, his thoughts went to the night his beautiful baby girl was hacked to death in front of her mother. He felt a lump form in his throat as a picture of Diane watching her baby scream out for help as the killer repeatedly broke into her tiny skull. Did she think of Banham in those final moments, and wonder why he wasn't there to save them? Did she curse him for not being there as that bastard then cut into her, blow after blow, sending her into unconsciousness and then death?

Then he thought of Alison. He had another chance, a life ahead with her. But what about Peter Byfield's life ahead? He couldn't bear the thought of Byfield following his pattern, losing his young wife and then spending years regretting and wondering if he could have done something.

Jim Carter lifted his hand as he walked back to Banham, 'Half an hour, approximately for the 'copter, I'm told,' he informed him. 'But possibly less.'

Banham clocked that Lorraine was down the street talking on her phone. He made a quick decision, which he had no intention of running past her.

Carter now had his back to him, talking to his own team. Only Crowther stood beside him, a detective sergeant under Banham, with no authority to argue or stop him. Banham's mind was made up.

He lifted the hailer. 'I have another offer to make to you,' he said calmly, and then carried on talking, without waiting for a reply. 'If I come in there, unarmed, hands in the air, no microphone or equipment, or weapon of any sort, would you swap me for the young PC, and let her go?'

Crowther's head shot round. 'Christ, guv, don't be so fucking stupid.'

Banham ignored him. He spoke again into the hailer.

'The helicopter has been confirmed. It is on its way. I will be your hostage, until the helicopter comes. And then, I will walk free, and you can fly to freedom or wherever you think it will take you.'

No one spoke. Jim Carter had heard the conversation, although Lorraine Cory hadn't. Carter had turned his head and now he walked swiftly over to Banham.

'Now I know you're an idiot,' he said, staring at him.

Banham ignored the remark. He spoke again into the hailer. 'I hold a high-ranking position. The powers that be will be sure to get your helicopter request moving quicker if they know I am with you as a hostage. In return you must release Hannah, and your other hostage, who is a big concern to me, as she is in urgent need of medical treatment.'

There was still silence from the warehouse. Crowther shook his head, then put his hand to his forehead. 'What the fuck, guv?' he said. 'Please don't do this.'

Banham put his hand in the air to silence him.

Crowther turned and hurriedly walked up the road heading for Lorraine Cory.

Lorraine was on the phone still, in deep conversation with Alison. She was totally unaware of what Banham was doing, and waved Crowther away.

Carter shook his head, but made no further comment.

'I'm waiting,' Banham said.

There was three seconds when no one spoke, then the voice of Sadiq shouted from inside the warehouse.

'Come on in.'

Chapter Twenty-four

Crowther hurriedly followed Banham as he walked towards the warehouse. 'Guv, for Christ's sake, you're being an idiot. The helicopter is practically airborne, it'll be over soon.'

Banham ignored Crowther. He stood in front of the warehouse and spoke loudly. 'Bring my officer to the door, and let me see her,' he shouted. At the same time he was unfastening his radio, and placing his loudhailer on the floor. Then he emptied his pockets and put his hands in the air. 'My hands are in the air, and I am unarmed. Go,' he said to Crowther.'

No one answered him.

'This is no trick,' he pushed again. 'Your helicopter is en route. I have agreed a straight swap, me for my officer. Bring her to the door, and let her walk free. I will walk in and take her place. No one will try anything from our side, that's a promise. My only condition, I must see her first, out here. As soon as she is outside the door, I will walk in.'

Carter tried again. 'You are definitely off your head, guv. I should refuse to work with you—'

The agonised shriek that came from the inside of the warehouse took everyone's attention.

Before Banham could open his mouth to ask what was going on, Massafur spoke. 'Nothing to worry about,' he said dismissively. 'That was an accident. My cousin can get a bit clumsy at times. He was helping her get up. She is on her feet now, sorry, her foot. She is getting ready to leave.'

'Guv, no,' Crowther stepped in front of Banham and tried to implore.

'Get the paramedics to stand by, right here,' Banham said, pushing him aside. 'I think she'll need help walking.'

Crowther shook his head. 'This ain't right, guv.'

'Just do it,' Banham raised his voice.

As Crowther turned around and headed towards the waiting paramedics to brief them. Banham called after him. 'Make sure Byfield is nowhere near. He can go straight to the hospital, but he comes nowhere near here. Got it?'

Banham then clocked Lorraine walking back purposefully towards him. 'Uh-oh,' he said half to himself.

Lorraine was looking furious. Carter was beside her. He had clearly gone running to her, like a teacher's pet, Banham thought to himself. He had to now hope he could still get Hannah out, and himself inside the warehouse before Lorraine used her power to forbid him.

'I've got some extremely interesting news and new evidence,' Lorraine said to Banham. 'The angle of the gunshot . . .' but she stopped in mid-sentence as Hannah appeared at the doorway of the warehouse. Sadiq was standing beside her, holding her up by her arm. Her head was hanging downwards, and it was clear she unable to stand unaided. Sadiq had his gun pressed into her temple.

Before Lorraine had time to ask or register what was happening, and then to forbid it, Banham had put his hands in the air, either side of his body, and walked up to the door of the warehouse.

'What the fuck?' Lorraine had now raised her voice.

'I'm coming in, unarmed, as promised,' Banham said to Sadiq. 'Now let her go!'

Lorraine looked over at Crowther. 'What the fuck? What does he think he's doing?' She then clocked the paramedics moving in.

'Get back here, Banham,' she shouted. Crowther said nothing. She then turned to Jim Carter. 'What the fuck?' Then to Crowther. 'What's he doing?' But her words fell on deaf ears.

Sadiq took Banham's arm, and quickly moved the gun to his head, and then nodded to Hannah.

'Jesus fucking Christ.' Lorraine put her hand to her forehead. 'What does he think this is going to achieve? The helicopter is leaving as we speak. They'll kill him.' Her other hand dug in her handbag again for her cigarettes. She put one in her mouth, lit it and inhaled, and then looked up to Jim Carter. 'For Christ's sake, don't just stand there, do something.'

Carter shook his head. 'Too dangerous to take a shot, ma'am,' he said, looking from Hannah to Banham, and then nodding to Lorraine to indicate Massafur at the window with a rifle in front of him, pointed straight at Banham.

'What can we do?'

'Pray for that fucker of a 'copter to get here before this cock-up ends in another death,' he said.

'It's about to take off,' she told him. 'It'll be twenty minutes at most. I just spoke to the station. And guess what? Ballistics don't think either of these two shot Martin Neville. The video from the CCTV shows the gunshot came from the right side of frame. These two were in the front at the centre of the frame.'

Hannah was blinking. Her one working eye was weeping and she couldn't see anything in the bright light she was facing.

The three paramedics hurried towards her, and two held her up before she crashed to the ground. The lifting of her foot to step on it had proved too much. Mary and Patrick held her and comforted her as Ainsley Kay, the beefiest of the three, placed the stretcher he was carrying on the floor for the other two to lower Hannah into it, quickly covering her with a foil blanket, and then an oxygen mask over her face.

Lorraine hurried over to her as they carried her to the ambulance. She was shocked at the state of Hannah's face, and could see her arm was broken and her foot swollen and badly damaged. 'It's all right, you're safe now,' she told her, speaking softly.

Hannah was struggling with her one working arm to get the

mask off and talk to Lorraine, but Lorraine placed a gentle hand over her hand. 'Don't, not now, pet,' she told her. 'Plenty of time for that later. We'll get Peter for you. He'll be at the hospital by the time you arrive, and we'll get you well again.' She looked up at Crowther. 'Go with her in the ambulance, and stay with her. When she is ready, get a full statement, but I want a police guard on her twenty-four seven.'

Lorraine then turned around, but Banham had disappeared into the warehouse.

Alison had taken Kevin McCaub's statement, and although she sympathised completely with him, she hadn't shown any sympathy. Instead she had given him a strong earful, and locked him back in a cell, telling him he would be charged with causing an affray, and carrying a dangerous weapon and a firearm. She had no intention of carrying that last charge through, but decided to frighten him. She was concerned that if he tried it again, his would be the next body in the morgue.

She was now back in the control room, in front of one of the videos that faced the warehouse. There was one camera recording from the roof of the warehouse down into Henry Street, where Banham and Carter and Crowther were gathered with the super, and another on the roof of the empty offices opposite, in front of the team of C019 officers. There were also the body cameras, which had sound attached. She stood still, listening intently, although the sound had rustling over it as the men moved and spoke. She couldn't believe her eyes, or ears, as she watched Banham offer himself, in exchange, for the release of Hannah. She turned with a puzzled and frightened look at Sam as Sadiq dragged Hannah out of the warehouse, a gun pressed to her head, and stood with her in the middle of the CCTV frame.

'What on earth's happening here?' she said, but then stopped talking as Banham walked into the frame, towards the warehouse, and then inside it.

'What the . . . ?' she said, turning to the other officers in the room. 'Are you all watching this? Wind it back. He's got no body protection on. No body camera, or a radio. He is unarmed and vulnerable. Am I going mad, or has he? He's gone into the building. He's changed places with Hannah.'

All the officers in the CCTV viewing room got up and crowded around the same video screening the CCTV cameras. All were aware that Alison had a terrible temper which could erupt any second. All, also, were shocked at what they were witnessing. A few eyes flicked worried glances at one another, but no one spoke a word.

After a long few seconds silence, Sam spoke at the same time as Larry. 'How long to the helicopter?' he asked, as Larry said, 'Is Peter with Hannah? He didn't get in the ambulance. Shall I call him?'

'Fifteenish minutes to the helicopter arriving and landing on the roof, but anything could happen in that time,' Alison told them. 'There is a briefed SAS team on board, on the floor of the 'copter, ready for a shoot-out. And of course they don't know that Banny has now changed places with Hannah. He'll be lucky if they don't shoot him. Jesus, what a mess.' Her hand went to her mouth as she lowered her eyes and shook her head. 'He's risking his life.' She then raised her voice, and her famous temper threatened. 'What does he think he's doing? He's supposed to share his life with me.' She pulled her phone from her pocket and stabbed Lorraine's number into the phone.

'Don't start. I know what you're going to say,' Lorraine said as she picked up the phone. 'And before you ask, no, it wasn't my idea, and I am as cross with him as you are. He is one hundred per cent on a disciplinary.'

'If he isn't dead by that time.'

'That won't happen, and don't say if you'd been here with him, none of this would have happened. Because it's hard to tell which of you two is the most hot-headed. So we have to deal with what we've got. Are we one hundred per cent sure the helicopter is coming?'

'I'm not God, so I'm not *sure* of anything, Lorry,' she snapped, then pulled herself sharply up. 'But, yes, I have been told it is.' Then she raised her voice in exasperation. 'This is what happens when I'm not there!' she shouted. 'That man has let his own emotional guilt cloud his judgement on this.'

'Can you calm down, please.'

'Come on, Lorry, you know I'm right. He isn't thinking straight. He feels, as he always does, that everything in life is his fault and responsibility. If I had been there, as I should have been, I would never have let this happen . . .'

'That's enough, Grainger,' Lorraine told her sharply. 'DCI Banham is my senior investigating officer on this. He makes the decisions. So pipe down, that attitude will help no one, least of all yourself.'

'Well, this is downright stupid.'

'Listen to me. Hannah Kemp has a broken arm, a bullet in her foot, and a face that is bruised to fuck. I wouldn't have let Banny do it either, but if the 'copter is airborne, we are talking less than half an hour.'

'Yes, and when it comes,' Alison shouted back, 'there will be a shoot-out. Banny is not armed, he is not wearing a bullet-proof vest, and he will have a gun to his head. Therefore, he is in great danger of getting killed.' Her voice had an emotional crack in it. She had now had enough. 'I am coming down there.'

'Excuse me? No, you are not.'

'If he's in the warehouse. He won't know I am there, outside. At least I'll be in a position to do something. I have a gun licence, so I'll bring one.'

'Grainger. You are going the right way to a disciplinary, too. I have told you to stay there. There are prisoners sitting outside the station in the vans. I need you to deal with that. I want full statements from all of them. As you say, there may be the person there who knows who shot Neville, if these bastards didn't. And I want to know what they say as they say it. Do I make myself clear?'

Alison didn't answer.

'We have a national emergency on our hands. We have to be seen to sort this. If these bastards didn't shoot Neville, as you have cleverly found out that they couldn't have done, then don't we owe it to

Edna Neville to find out who did? Because someone did, and that gang sitting outside the station in those meat vans may well shine a light on that. They were there, so they must know something, or one of them may well have shot him by accident. This is important. I know you can get that out of them. Also, I need you to sit on the Home Office, and keep me up to speed with the helicopter situation. I've got every paper and every television and radio station hanging around here waiting for a chance to make a story of our inadequacies and I feel very sure we are not going to come off well.'

'All is not lost on that front,' Alison said, now sounding calmer. 'If we can get permission to dig in that Catford park and the surrounding area, where Kevin McCaub has told me the other woman is buried, I feel sure we will be able to bring five additional murder charges against those men in there, alongside killing McCaub, hostage-taking, and grievous bodily harm. That will do us some good.'

'Print out some pictures of Massafur Khan and Sadiq Ashraf. If they get shot down, which I fear they will, we can run the pictures past Hannah when she is in a better state, and double-check those facts before we start asking permission to dig the park up.'

'You know, I'm on holiday, officially,' Alison said suddenly, 'so I can be where I choose to be. And I choose to be down there, helping save the life of my fiancé. So I am on my way.'

'So being back in uniform appeals to you, does it, ex-DI Grainger?'

Alison hesitated at that.

'No, Alison,' Lorraine said. 'I have said a firm no. That is an order from me. Please don't ruin your very promising career. You are an excellent detective and I would hate to lose you, but if you disobey me, you will be back directing traffic, and that's a promise.'

Alison hung up.

Once inside the warehouse, Banham's hands were pulled behind his back and tied, tightly, with rope. The rope was then tied to the rusty radiator on the same side of the room as Farzila Khan. Near her, but too far away for Banham to read clearly if she was actually dead or unconscious. The part of shirt that Hannah had tied over the remaining third of her finger was soaked in blood. Blood had also pooled over her hand, around the remains of her finger. Banham tried, but was too far away to see if she was still bleeding.

He had seen a lot of corpses in his long career, and even from the distance he was, he felt sadly confident that this woman had died. He stared, studying her unmoving body. Then his own demons stirred inside him.

This woman was young, and, he felt, beautiful: long, flowing, shiny dark hair and, Banham suspected, normally perfect features, although her nose was bloodied and probably broken judging by the swelling and puffy eyes.

His stomach turned; he was nearly sure she was dead. He looked, desperately, for some sign of life. If she was alive, then it was barely, and she wouldn't be for long. But then the helicopter wouldn't be long now either. He prayed she just might hang on.

He was also working out how he could lift her safely out of the warehouse when the helicopter came. If there was a fragment of a chance of saving her, he had to find it. He had got Hannah Kemp out, now he prayed he could save this innocent woman.

'The helicopter is only about twenty minutes away now,' he said to Massafur. He decided to work on the weaker of the two and knew that was Massafur. If there was any chance of getting his hands untied, it would be from him. Try as he was, he couldn't move the knots around his own wrists.

Alison was the one for knots, he thought to himself, she could undo anything. He blinked, as he thought of her alone in a taverna, unmarried, and waiting for him. He had risked his life in here and might not get out to join her. Then he would have let her down, as he had Diane. He told himself he would get out and, with luck, so would Farzila. The paramedics were outside, her finger was on ice. She had a chance, a very slim one, but there was one there.

Massafur had been standing at the back of the warehouse with Sadiq. They were checking the back door was still secure after the pounding it had taken. When Banham spoke, Massafur turned to listen.

Banham indicated with his head to Farzi. 'I know you are taking her with you,' he lied. 'I presume you have plans for her. If you want to take her, you should try to keep her alive. She doesn't look in a good way. I have a bit of medical training. Want me to check that wound?'

'Just shut the fuck up,' Sadiq snapped quickly back.

Banham had expected a bridge to go up with Sadiq, but he had worked out the other one was malleable. Get through to one, and that one could crack the other. Massafur wasn't only listening, he seemed concerned. And he was obviously stupid enough to believe the police would just let them pilot themselves off in a helicopter, with a hundred grand, and not care that they had murdered multiple people.

Banham persisted. He shrugged casually. 'Give me something to do. Why would I try and escape when I gave myself up to you, and knowing the helicopter will be here, and I'll be free in twenty minutes. I've got medical training, I can help her, which will be of help to you.'

When neither answered, Banham pushed on.

'A lot easier for you, if she is conscious when the helicopter arrives. It'll make your getaway quicker. She's very much not conscious at the moment. Want me to try and bring her round?'

'Throw a bucket of water over her, that'll do it,' Sadiq said to Massafur.

Banham didn't give up. 'I know you want to take her with you.'

He could see Massafur was thinking.

'This isn't a trick,' Banham lied.

'You ain't getting your hands untied,' Sadiq snapped. 'Just shut the fuck up, or you'll get a bullet in them.' He marched over to Farzila. Banham watched carefully as he pulled her roughly by the wrists, and then slapped her face. He still couldn't see through the blood-soaked piece of Hannah's shirt whether the amputated finger had been bleeding out. He thought of Diane again, then pushed that thought from his head. His job now was to keep himself alive so he could help this woman, if it wasn't too late, and then give evidence to a judge to put these bastards behind bars, never to see the light of day again. And then to get himself off to Greece where Alison would be waiting for him.

Vernon White was an SAS captain as well as an experienced and qualified pilot. He had been hand-picked for this job. He had then speedily pulled together half a dozen of his best men. They'd had a briefing at the Epping head office, and knew exactly how they would carry out the mission without harm to any nearby civilians. White was piloting, so his next in command, Sergeant George Slater, was on the phone updating Jim Carter as the 'copter took off.

Carter moved his gun team into place and they were again on standby, ready to go in. They had been told about twenty minutes. Fifteen to get there, and five to circle the area, to make the hostage-takers aware they were there.

The plan was to get the hostage-takers out of the warehouse and onto the roof. The two hostage-takers would then be handed the hundred thousand pounds, all counterfeit notes, that Slater held in a large brown case. They would then be asked to free the hostages, which they hadn't yet learned was the pregnant woman and DCI Banham, and not the young female PC. The briefing had informed them that the hostage-takers, in all likelihood, would not release the pregnant woman but attempt to take her onto the helicopter with them. This was where they were all going to play very carefully. The woman, they knew, would be in the centre of the firing line, and they couldn't take any chances with her life. Where they stood with the police officer, no one was guessing, they might also attempt to get the PC on the helicopter. The SAS were on the ground of the helicopter to make sure that wouldn't happen. The clear instruction was: one move of a hostage-taker's hand to their gun, and the SCO19 team would take them out, one bullet each.

Jim Carter was going to be told to tell Massafur and Sadiq that his SC019 team had been instructed to stand down. They would in fact have moved completely out of sight, but have eyeball on the killers, and if they could get a clear shot, with one hundred per cent guarantee that neither of the hostages could get wounded, then they were to take it. Their instruction was to move quickly, keep to the plan, and stand still if anyone other than these hostage-takers stood to get in the way of the shot.

'We should be with you in under twenty minutes now,' Slater told him. 'Make sure everyone is out of sight, and in position.'

'Understood,' Carter replied and then added that DCI Banham was now a hostage and not the young PC.

'OK, that will make things easier, we suspect,' came the reply. 'Keep us informed on movements.'

'Will do.'

Carter turned and relayed everything to Lorraine Cory, who immediately dialled Alison. It went to voicemail. She then rang the station line and was told Alison had gone to the loo. She took a deep breath and rolled her eyes to heaven. Gone to the loo, now Alison was playing games.

A few minutes later she tried Alison's mobile again. No one answered. Lorraine left her a message. 'I sincerely hope you have got the trots,' she snapped into the phone. 'But if you haven't and you are on your way down here, then you will be sent straight back to the station. Got it?' She paused and then added. 'In handcuffs, and on a disciplinary charge. I hope you are not that stupid. This is an extremely sensitive and delicate operation. It is coming to a head.' She sharpened her tone. 'Do not fuck with my orders. Just do as you are told. Phone me as soon as you get this, and let me know you are obeying instruction. Should it be that you are out the back sorting out the prisoners in the meat vans, then keep me informed, and ring me back as soon as you get this. Finally, consider this a warning. I will not be disobeyed.'

The hospital was heaving. There were many in A&E, still waiting from last night's riots, some needing stitching, or X-raying, or plastering from the stampeding and the fighting in Henry St.

Hannah was rushed straight past everyone and in as an emergency. Crowther was with her, assuring her, even though her eyes were now closed, that Peter was on his way. He was also barking at everyone who walked speedily by her stretcher, as she was hurried into a bed and screens pulled around her, what and where her injuries were.

Peter Byfield arrived within minutes. He looked pale and drawn and not far from tears as a nurse brought him a chair to sit beside Hannah's bed. She had once again lost consciousness. The paramedics assured Peter it was trauma, she had been in and out of consciousness, they told him, during the short drive to the hospital. Her arm was broken and the pain had knocked her out. The painkilling injection hadn't had enough time to take effect, so she was sleeping. Her body had closed off, temporarily. She was going to be fine, they reassured him, with a gentle tap on his back. They intended taking great care of her.

Crowther knew there was no way he could talk to her now. A statement from her was out of the question, it would have to wait for a while. He spoke to the doctors, who agreed to let Byfield stay close by her side during the X-raying of her body and as she was put through various tests and assessed. He would be the police guard that Detective Superintendent Cory insisted was with her at all times for now.

He left Peter with her and walked up to A&E and enquired about the older lady and gentleman who had been brought in from the siege and rushed here by ambulance. It was overflowing, and the very tired nurse he spoke to said the couple were fine, they had been discharged. They had been checked over and given an all clear. She said she would pass the notes on, email them to him, as soon as she could put her hands on them, but assured him they were in good health, and the gentleman had been given his medication.

Crowther asked for their home addresses. As the nurse went off to get them, Crowther made a call to Lorraine Cory. He updated her, told her the two hostages were fine and Peter Byfield was staying with Hannah and wouldn't leave her side. He requested to be able to return to the scene and be on hand to help there. She agreed, as long as there was a police guard on Hannah. She reminded

Crowther to get the addresses of the other hostages, so a statement could be taken later in the convenience of their homes, once they were a little less shocked.

Alison had listened to Lorraine Cory's voicemail and knew, from the tone in the message that she was serious about the threat of being back in uniform if she turned up at the scene. She also knew Lorraine wouldn't be messed with and she would face a disciplinary hearing. She was furious. Banham was supposed to be her husband, so who would blame her, even at a disciplinary, if she disobeyed orders to help him. There was no doubt, as everyone knew now, that the hostage-takers were killers, and now her fiancé's life was hanging by a thread. Bollocks to the super's orders, she thought, but then again, supposing her turning up caused Banham to take an unnecessary chance?

The super's opinion didn't come into how Alison felt at this moment, this was about Banham. He was her man, and she would certainly not take any risk to put him in danger, but she would take any risk to get him out of it.

She hadn't had a cigarette for years now, but having blagged one from PC Alan, along with a box of matches, she stood outside the station weighing up what to do. She told herself she would make her mind up while she smoked the cigarette. One little Benson and Hedges wouldn't start a smoking habit again, surely?

The nicotine tasted good as she inhaled for the first time in a couple of years. Before she had finished the much-wanted smoke, she'd had an idea. She had photos of the men they believed were guilty of murdering the bodies found in the park. She had also the statement from Kevin McCaub saying as much. If she could get a photo identification and witness statements from the older hostages who had been freed, and from Hannah Kemp, proving the hostage-takers were these same men, then she had evidence to apply to get the park dug up. And if that dig found the missing body, then she would have cracked a very difficult case, and could get these men on those other unsolved murder charges. Technically, she knew they were guilty of Martin Neville's murder, but as they possibly hadn't fired the gun that shot him, they might get away with manslaughter, and she wasn't having that. She owed it to Martin to get them put away for life. And she intended to do that for his widow too. She ground her cigarette butt into the overflowing concrete ashtray in the station car park.

PC Albert Lipton had been with the hostages, who he now knew as Mariam and Buisha, in the hospital. They had been checked out. Neither were suffering from anything but shock, although Buisha needed the medication he was carrying in his pocket but had forgotten he had. Lipton was going to drive them home, make them a nice cup of tea, and then take their statements, but first, while they got themselves together, he would pop down to see his colleagues Peter Byfield and Hannah Kemp.

Alison arrived at the hospital within ten minutes. She parked in a side road, and as she approached the hospital front entrance by foot, she was taken aback by the crowds of reporters and cameras standing waiting. She knew they were waiting en masse outside the station, which is why she had slipped out the back door, but hadn't realised they knew Hannah and the other older hostages were here, and, like the vipers Alison thought they were, they were, insensitively, waiting to get statements from the wounded and shocked hostages.

She pushed her way through, careful to keep her head down, hoping no one would recognise her from any of the many television appeals she had done in her time.

No one did.

Once inside and at reception, she flashed her warrant card, and asked to be directed to both Hannah Kemp and the older couple. She was directed to Hannah and Peter, and told they thought the older couple had left, and were being driven home by the PC who was looking after them.

Alison hurried to the private room the hospital had allocated Hannah to give her some peace and quiet. Hannah was drowsy but awake. Peter was holding her hand and Albert Lipton sat the other side of the bed. Peter looked drawn and ill.

'When this is all behind us, maybe we'll have a double wedding,' Alison tried joking. 'How are you? What's the damage?'

'Her arm has been X-rayed, it's broken in three places,' Peter said with a resigned shake of his head. 'They removed the bullet from her big toe, but she can't stand up. And we don't know yet if there is any internal damage, but look at her beautiful face . . .'

Alison didn't let him finish. She leaned into Hannah. 'We'll get them,' she said gently. 'I promise you. And I'll make sure they fall into a few walls before they get to court. And your face doesn't look too bad,' she lied, covering her anger as she stared at the swelling and congealing blood over the woman's eye. 'That'll heal quickly.'

'The DCI—' Hannah started to say.

'I know,' Alison interrupted. 'He's a big boy, he'll be all right. Hannah, can you help me? Can you see?' She pulled the photos from her bag. 'Are these your hostage-takers?'

Hannah shook her head.

'She can't see, everything is blurred for her at the moment,' Peter said.

Alison nodded. 'I'm sorry to push, I want to make sure they get what they deserve. I probably shouldn't.' She turned to Lipton. 'Did you drive the older hostages home? I am told they're in reasonable shape. I'll need a copy of their statements when you take them, and I'm sure they'll recognise these pictures.' She handed him the pictures.

'They haven't gone yet,' Albert told her. 'They are getting themselves together. They were put in private rooms, away from everyone, as so many press are trying to find them. I'm going to drive them home in a few minutes.'

'Oh, well, I'll show them the pictures before they go,' she said. 'Do you think they are up to giving us a statement now?'

'I had told them I would take them home first. The hospital staff are arranging for them to leave by the laundry door, because of the press. But we can ask them. I'll take you to them.'

'See you soon,' Alison said touching Hannah's hand as she left the room.

They walked along the corridor and up the stairs and Albert

turned into a corridor. 'They took us up here, to avoid the press that were trying to barge in on them. Insensitive bastards. It's just down here.' He then opened a door.

The room was empty.

He stepped back out, and opened the next door along. That was empty too. 'Ah, they'll be downstairs waiting for me. I'd better not keep them waiting.'

They both hurried back down the corridor and down the stairs. All the while Alison's phone kept buzzing in her pocket. She pulled it out. It was seven missed calls from Lorraine. She hesitated, then dialled the helicopter port, and was told the 'copter had taken off and would be arriving in twelve minutes. She checked her watch, and pushed her phone back in her pocket.

The older couple were downstairs in the visitor's room, the nurse told them. The doctor had checked them over, had given them both prescriptions for sedatives, as well as giving the older man another prescription for his schizophrenia. Other than that they were both in good shape and were being completely discharged. They would have to wait first for the chemist to make up their medicine, then they could go.

Alison and Albert found the visitor's room.

Alison asked after their health, and settled beside them in the visitor's room. 'Albert is going to drive you home,' she told them, watching them closely. They both looked in shock. 'And you can go out the back just as soon as you've got your prescriptions. Can I just ask you to look at these photos and tell me if these were the men that had taken you hostage?'

The woman, Mariam, nodded, and smiled at Alison. 'We are OK. We are lucky,' she said as she took the pictures and studied them carefully. The man looked blankly at Alison. He then started mumbling nervously. The woman patted his hand. 'You are safe, I keep telling you, these are police officers. We are safe now.' She looked over the pictures and said to Alison. 'He had his medication late, so his mind wanders.' She looked back down at the pictures of the men Alison had printed out from the computer.

'These men are wanted for other murders, Alison told her. 'So I need to know if they are the same men that took you hostage.'

Mariam shook her head. 'No, it's not them,' she said. 'These weren't the men who took us hostage, were they, Buisha? They were older.'

'These are older pictures,' Alison told her. 'So in the pictures they would be younger. Is there any chance they could be the same? Can you look closer?'

The woman did, and still shook her head. 'Mrs . . .' Alison looked at Albert to tell her the woman's name.

'Call me Mariam,' the woman said.

'Mariam, are you sure?'

'Yes, quite sure.'

Alison's heart dropped to her boots. So her theory was wrong. The bodies in the park, with the missing third fingers, were just coincidence. She had been barking up the wrong tree. But, it was a big coincidence, or was Kevin McCaub setting these men up for other murders to get back at them for going after his brother? Alison was annoyed with herself for being taken in by him. But how did he know there were bodies buried in the park?

Alison's phone buzzed again. She pulled it from her pocket, and knew she had to take Lorraine's call. She walked outside the door.

'Lorraine. All in hand,' she said. 'I couldn't stay at the station, I felt like a cooked-up hen, so I am now down at hospital. I wanted to show the photos to the hostages, and Hannah, but Hannah is out of it for a while. They say she will be all right though, thank goodness. She looks in a bad way though. She has taken a beating, So it will take time.'

'I saw her. Did you show the pictures to the older hostages?'

'It's a no from them,' she said. 'But I think they are in shock too. It's a mighty big coincidence, otherwise. Or else Kevin McCaub is having us over.' There was a few seconds pause. 'How is Banny?' she asked.

She listened while Lorraine told her nothing more had been heard from inside the warehouse. That they were all anxiously waiting the helicopter's arrival, and obviously very concerned. Then

Lorraine quickly added, 'Of course, Banny knows what he is doing. He'll be fine.'

Alison wanted to argue that if he knew what he was doing he wouldn't have been stupid enough to change places with Hannah in the first place, but decided to say nothing. She knew why he had. 'The helicopter will be there within minutes now,' she said calmly. 'I just spoke to them. Good luck with it all.' Then she hung up.

Her insides felt like she was riding a funfair ride if anything happened to Banny . . . She couldn't bear to think about it. She loved him there was no doubting that, and would dress up, again, as a fancy poodle and marry him, if this all turned out OK.

As she turned to go back into the visitor's room her phone trilled again. It was Lorraine. She picked up.

'Why don't you come over and be here to greet him when we get him out.'

Alison nearly jumped through the roof. 'And no disciplinary?' she asked.

'Nope. Just get down here and don't mention anything until it's all over.'

Alison felt like crying with relief as she thanked her, but she kept a grip, she had two older people there who had been through a lot more than herself that morning. She clicked off and said to Albert, 'I am on my way to Henry Street. I'm going to be there when the SAS jump the 'copter and take the hostage-takers down, and Banny gets freed. I will leave you to look after this lady and gentleman, take them home, and get a full statement when they are both safely in their homes. Oh, and arrange police protection for them. They'll need a patrol car around their street for the rest of the day, to keep the press at bay.'

'I'll drop you on the way,' Albert told her.

'Thank you for your time,' she said to Mariam and Buisha as she left the room.

She then ran straight into the pharmacist, who was holding bags of prescriptions.

'Are Mr and Mrs Khan in there?' the young, pretty pharmacist asked Alison.

Alison stopped at that remark. 'Did you say Mr and Mrs Khan?' She asked. 'Are they a couple? I hadn't realised.'

'Oh, I'm not sure. Maybe just related, but they have the same surname, that's all I know. I'm just delivering their prescription.'

'I'll give it to them,' Alison said taking it, and checking for an address on it. There was none. She went back into the room. 'I've got your prescriptions,' she told them. 'I noticed you both have the same surname.'

'He's my brother,' Mariam told her.

'How did you come to be in Henry Street last night?' Alison pushed.

'We have a grocery shop, on the corner,' Mariam said. 'My brother is not completely well these days, so I go in and help out. We were in there when the riots started. I'm afraid Buisha gets confused. I told him to stay in the shop, but he went out when the explosions started, to see what was happening, and, of course I went out after him. It was very busy and crowded, I was hanging on to his arm trying to pull him back in the shop, next thing I knew, an arm reached out and grabbed me. I held on to Buisha. That's when we were both dragged into the warehouse.'

Alison thought back to the CCTV image she had been watching, and she remembered seeing Buisha wandering into the street. She looked at him. He was shaking.

'Let's get you both home,' she said.

'I will go home with Buisha, he cannot be alone,' Mariam told her. 'He missed his meds and is still suffering the confusion that comes if they are missed. I'll stay with him until he seems better.'

'What about your family? You said you didn't want anyone contacted.'

'He is my family. All the rest are in Pakistan.'

'Let's get you both home,' Alison said, gently.

Vernon White had been circling the helicopter above Henry Street. George Slater had binoculars in front of his eyes, surveying the roof of the warehouse and its surrounding area, as they circled.

The plane had descended towards the roof, but Slater had stopped him landing after the long lens of the binoculars told him the roof might not be safe.

'I'm not convinced the roof will take our weight,' he'd said. 'It could disintegrate beneath us, then we'd be inside the warehouse. That would take them by surprise! But wouldn't guarantee the hostages' safety. What do you think?'

White lowered a little further and then took the helicopter up. He shook his head. 'Not landing there,' he said. 'SC019 are in place in the outer guttering. Definitely not chancing any of our boys getting hurt if the roof gives way. We'll have to land on the road surface. That puts us at a disadvantage though. We'll be in full view of the warehouse. Let's have a look round the back.'

White ascended again and started circling. He was watching either side of the road. 'We'll land it right in front of the warehouse,' he said decisively after a few seconds. 'I'll just circle the outer roads, check them out, but they'll know we are here, so let's go from the front.' He turned to Slater. 'Ring through to Carter and tell him, we are re-planning. Everyone ready to go?' he shouted over his shoulder to the SAS team who were crouched on the floor behind him.

They were.

He turned the 'copter around and moved over the back and side roads. 'A lot of press around,' he said to Slater. 'Tell Jim Carter to relay the message to the police team to make sure everyone except SC019 stays clear of the back of this warehouse. My thoughts are they'll duck back in if shooting starts and make an attempt to get out the back. Watch out for press and nosy civilians.'

'On it, sir,' came the reply.

Alison was in the front of the police car, next to Albert Lipton. The older couple were in the back. Both had fallen asleep. When Alison's phone rang, she glanced in the back to make sure it hadn't woken them, and picked up quickly.

She listened as the SAS team, SC019, and Lorraine Cory had a three-way chat led by George Slater.

'We are on our way there,' Alison told them, letting them know she was joining in on the conversation. She then clicked her phone off quickly and turned to Albert. 'The helicopter is there. It's circling, looking to land in the street any minute, not on the roof, apparently. And SAS are in place. They intend to move in as soon as it lands. As the warehouse door opens with the hostage-takers, SC019 will move in. If the hostage-takers get to the helicopter, with or without the hostages, SAS will take them down.' She paused and took a breath to swallow her anxiety. 'And, fingers crossed, Banny will be safe.' She turned to look in the back again. 'They are asleep. We'll go straight to Henry Street, I have permission, and I need to be there ASAP. You can drop me, and then take these home.'

'I'd rather come with you and watch the action,' Albert said.

As she opened her mouth to tell him, no, but he could come straight there after he dropped the couple off, she felt something cold and hard being pressed into her temple. It took a couple of seconds for her to realise it was a gun.

'The only place you are going is Hell,' Mariam said between grated teeth.

Albert immediately slammed the brake on.

'OK, OK,' Alison said, speaking very calmly and throwing her hands in front of her and into the air. 'What's all this about?'

Mariam obviously hadn't been asleep. She had heard the conversation and had sprung to life. Her unsearched handbag had contained a gun. She was holding it now, the muzzle a millimetre from Alison's eye.

'Whoa,' Albert said. 'What's your problem here?'

'Just drive the fucking car,' the woman spat at him, jerking at Albert with her elbow. 'And don't ask questions. Now move it to that warehouse, or you'll both be without your eyes.'

Albert had started shaking, but nodded his head as if it was battery-controlled and wouldn't stop. He then went to press his personal emergency radio button, but she grabbed it from him, and threw it on the floor in the back.

'Don't try and be clever,' she spat. 'Unless you want your head blown off. Get your foot down and your siren flashing and get to that warehouse,' she commanded him.

'Why all this—' Alison started to ask but was interrupted.

'Shut your noise, or I'll shut it for you.'

The next second Mariam's other arm appeared, holding a second pistol which she pushed into the side of Albert's temple. His automatic reaction was to throw his foot on the brake.

'I said drive,' her false teeth knocking against each other as she shrieked. 'Put the siren on. Do it.'

'I'll do it,' Alison said, reaching down with one hand to tap the pistol and knife which she had packed tightly when she had decided to disobey orders and go to the location and help Banham. The weapons lay, one in each of the boots she wore. She felt them, then pushed the siren button to *on*, feeling relieved she had the presence of mind to bring them.

'You will do exactly as I say,' Mariam said to Albert. 'Got it?'

He nodded, and then his fear took over and his nodding continued.

'One false move and I will pull both triggers. Drive over to the warehouse.' She nudged the gun harder into the man's trembling head. 'And you will keep your siren on, and get there, pronto.'

He attempted to say yes, but it came out as a snort.

Alison thought about the knife in her right boot. It was in a holder, so she knew she wouldn't get it out quickly enough before Mariam caught on that she was up to something. But the gun wasn't in a holder. She merely needed to lean forward and she could easily pull it from her boot. However it was a while since she had been to target practice, and she knew she wasn't SC019, so couldn't take chances. If she fumbled, this mad woman could blow both their heads off. The man Buisha was still sitting beside Mariam. He was staring into space, but Alison was fully aware that could be an act too. She decided to play it safe and wait her chance. Henry Street wasn't far away. She glanced in the wing mirror. Buisha was still sitting there like a dummy.

'Put your foot down,' Mariam shouted again as Albert swerved in and out of traffic at about sixty miles an hour.

Mariam then turned her attention briefly to Buisha, nudging him in the ribs with her elbow. Alison thought about taking that moment to pull her pistol, but decided it was too risky. She'd need three seconds to bend and pull her gun free, in that time this unbalanced woman could have shot and killed them both.

Mariam nudged her brother. 'Get the phone from your pocket, and press S,' she told him. 'When it rings, press the bell picture, below the green sign, so it will go to loudspeaker and I can talk to the boys without using my arms.'

Buisha seemed confused. He had the phone, but was dithering about what to press.

'S,' she shouted at him. 'Press S, for son.'

Alison's brain went into overdrive. So this woman was the mother of one of the two hostage-takers. The whole family were murderers then. No wonder she had denied it was them in the photographs. Her Banny was in the warehouse with two sadistic killers and she was in this car with two insane people, one holding guns. And she had been nervous about a wedding ceremony. *Stay calm*, she told herself.

What best to do, though? This woman would likely pull the trigger at the drop of a hat. If Alison went for her gun, in those three seconds, the woman had the time to shoot either her or Albert. She had to do something. Her mobile was on her lap. She only had to press one letter, and it would go through to Lorraine, who might or might not hear the conversation, and would know that the helicopter, and the team of SAS soldiers, had been rumbled.

Albert, meanwhile, was still ducking and diving through traffic. She reckoned she had about three minutes. Or, if they were lucky enough to have to slow at traffic lights, maybe someone would see the guns at their heads and ring 999.

Alison checked the mirror. The woman's attention was now on her brother. She was getting irritable with him. He was not doing too well trying to find the letter 'S' on his phone. Mariam Khan snatched it from him, and in doing so had had to take the gun away from Albert's head, although her other hand still held the gun at

Alison's temple. The thought crossed Alison's mind to grab Mariam's elbow, and twist it till the gun fell free. She was stronger and fitter than this woman, that was for sure. She decided against it, Mariam's gun could go off. She watched in the mirror as the woman put the other pistol in Buisha's hand, telling him to hold it at Albert's head, but not to pull the trigger unless she said so.

Alison and Albert both, simultaneously, snatched breath as she said that. If this man couldn't find the letter 'S' on a mobile, he certainly didn't have the common sense to hold a gun to Albert's head and be trusted not to kill him, even by accident.

Mariam now had the phone to her ear. She had pressed 'S', and was talking to her son. Alison glanced at her own mobile on her lap. Her hand slowly moved towards it, but Buisha was surprisingly observant. 'Touch that, and I'll blow his head off,' he said with an energy that took Alison by complete surprise.

'The helicopter is a trap,' Mariam was speaking on her phone, she looked up as Buisha spoke. 'What is it, Buisha?' He said nothing, just licked his lips. Mariam then said, 'He's not very well at the moment, I warn you,' she told Alison. 'He will kill you both in an instant if you upset him.'

'Quite the quick on the draw man, aren't you?' Alison said to him, her brain ticking over quickly. 'You are obviously very good at this.' Then a thought flashed into her mind. 'So did you shoot the other policeman, was that you?'

Buisha merely burst out laughing.

Alison then listened as Mariam spoke into her phone. 'You must stay in there, with your hostage, no matter what they say or promise. Do not go out of the warehouse. You have a good hostage there. He is a high-up policeman. I will get more help. I'll get the cousins. We'll work something out. Have you got Farzila? Good. I'll get some more of the family. When the helicopter lands and they tell you to come out, you stay put. It'll take five minutes or more before they move into the warehouse, I will have rounded up more of the family and we'll be there, with these hostages to stop them. These are police hostages. They will do nothing to you with my gun to their heads. You will drive the helicopter, and we will take all the hostages with us.'

Alison lowered her eyelids. She had to think. If she could get her phone to record this, she could warn everyone. Also if she could get her phone on, she would ask them about the bodies in the park. They might be proud and mad enough of themselves to drop themselves in it, then she would have enough proof to request to excavate the rest of the park, and find the last missing body.

The next moment Buisha turned his attention for a second to his sister, and Mariam turned to him, Alison took the risk and quickly pressed the button to ring Lorraine, then the silence button, then the 'record conversation' button.

Mariam was still on the phone to her son, so if Alison managed to record that conversation, it would prove, without doubt, that Mariam and Buisha had been part of the set-up and not hostages at all. If Lorraine knew that, she could avoid walking the SAS into a trap with them. Alison knew Farzila was the sister of Massafur. So this was their mother? A woman who had allowed and watched her daughter endure the torture she had been put through? They had the girl's DNA, from the finger that had been taken, so they could prove the relationship, as well as any relationship to the bodies in the park. The evidence of those would be on file in the basement. Alison also had a written statement from Kevin McCaub saying that the bodies of the women found buried in the parks were part of the family, and the murdered men, their husbands. So it was all the same family. Farzila was only guilty of marrying the man she loved, and this family intended murdering her for it. And didn't mind who they had to kill on their journey to doing it. Alison shivered; not only was Banham in grave danger, but now she was too.

'We are nearly with you,' Mariam spoke into the phone. 'If anyone shoots at you, cut the finger from the new police hostage, and throw it out the window. They will know not to mess with us then. We will be there soon.' She then hung up, redialled, and spoke at the rate of knots in her native language. Alison knew she was calling up the cousins.

Alison chanced a glance down to her phone. The red light was on. It had been recording. She had to pray Lorraine would get that conversation and could stay one step ahead. Alison's temper was now boiling, If they touched Banham's finger, Alison vowed she would get her gun and shoot the woman herself. She pressed her ankles together, she could feel the gun and knife, and first opportunity she would have them out.

Alison's thoughts then turned to Lorraine. Had the super picked up her end, and had she heard the conversation? Would she be expecting them? If not, then, when this patrol car tore into Henry Street, and Lorraine saw the guns held at her officer's heads, she would be furious with her. Lorraine had finally given in and invited her down there, to see the end of the siege and Banham walk to safety. Now Alison being there, with a gun to her head, would put everyone's life in danger. She thought of lying on a beach, sipping a large vodka and tonic, with sun block rubbed into her skin by Banham, and their peaceful villa, with no one to bother them for two weeks. Sun, sex, and Banham. How could she have doubted all that. And how the day had turned out, instead!

Mariam broke her thoughts. 'Turn right just here,' she ordered as they turned into Burton Street. Albert obeyed and turned again into Hazel Close.

'Pull up here,' Mariam ordered again, pushing the muzzle of her pistol aggressively deeper into the terrified man's temple.

Albert immediately obeyed, although the car jerked to its halt as his unsteady legs too, were obviously shaking. Alison would have liked nothing better than to have punched the woman hard in the face. It was clear Albert was terrified and had never been in any situation like this in his long policing career.

Because Alison had been standing in the CCTV room at the station for hours since this morning, watching the goings on in and around Henry Street, she knew every inch of the geography of the area they were in. She was fully aware of exactly where they were: off Burton Street, which was parallel to Henry Street, but held a good view of the area above the warehouse. That had to be a plus.

She would bet this woman would also have a good idea, and Buisha too – if indeed he was sane, which Alison was still trying to fathom out.

Mariam had said they owned the small grocery shop on the corner. Or was all that just a smokescreen? Regardless of that, knowing the geography of the area well possibly put her in a better position than the two holding the guns. And if she kept her wits about her, she might be able to get another warning to Lorraine before Mariam's family arrived and started to cause mayhem.

She weighed everything quickly in her mind. Her phone was still recording, although she still didn't know if Lorraine had heard any of it, or even knew they were there, or that trouble was expected. On that she could only hope.

Alison had, possibly, more experience using a pistol and a knife them than this woman, although on that she wouldn't take bets. This woman seemed to enjoy cutting off fingers, and letting victims slowly bleed to death, so shooting a stranger would probably mean nothing to her. But how experienced was she at hitting her target?

Alison was now aware there were journalists and TV vans all along the street. Mostly they were standing around drinking coffee, watching the helicopter circling, and waiting for some action. Some were filming it. They all seemed involved in conversation with each other, or on their phones. Or reporting into live television cameras about the current goings-on. If only she could get the attention of one of them. She spent her life avoiding them as they hounded her for stories for their papers. Now, when she wanted their attention, it wasn't happening. They surely all knew who she was, from her countless press conferences, maybe one of them might notice her.

Mariam, too, was aware of the camera crews around and immediately lowered the gun she was holding. She pushed Buisha's hand down too. One gun dug into Alison's side and the other into Albert's back.

Alison glanced at the passenger door handle.

'These guns are loaded,' Mariam told her, obviously noticing Alison looking at the door handle. 'I will kill you both, without hesitation, if you move from your seats.'

218

So she was as sharp as she was cruel, Alison thought. 'We won't,' she answered to the woman, but didn't add that she too had a loaded gun, and full access to the locks on the car.

Mariam then looked up at the circling helicopter. Alison nearly went for the handle at that moment, but knowing she had the petrified Albert to take into consideration as well as herself, she stayed still.

'You don't move until I tell you to,' Mariam spat at her, with another spiteful dig in Alison's ribs with the gun.

'OK. OK. I hear you,' Alison said.

Chapter Twenty-five

Having his hands tied behind his back and around the end of a radiator made it difficult for Banham to even sit, but he had managed to slide to the floor and sit uncomfortably. He was a little way away from the pool of congealing blood around the unstirring Farzila. He could see the bandage tied over her missing finger, but, as far as he could see, no blood was leaking from it. Either Hannah had done a good job stopping the flow of blood with it or this young woman was dead. She was very still, and the blood leakage was vast. He was trying to make out if there was any sign of breath coming from her, but he wasn't quite near enough to be clear, and from where he was, the body seemed very still. A few yards across the room, the dirty concrete floor was stained with another large pool of dried blood: obviously where Martin Neville lost his life, Banham thought sadly.

He could hear the helicopter circling overhead, and watched the hostage-takers as they watched the plane from the window. They had just taken a phone call, but with the noise of the helicopter, he hadn't been able to hear what was being said. They were now speaking to each other in low voices in a foreign language.

He sensed their anxiety as the helicopter continuously circled but hadn't managed to land.

Banham had learned from his training that when a hostage-taker became anxious, especially one as unpredictable as Sadiq, they often panicked, and then lashed out and hurt someone. He was the only person left to take it out on. He decided to try and keep them calm.

'It'll find a way to land,' he told them gently. 'It's always like that when a 'copter has to land in a built-up area. It's not easy and they have to take their time. It will be fine. Not long now, and you'll be out of here.'

When neither answered, and Massafur wiped the perspiration from his face with the back of his arm, Banham carried on talking. 'As I say, it's always like this, nothing to worry about,' he repeated. 'You have to think of the people around, the propellers go on for a bit after you turn off the engine. So they have to be very cautious when they land to avoid casualties.'

Massafur's phone rang at that moment, and took their attention.

Mariam pressed the letter 'S' on her mobile again. Her eyes were moving in a darting fashion, like a predator watching its prey, from Alison to Albert. The gun was held firmly in her wrinkled hands, and there wasn't any sign of nervousness in her body language. Buisha held the other gun at the back of Albert's neck again.

Alison listened to the phone conversation, but kept her face to the side window, scouting the street. She was still hoping someone from the press would come and knock on the window and ask for a story. That would be her chance.

'We are at the back, in a side road,' the woman said into the phone. 'In a police car.' There was a pause while she listened. 'He's doing OK. He has taken his medication, but it was very overdue, so he may be a bit unpredictable.'

Alison sucked in air at that remark. So the man genuinely was unbalanced. She prayed he wouldn't shoot Albert by mistake.

'Now listen to me,' Mariam said. 'The helicopter is circling. I can see that from here. We are at the back of your building, but a few streets away. You know this is the trap. Do not go out into the street. The helicopter is there to lure you out.'

Alison took a deep breath. This was all her fault. She would get such a bollocking over this, all the budget and manpower taken to set this up, and it had all gone tits up.

'Do not leave that building,' Mariam said. 'As I have told you, they have soldiers with guns inside the plane, and they intend to kill you all. Stay inside there. Have you got the bitch?'

Banham was listening to Massafur. He was watching his reaction to the call, trying to work out what was being said on the other end. 'How far away are you?' he heard the man say. Sadiq was now standing beside Massafur, listening in to the call. 'Keep the guns close to their heads. Only fire if you have to,' he said into the phone.

Banham's ears pricked up at this. He now knew they were holding someone at gunpoint. But who was it? It wouldn't be Lorraine, or Crowther, surely. So it was either SC019 officers, which he doubted, or some of his uniform team. He knew his PCs had little experience of firearms, and would be terrified.

'Mama, just be careful. It matters not about them, we've killed already.'

So now, Banham realised, they were talking to their mother. And their mother was holding someone at gunpoint?

'What? Who is in the helicopter?' As their mother answered that question, both Sadiq and Massafur looked at each other and then turned slowly to look at Banham.

Banham immediately realised that the police this mother was holding at gunpoint knew about the SAS in the helicopter. So who could it be, he wondered? Who knew there was a team of SAS out there? Word must have gone round, and it was one of his uniformed officers. He prayed there weren't more police killings imminent. This whole episode was about family honour. It had been a set-up all along, and Martin Neville had lost his life over it.

'OK. Then we need you to get back here. Bring the hostages with you. We will have three then, and all feds. That will help a lot. No, no good coming in the back way. That helicopter will see you. It will see everything from where it is. Bring the hostages with you in the front, in full view of everyone. Keep the gun to their heads, and walk up the street. We will use them, as bait, to empty the helicopter.' A pause. 'Yes, I will fly it.' He looked at

Banham. 'I will also send another finger out, to let them know not to mess with us.'

Banham felt the blood drain from his face.

Alison was straining to hear the conversation on the other end of the phone, as she pressed her face to the window, trying to attract attention from any of the journalists or photographers around the street outside. She knew Buisha was leaning beside her, the gun at Albert's neck. She didn't dare go for her own pistol, she couldn't risk his insanity. He could shoot Albert without a second thought. She sat bolt upright as the woman said, 'Yes, that's fine, but don't cut his whole finger off, he'll bleed too much. You could lose him, and we need him alive. Cut part of his ear, or the end of his finger.'

Alison flicked an angry glance at Albert. Her temper was now really bubbling. She was going to get out of here, and shoot this woman, she had made her mind up. That had to be her Banny, there was no other male hostage, and no one was touching her Banny.

Next thing, she had the gun back against her temple. 'Get out of the car, and get walking,' the woman ordered. She then nodded to Buisha. 'Gun to his head, and get him out of the car,' she ordered to him.

This made Alison very nervous for Albert, as she watched the dithering and eccentric old man push its muzzle into the back of Albert's head.

Alison thought that if this wasn't the most degrading, worst thing that could be happening, it would be like a bad television show. Lorraine Cory, who had insisted she shouldn't come anywhere near the scene of crime, was about to see her with a gun to her head, being marched into the warehouse as another hostage. Worse still, she would know it was Alison who had given the game away over the SAS helicopter. She could kiss goodbye to any sight of promotion in the near future. But then, she thought, maybe she had no future. Maybe her future was about to be cut short by a bullet in her head. And if there was a future, it would be back in uniform, directing traffic. She half wished she had listened to Banham and was now in Mykonos with her factor 60.

She kept her eyes on Albert as they were pushed out of the car and then marched, guns at their heads, past the circus of media, including television cameras and photographers, who immediately started filming as they were paraded down the road and into Henry Street.

Jim Carter was the first to see them. 'What the fuck?' He had caught sight of them just as the helicopter was about to come down in the street. George Slater had seen them at the same time, from the air. 'Take her up again. Quick,' he shouted to Captain White, pointing to the four walking up the street.

As the helicopter zoomed speedily back into the air, Lorraine Cory turned. Her gaze caught Alison's, and stayed, staring at her.

Alison could almost feel the degradation of a PC's uniform, and knew she would be lucky if she lived long enough to bear that degradation.

Then there was the sound of a shot. Alison turned, heart in mouth, to see Buisha aiming his gun in the air, and in the direction of the helicopter. 'Come and get us,' he shouted, then jumped in the air and whooped.

Alison was worryingly aware that Albert was now shaking badly.

'Shut up,' Mariam quickly turned and hushed her brother. 'Shut up, and keep walking into the warehouse.

Alison's brain then went into overdrive. Should she stagger, and then lift her foot, and pull her gun from her boot? She knew the SC019 team were there and if Mariam's hand moved over the trigger they would shoot. But then she thought about Banham. He was inside the warehouse, unarmed. If she tried anything, and SC019 took Mariam out, the hostage-takers would surely shoot Banham. She decided against doing anything for now, and walked on bearing the fear and degradation of Mariam's gun pressed into the back of her head.

'Stand by,' Carter shouted to his team.

'Nobody shoot,' Lorraine shouted quickly to the SC019 team, as they stood from their positions of hiding, and their guns flew out in front of them, pointing at Mariam and Buisha, waiting for the next command. She then turned to Jim Carter, her voice nervous but commanding. 'There are officers' lives in jeopardy,' Lorraine said, as Alison and Albert were pushed, only yards from her, towards the door of the warehouse, and with a team of firearms officers, and an SAS team in a helicopter, plus the national television cameras and a fleet of photographers, watching their every move.

'Lower your guns,' Mariam shouted. 'Or I will kill this woman and man.' She raised her voice, and cocked her pistol at the back of Alison's head. 'Now.'

'Tell them to back off,' Lorraine shouted to Carter.

'Hold your fire,' he yelled the order.

Lorraine took a step forward towards Alison.

'Get out of my way,' Mariam shouted, as she pushed Alison within inches of Lorraine, spitting at Lorraine as she passed her. 'Massafur, open the door, we are coming in,' Mariam yelled.

Lorraine stepped back, avoided the spittle, but caught Alison's eyes as she moved. Her expression gave nothing away.

The door to the warehouse opened, and the terrified PC Albert Lipton, followed by a very angry and pent-up Alison, were pushed in.

Jim Carter was standing next to Lorraine Cory when the voice of Vernon White came through on his radio.

'OK, we have three choices,' he said in a voice that was clipped and abrupt. A voice of a man no one messes with. 'First, are you receiving me?'

'Go ahead, mate,' Carter said to him. 'We have you loud and clear.'

'We can land on the roof, and chance it caves in. We are pretty confident it will. The roof would collapse inwards into the warehouse, but it would take them by surprise, we'd be out of the cab and in there within seconds. However, we have no eyeball on the inside of the building so don't know the whereabouts of the hostages in there. We'd say they're tied up, so that puts them at a big disadvantage. They could get hurt.'

Lorraine had stepped nearer to Carter. 'Or?' she pushed. 'Option two?'

'Or?' Carter repeated. 'Guv'nor says, what's the next option?'

'Or we bring the 'copter down in the street, jump out, forming a speedy line, which will take three seconds. They will see us, and have those upper-hand three seconds to shoot the hostages, or as they have threatened, to blow up the building.'

Lorraine turned to Crowther. 'Get the press out of here. Now,' she snapped, noticing a few stray journalists and a television cameraman who had sneaked back in. 'Tell them we'll arrest anyone who isn't away from the street within the next sixty seconds, and mean it. Three hostages are in there, all police officers.'

'Or,' came the voice of Vernon White again.

'Or?' Carter asked tentatively.

'Or, we land in the street. The team stay put in here, and we bluff it out. Tell them their info is wrong. There are no soldiers in here, and they are free to go if they free the hostages first. All options are chancy.'

Lorraine then turned to Carter. 'Well? Make a decision, Banham's not here, so it's down to your expertise. Taking into consideration they probably now know that this is a trap.' She turned away and shook her head. 'Christ, what a fuck-up this is.'

'Land on the road,' Carter said into the radio, at the same time signalling his men to surround the warehouse. He then turned to Lorraine. He was holding the hailer in front of her. 'Now I run this op.'

Within that minute, the 'copter stopped circling. It then slowly started to descend. 'Everyone stand back,' Crowther was shouting, as everyone moved clear. 'Stand clear now. Now,' he yelled. The press had left the road immediately they were told, and the uniform presence now spread out to allow room for the helicopter to land. Its lowered wheels touched the road, but the propellers were still turning.

Lorraine took the hailer as Carter moved, stealthily and quietly, with his team to the rear of the building.

'We have your money, and your helicopter,' Lorraine spoke loudly and firmly. 'You now bring the hostages to the door, and you may walk out to the helicopter. The money is inside.'

It was like a slow burn for Banham. He stared in disbelief as Alison was pushed into the warehouse, with a gun held to her head by the old lady he had believed was a hostage.

He opened his mouth to speak, but was interrupted.

'Over there, get over there,' Sadiq said to Alison. Then he turned to the trembling Albert. 'And you, over there.' He pushed the PC into the far corner of the large space in the warehouse and started to tie his hands to another radiator.

Massafur turned to Alison. 'Sit,' he commanded her as one might a disobedient dog. Then he pushed her to the ground, next to the pool of congealed blood and the very still Farzila. Alison was aware Banham was staring at her. If only she could tell him she had both a gun and a knife in her boots and no one had bothered to search her.

'Please don't tie my hands tightly,' she said meekly.' She was praying Massafur wouldn't search her, and decided her best chance was to play meek and get his attention somewhere else. Her mind was on getting to that gun in her boot and shooting Mariam, not to kill her, but to graze her, and teach her how it would feel if they cut her ear off. She briefly snatched a glance at Banham's ear. If this had happened any other day but this day, she would be in bed with him now, on honeymoon, making love, feeling his tenderness, and kissing that ear. 'I'm hardly able to fight anyone,' she lied, in a whinging tone, 'my wrist was broken last month and it's only just mending.'

'Shut the fuck up,' Sadiq snapped at her, as Massafur pushed her against the opposite side of the radiator to where Banham was tied.

Massafur then took the rope from his pocket and started tying her hands. And he wasn't tying too tightly. She was extremely good at freeing her hands from knots and felt confident she could get out of these, given the time, and with no one watching her.

As soon as he moved away, she started moving her wrists around to loosen the ropes, before freeing herself from them. There was just a radiator between her and Banham. Their hands could be touching, if they weren't both tied.

She would work on her wrists, then she intended to get to Banham. She had the knife, but the bugger was, it was in a holder, and would take a few seconds to get it out. But it was there, and once out, would free Banham in seconds. She stared at Farzila. The woman was lying curled up, in a pool of blood. Her face was distorted with swelling, and her nose and mouth were stuck together with blood. Had she choked on her own blood or bled to death from her finger? She was definitely dead. She looked so young, too. What a way to die, Alison thought. How could Mariam do that to her own daughter, all because the family didn't approve of her choice of man? She turned to look at Banham. He was staring back at her. She couldn't work out if he was pleased or furious to see her. She just wanted to lean across and kiss him.

Chapter Twenty-six

Lorraine's voice alerted them. Both Massafur and Sadiq moved quickly to the window to watch the goings-on in the street.

'The helicopter is out there, it's landed,' Sadiq said to Mariam and Buisha. 'It's full of SAS soldiers, you say?'

Mariam pointed to Alison. 'She said it to someone she spoke to on the phone. Ask her. Go and ask her! Bitch.'

Sadiq marched over to Alison. She had been fiddling with the ropes that had tied her hands, and was doing pretty well. She needed less than a minute now to get free, but needed nobody to be watching her. She was aware that Banham had clocked her actions. He knew she was good at this. He had turned away, deliberately not watching her, not wanting to draw any attention to her. He had kept his attention directed at the window. What he didn't know, and she had no way of telling him, was that she had a loaded gun in her right boot. And what she didn't know was whether he was pleased she was there, or angry with her. Banham had one of those faces that gave nothing away. Well, she was here, and they were fighting these bastards together, everything else they could sort out later – if they lived to have a later.

Sadiq barely glanced at Farzila. He marched over to Alison. He stepped over the pool of congealing blood and stood in front of her. She immediately stopped fiddling with her tied hands and became still.

He dug the butt of his rifle into Alison's shoulder, and narrowed his eyes.

'What do you know then, bitch,' he said to her, butting her hard again, and then again, with the rifle. 'You tell me, and don't try and lie because I will cut your throat if you do, but first I will rape you.'

'Oi, calm down,' Banham spoke, angrily, before he thought. When Sadiq turned to him with a raised rifle, he became calmer and said. 'You asked her a question, but haven't given her time to answer.'

'He asked her,' Mariam shouted. 'Not you. So you shut your mouth, or we will kill you before we get on the helicopter.'

Alison had got the message, loud and clear, that this family were totally unbalanced, and killing came very naturally to them. She knew she would have to tread carefully. She had a very bad temper, and unlike Banham, found it hard to keep it in check.

Banham slightly bowed his head. 'Understood,' he said. 'I was employed to help you. I negotiated the helicopter for you, and I am trying to help get you on it, with as little violence as possible.'

'Then get them to bring the money in, and tell them to leave the helicopter running,' Mariam said.

'I'm not sure they'll listen to me any more,' Banham said calmly.

'They will if we send out your ear with the demand,' she answered.

That sent an angry shiver through Alison. She started fiddling again to get her hands free. This family were all insane, and Buisha was probably the most dangerous of all of them, he was certified, and hadn't had enough medicine. She was also confident now that the shot that killed Martin Neville came from either Buisha or Mariam, and she was determined to prove it and then get them to pay for it. This could all be proved in the ballistics lab, as one of the guns the two were holding now was probably the one that shot Neville.

'I was at the station, and there were rumours going round that there would be SAS here soon. I may have confused that for SC019, that's a gun team,' as they are definitely here,' she lied, fully aware that the hostage-takers knew there was a gun team outside.

She was also now aware of the activity moving around outside, and knew it to be SC019 getting into place. It wouldn't be long and this was all going up. She had to get her hands free and then Banham's.

Massafur moved to the window. 'There is a gun team surrounding us,' he nodded.

She knew she needed to get Sadiq to move away from her then she could finish unknotting her own hands. If she was tied, they would all be sitting duck targets. Once hers were free, she could then release Banham and Albert. The last knot was proving difficult, it needed at least a full minute, and with Sadiq standing over her, and the gun team getting into place, she was aware that time was against her. She couldn't dare pick at it.

'I was only repeating what I heard,' she said, playing meek. 'I heard in the station, that they had asked for a helicopter. They said they would have soldiers there, who were armed. I only presumed it was the army, or the SAS. I'm sorry, I don't know anything much, I'm—'

Sadiq didn't give her time to finish the sentence, he brought his hand back and hit her hard across the mouth. 'Lying bitch,' he said, as Alison reeled back in shock.

'That's not necessary,' Banham said in a raised and angry tone.

'I can only tell you what I know—'

'There are a lot of gunmen outside now,' Mariam interrupted, cutting Alison off in mid-flow and moving to near the window. Sadiq and Massafur followed,

Alison caught Banham's eye. She lowered her eyes and nodded her head to let him know she was nearly free. She then started frantically fiddling and pulling with her hands behind her back. All the attention was on the goings-on outside, so grabbing the moment, she fiddled as fast as she was able.

She turned to Albert. He looked petrified. He was all on his own down the far end of the large, barn-like, space.

She only wished she could reassure him. She was angrier now than she had been when they threatened to take Banham's ear or finger the first time. These men were complete sadists. She glanced at the dead girl in front of her. She would happily have shot them both for what they had done, and sod justice. Maybe she would as soon as she got her hands free and on her gun and knife. With luck the SAS would do it for her. She was already in enough trouble. She also knew her Banham would be seething and would want to kill Sadiq for threatening to rape her. After what happened to Diane, she knew he wouldn't hesitate to shoot Sadiq if he touched her, and if he had access to a gun. She was so angry, she nearly broke the rope with her energy.

Mariam turned back from the window. 'They are pointing their guns and surrounding us,' she said. 'Why don't you cut her finger, or her ear, and throw it out to them,' she indicated to Alison.

Alison's heart leaped into her mouth. If the woman attempted to reach for Alison's hand, for access to her finger, she would know she was untying herself. Her wrists were so nearly free of the rope that bound them to the radiator. She was going to be caught red-handed.

'No,' Massafur said. 'No finger or ear.'

Sadiq walked over and lifted Alison's long, waist-length, reddish-brown hair. He then pulled his knife and quickly slid it through her long hair, slicing half of it away.

Banham and Alison both gasped in unison.

'I could fly the helicopter. She doesn't look as if she would struggle,' Buisha suddenly spoke, pointing to the dead Farzila.

No one answered him.

Mariam snatched the handful of Alison's long hair from Sadiq. 'I'll throw it out,' she said. 'Let them know if they come near us as we go to the helicopter, we mean what we say, and we will slice her.'

'This man is very high up,' Massafur said, indicating Banham. 'With him, we are safe. We can get on the helicopter, and if anyone attempts to stop us, we will slice some of him.'

Alison gasped. Sadiq then moved to her and with one hand, he grabbed her by the throat, pushing her back into the radiator. Her hands were now squashed into the wall behind her with the force. She managed to pull one on top of the other. She was nearly there, and then she would go for her knife.

'Who is on the helicopter?' he spat at her, squeezing into her throat harder. 'I know you know, so tell me, now, or I will hurt you.'

'I . . . I . . . honestly,' she stammered, 'don't know for sure. Her hands were now almost there, but because he had her neck in such a tight grip, and it was taking all her strength not to let him break it, and she just didn't have the force to pull the last piece of rope from her hands.

Banham was watching. His breathing was getting heavier. He turned to the window and then back to Sadiq and Alison.

'I think the helicopter is empty, apart from the pilot and co-pilot. It looks like it from here, anyway,' he said, speaking very calmly to Sadiq, in an attempt to pull focus from Alison's situation, giving her the chance to completely free her hands. 'I asked for it for you, if you remember. And no one said anything about soldiers to me. It has a pilot. I can see him, and I think a co-pilot. They'll know to leave when you release us. That is what I ordered, and from what I see, that is what there is. No tricks.'

Sadiq was nearly choking Alison with his strong hands as she struggled to speak.

Massafur walked over and leaned with his back flat against the wall to peer out. He then nodded. 'He's right,' he said. 'I only see a pilot and co-pilot.'

'You can drive it,' Mariam said to Massafur. 'We'll take the hostages with us. She's dead.' She nodded in the direction of Farzila. 'But we'll take her, carry her out, and burn the devil from her when we land. No time to worry about whether the money is in the 'copter. Untie the hostages, and let's go.'

As Sadiq bent to lift the dead Farzila, everything went up. There was a crash and the SAS and SC019 teams seemed to appear from everywhere: roof, back door, back window, front door, all holding guns in front of them.

'Freeze. Drop everything, now. Hands in the air, or we'll shoot,' came the order.

At the same moment Alison pulled her hands free. She turned to see Sadiq lift his gun to fire at the soldiers, but having been warned, he was blown to bits by SAS soldiers in different parts of the building, and the firearm officers who had seen him go for his gun.

'Police,' Alison shouted, with one hand in the air and one hand pulling her knife from its holder as she hurriedly turned her back to free Banham's hands. Massafur then turned to her, his gun in his hand intending to shoot Alison in the back, but he too was blown to bits in front of their eyes from a tirade of gunfire coming from all directions.

'Hands in the air,' Jim Carter shouted. 'Anyone moves and we'll shoot.'

Alison was slitting Banham's ropes, and quickly freed him. 'Police,' she shouted as she worked at his ropes. She then pulled her gun from her boot, still shouting, 'Police' and threw it to Banham.

'Police, police, he's police too,' she shouted as she ran to Albert with her knife.

In the same moment Mariam had fallen to her knees, hands in the air and was screaming that they had killed her son.

'Hands in the air,' Carter warned Mariam as she turned to crawl to Sadiq's body but snidely reached across for his gun.

'Freeze,' one of the SAS soldiers yelled at the same time that Banham saw Mariam reach for the gun, and praying that the gun that Alison had thrown to him had bullets in it, he pulled the trigger and fired. Alison had loaded her pistol, but it wouldn't have mattered, Jim Carter had seen it too, and both he and Banham had filled the woman with bullets within seconds.

The SAS team had also opened fire, but Banham's bullet had hit her in the back of her skull. Mariam was already dead before she received any others, although machine-gun bullets were still penetrating her body like flashes of lightning. Her body jerked up and down and spurted blood. The blood was landing on the now congealing blood around the daughter that Mariam had been responsible for murdering.

'Hands in the air, Buisha,' Banham tried to say, but again the man had turned defiantly with his gun in his hand, and before even pointing it in the direction of the SAS team, he too, was down and dead, one bullet between his eyes.

★

Peter Byfield was sitting next to Hannah in her private room in the hospital, holding her hand. Her bruised and swollen face was covered at the mouth with an oxygen mask, and the half a dozen tubes that bleeped around her were inserted into different parts of one of her arms and hands. The other arm was bound in a pink plaster cast and then held with a leather strap around her neck. From her forehead to the top of her head was covered in bandage. She was awake, but drowsy and full of painkillers.

'I just heard the hostage situation is over,' Peter told her, as he clicked his phone off. 'The DCI is out and unhurt. All police are safe and all the hostage-takers dead.'

She nodded, tried to smile, and lifted her plastered hand and arm, intending to pull the mask from her face and speak, but then winced in pain, and closed her eyes and fell asleep.

Byfield rearranged the pillow behind her to make her more comfortable. 'Three breaks in your arm, one shoulder badly dislocated, a broken nose, multiple bruising, a bullet extracted from your foot, and a cracked forehead. Oh, and a rainbow-coloured and very swollen eye. But still looking beautiful. I'd say six months to a year off work.' He kissed her fingers very gently, and then any part of her bandaged head where he could find a piece of peeping skin to kiss.

She opened her eyes again, and weakly attempted to pull the oxygen mask down from her mouth and nose. He placed her hand back and pulled the mask gently from her to save her energy and so she could speak. Her speech was nearly inaudible. 'And a wedding in less than a month,' she said, screwing up her face in agonising pain.

'You are beautiful, and I want to marry you,' he reassured her. 'On crutches, with a sack over your head, an arm in a sling, hopping down the aisle, whatever, you want. In here if you like. I want us to go ahead with the ceremony. And, the upside is you'll have six months to a year off. We can get into our new house, and slowly get it the way you want it, and you will be there to oversee all the happenings.'

'I'm not getting married looking like this,' she said as carefully as her injured mouth would allow. Then she attempted to cry, then to laugh. 'Imagine the wedding pictures! What will our grandchildren think? They'll think you married a monster.'

'Whatever you want, darling,' he said to her. 'I'm just glad we are here, and together.'

'So much is booked, though, and paid for.'

'Don't worry about that.'

'I won't be able to wear my dress. I so love it. I know you haven't seen it, 'cos it's unlucky, but the sleeves are tight and fitted, and it had shoulder flaps.'

Peter thought about saying they had already had enough bad luck to last a lifetime, but changed his mind. 'So get another one, or marry me in a sack,' he offered.

'You know DI Grainger was marrying the DCI, and that got cancelled because of the riots? I'm sure they'll have their wedding again, and Alison and I are probably the same size. I could give my dress to her. I know she didn't like the one she was marrying in. Mine was lovely. I'm sure she'll love it. I could just get a very plain loose one, down to the floor, and then I *could* hop up the aisle with a crutch. Or in a wheelchair, when the bruising goes down from my face.'

'I'll marry you in a dustbin. Whatever will make you happy. The best bit is, the doctor said you will make a full recovery, but it will take time. Let's get married in hospital. It has been done before. The vicar comes here.'

When Hannah didn't answer, he realised her eyes had closed and she had fallen asleep again. Within a minute she was snoring loudly. The pressure of the bandages that covered her fractured nose made her sound like a warthog. Peter sat back in the armchair by her bed and put his headphones over his ears.

The cacophony of screaming sirens would have been heard all over the south-east. Fire engines, ambulances, more police cars, and a half a dozen coroner's vans were all squealing into Henry Street.

It wasn't easy keeping the press at bay, but the new team of police that had come in from surrounding areas had cordoned off the street, and were guarding the area like a team of Rottweilers.

Lorraine Cory had been the first on the scene, after Jim Carter had come to the door and shouted all clear.

'None of our lot is hurt,' he said. 'Everyone else, dead, ma'am.'

She had merely nodded and hurried in to see for herself.

Banham was facing Alison. He opened his mouth to speak, but she put her hand in the air to stop him.

'Can we argue about this later?' she said wearily. 'I know I should have been in Mykonos, and you are my superior officer, but I've been at the station and discovered new evidence on the bodies in the park. Remember the ones with the women with missing fingers, their left hands, third finger?'

Banham said nothing, but he was listening.

'Well, I have statements, from Kevin McCaub, that this family were responsible for that. I think we will find they were all related, as McCaub said, and that it was the same scenario as this one, the women not marrying the family choice. An unfound body is in the same park in Catford, apparently. I am going to request a digging team.' She paused. He didn't speak, so she carried on. 'Also, and more importantly, the bullet that killed Martin Neville is in ballistics, but while studying the CCTV in the computer room, I noticed that the angle from where he had been shot, couldn't have been from a gun fired by Massafur or Sadiq, they weren't standing in the direction that the bullet came from, but from the angle that Mariam stood with Buisha, so I am confident we will prove it came from the gun that was held to my head by Mariam.' Again she paused and waited for him to speak.

He still remained silent but listening.

'I broke the rules by not following orders, and for that I apologise, but I have found all that out. Oh, as well as saving your life.'

Banham blinked and shook his head. 'Excuse me, actually, I just saved yours. I actually shot that woman. She was going to shoot you in the back.'

'Yes. But I gave you the gun, so I saved yours first—'

'Shut it, both of you.' Lorraine Cory's intervention stopped them in their tracks. 'There are ambulances outside. I want you both checked over, and then you report to me, back at the station. In my office.' She looked at Banham. 'And I'll take that pistol from you, before you do some more damage. I'll forget I just overheard that conversation. SC019 shot that woman, I believe.'

'Don't dump the dead woman's gun,' Alison said quickly. 'I think it may turn out to be the gun that shot Martin Neville.'

'Oh, and who's the cleverest of them all,' Lorraine said sarcastically before shaking her head. 'And it never rains but it pours. My office, both of you, after you've been checked over.'

By the time they got to report to the super's office, they had both been told there was no damage to either of them, except a bruise on Alison's face from the wallop Sadiq gave her, and fingermarks on her neck from the pressure of his fingers. They were both given very large brandy-coffees. Alison had told Banham everything she had found out while working on the case from the station.

Neither had mentioned getting married, or weddings.

'How are you both feeling?' Lorraine asked them as she offered them the two seats opposite her in her office.

'Fine. I was a little taken aback when I realised Mariam was with the hostage-takers and not a hostage, and more than a little worried that the whole operation would get blown because she knew about the plans for the helicopter, but—'

'But at least you got into the action,' Lorraine interrupted, with more than a lacing of sarcasm. 'Even though you nearly got yourself killed.'

Alison wasn't one to take being told off, discreetly or not. She quickly answered back. 'And I found out where the angle of the shot to Martin Neville came from. Has ballistics got the gun?' she added.

'Yes. You say Mariam fired the gun, or Buisha?' Banham asked.

'I know it couldn't have come from Massafur or Sadiq,' Alison told him. 'I closed in on the CCTV. They weren't on the side that had fired the shot.'

'Indeed they weren't,' Lorraine said. As Alison turned to Banham looking pleased with herself, Lorraine added, 'However, you are wrong on that score. And, yes, the report is back from ballistics. And, yes, we have the gun that fired that shot.' She sat back in her chair, savouring the moment of putting Alison in her place. 'It actually came from Kevin McCaub's gun.'

'What?'

'The gun was confiscated when his gang were arrested. A Bernie Doolan had it in his hands, when they stormed the back of the warehouse. McCaub had given the gun to him for protection when they went to the warehouse. We confiscated it when Bernie Doolan was arrested. We sent it over to forensics to see if it had been fired for any other convictions. And it turns out, that was a match to the gun that fired the shot that killed our Martin.

Alison turned to Banham, as Lorraine continued. 'The plot thickens, as it also had Devlin McCaub's prints over it, as well as Kevin's and Bernie Doolan's. We spoke to Kevin McCaub again, and he told us Devlin shot Martin, by mistake. He said he was aiming at Sadiq, but Neville jumped in the way. When Kevin and Devlin were arrested Devlin passed the gun to Doolan.

'We then questioned Bernie Doolan. He told us the same: that he took the gun from Devlin, after Devlin fired it as he was arrested, Bernie then ran into the crowds to avoid arrest. He then gave it to Kevin when they went to the warehouse earlier, and then took it back and was using it. Hence the fingerprints of the three of them on the gun.

'Not for a minute wanting to take Doolan's word for it, we then had forensics check Devlin McCaub's clothes, and his hands in the mortuary, and lo and behold, they are covered in gunpowder residue. Devlin McCaub shot Neville. He didn't mean to, but he did.'

'Where is Bernie Doolan now?'

'Giving a statement to that fact.'

Alison turned to Banham. Banham shook his head.

'So, you aren't that clever, you got that wrong as well as disobeying my orders,' Lorraine said in a harsh tone to Alison.

Banham quickly jumped to Alison's defence. 'I have to say I was glad to see her, she was able to untie my hands, which probably saved me getting shot—'

'No one is asking you what you think, either,' Lorraine snapped at him. 'You two are both on a disciplinary.' She turned to Banham. 'You were given the job of hostage negotiator, not hero, and you too, disobeyed my order.'

'Jesus, Lorraine,' Banham said. 'We both did what we did—'

'Shut it, both of you. You are both suspended from duties pending your disciplinaries. I will let you know when they are coming up.' She then changed her tone, and said flatly, 'Well, it'll be at least a month, maybe longer.' She looked down as she added, 'Time to plan another wedding.' She then looked up at Alison over her long, bleached fringe.

Alison gave nothing away.

'I understand your hair isn't at its best, but the wedding photographer could shoot you, sorry, bad phrasing, could photograph you, from the front only. And Hannah Kemp has very kindly offered you her wedding dress. She said she knows you didn't like yours. She said you will love this one. It's pink and frilly.' Lorraine managed to keep a straight face as she watched Alison's grow longer and her eyebrows higher. Then Lorraine added, still looking at Alison from the drooping fringe. 'I know you won't refuse that kindness. The best bit, of course, is that Hannah won't be able to travel for a long while, so they have also offered to give you their honeymoon in the Seychelles.' She looked at Banham, and added, 'It is a present for saving her life. If I were you, I would make the most of that one.'

Banham and Alison turned to each other, both looked delighted. Then Alison turned to Lorraine.

'And will we have jobs to come back to?'

'Well, of course you will have jobs to come back to, but maybe not what you would like. You, for instance, might have to get used to the feel of the itchy uniform of a PC for a while, and Banham, I know how you hate being in the office full-time, but there's a lot to learn about computers as you get older, and it might just be the right time for you to do that course that you have been putting off.'

As Alison and Banham turned to look at each other, she added. 'Now go. I don't want you hanging around and trying to gain sympathy. You both made your beds, and you can jolly well lie on them, together or separately.' With that she turned away and opened her filing drawer, as if to get on with more important things.

Once out in the corridor, Banham was the first to speak.

'Have you got your car?'

'Yes.' Alison turned, and carried on walking.

'Do you want to leave it here, and go and have a drink?'

'I can't. I don't know if my parking space still belongs to me. It is in the spaces for CID cars only. I'd better get it out. And, I think we've had enough to drink in that coffee.'

'Let's get something to eat then.'

Alison sighed. 'Do you know what, I'm so tired, I think I'd like to go home and just sleep.'

'Go home where? You are in the middle of moving. Half your stuff is at mine, and the other half still at yours.'

Alison lifted her eyes to meet his.

'So go home where? Where is it you want to be, Alison?' Banham asked holding her eyes with his.

Alison looked away, shrugged, and shook her head.

His hands flew to his face. He then moved his hands from his face and put them on her shoulders, so she was facing him. 'I love you, Alison. If you love me, that is all that matters. We'll get through this, you know we will. We've got through worse.'

'Nothing is worse than demotion,' she said quietly as she walked on.

They were at the door that led to the car park. She turned to face him. 'I do love you, Banny, I truly do.'

'But?'

She shook her head. 'No buts, I love you.'

'Sure?'

'Positive.'

'So we take this break, and we plan another wedding?'

She held his gaze, her forehead crumpled, and then shook her head. 'Let's do the honeymoon in the Seychelles, and then play it by ear. I don't want to get married with half my hair missing.'

'And there was me thinking it was the pink frilly dress!'

Acknowledgements

Many, many thanks to all the police who have helped me with all the technical jargon in this story. I know I can't name you, but I can say – without you, and your generosity of time and knowledge, this book would be a lot weaker. Any mistakes are all mine.

A sweeping salute to Accent Press and the wonderful crew at Headline. Thank you.

My wonderful agent David Headley, and all at DHH. Summed up and simplified – YOU ROCK.

Lastly, but certainly far from least, to all the readers who read me, and write to me. You are all stars and I am so grateful for your support. Thank you.